LOST SOULS

The Cube of Asgard

Kevin Oxland

To Beth + Victoria,

I hope you enjoy it

Kevin ☺

First Published in the UK by Peachstone Publications 2011
First Published in the USA by Peachstone Publications 2011

www.peachstonepublications.com

ISBN 978-0-9570242-0-5

First Edition

To Emma, Rebecca and Jessica Oxland

PROLOGUE

Drake Jones entered the brightly lit chamber. The cold steel pressed into his skin as he cupped the ancient realm cube in both hands. He reached out, placed it gently on the stone pedestal and stepped aside. The chamber lights dimmed to a hazy glow. On the sides of the cube, a green radiance seeped from the mysterious symbols. From the ceiling, a glass dome descended to cover it, sealing it in its own airtight cocoon with a fading hiss.

Pondering the cube's hidden wonders, Drake smiled. "We must convince the boy to attend the academy, Angeline," he said. "We cannot allow him to continue along his path of self destruction."

Angeline pushed her dark rimmed glasses up the ridge of her nose and stared at the cube. Her smooth skin and protruding cheekbones were flushed with a green hue. She nodded. "Indeed.

A year has passed. We must move fast before it's too late."

"But I don't understand," said Drake. "It should already be too late. Why is he still alive?"

"He is not like the others here, Drake. He is special…very special, but I think you already know that," Angeline said as she turned to look at him with a raised eyebrow.

"If we do this, I expect the parents to be a problem and they may not agree with our intentions…especially his father."

Angeline shook her head slowly. "The mother will be of no concern, I can assure you of that. But you're right; the father could present a problem. I will personally take care of him myself, so don't worry about him. You do whatever it takes to get the boy here, but he must come to no harm. As you know, four sets of twins have been abducted over the past few weeks alone. I'm afraid it may be too late for them now, so time is of the essence. We cannot lose anymore. Is that understood?"

Drake nodded once, turned and left the chamber. Angeline followed, glanced back at the cube and closed the heavy metal door. She reached over and tapped the security code on the keypad.

The door hissed and sealed.

CHAPTER ONE

Hanging by a Thread

Spencer Quinn plunged his hand into his pocket and pulled out a strapless watch. It read 3:31 P. M. He knew that if he waited any longer he would miss the bus.

The Friday afternoon was unusually hot for July. All the schools in the country were closing for the long summer vacation, and Spencer anxiously watched the students pour though the doorway and spill onto the playground. As they passed, he surveyed them carefully, but Frankie wasn't among them.

He heaved his bag onto his shoulder, threw one last glance down the corridor and pushed through the doors. He walked across the gum-mottled playground, his head down. He strolled past a row of small trees, but no matter how hard he tried to blend in with the crowd, he couldn't shake the feeling that a gigantic arrow was floating above his head, pointing down at him.

Halfway to the gates, he heard the voice he dreaded.

"Hey look who it is. It's Freak Boy," bellowed Billy Hood from across the playground. He was a tall boy with brown hair, rosy cheeks and the build of a football player.

"Oh great," muttered Spencer. He didn't look at Billy. He

gripped his bag strap, fixed his eyes on his scuffed black shoes and picked up his pace toward the school gates.

He heard another jeer.

"Hey, weirdo, where's your girlfriend?" snarled Arnold Baines, one of Billy's henchmen. He was a short, skinny boy with flat, blond hair and a gap in his overly large top teeth. Wherever Billy went, Arnold was sure to be loitering in his wake.

Ten paces from the gate, Arnold ran in front of Spencer, his arms out to his sides. Spencer avoided eye contact and stared at the ground. He tried to get around but Arnold mirrored every move he made.

"Go on, Arn, hit 'im. See if he does it," goaded Billy, now standing behind Spencer.

Spencer looked up at Arnold, smiled and narrowed his eyes. He knew Arnold was a coward at heart and Spencer wondered whether his spineless core could be manipulated.

Arnold hesitated. He glanced over at Billy and then at Spencer with an uncertain look on his face. "But what if…" he began.

Billy interrupted him, "Just do it, or I'll do you."

With that, Arnold reached out and pushed Spencer hard in the chest, forcing him to step back.

"You really don't want to do that," said Spencer calmly while shaking his head.

"Do it, Arn, go on, do it again," demanded Billy.

Arnold did, but it was much harder the second time. Billy quickly followed with a jab between the shoulder blades, shunting Spencer forward. They did this repeatedly while chanting, "Freak...Freak…Freak…"

Anger coursed through Spencer's veins. His muscles tensed. "Leave me alone!" he said through gritted teeth. "Please, go away now and you'll be okay."

Arnold started laughing. "Look, he's shaking. He's going to do it, Billy, he's going to do it," he said and pushed Spencer again.

The pain in Spencer's head swelled to bursting. His body trembled. He clenched his fists tight, forcing himself to concentrate on the pain of his nails digging into his flesh.

Arnold's expression changed to panic.

Spencer's vision blurred and a blazing heat boiled in his chest. A pain shot through his temple like a scorched needle piercing his skull. He retched and staggered helplessly. He squeezed his eyes shut, clamped his hands to his head and yelled out as the pain drilled into his brain. But as quickly as it took hold, the pain eased. A white light flooded his mind's eye and every thought and feeling drained from him. The world melted into darkness. A cool ripple washed through his body and the last thing he heard was Arnold's wild screams.

~ ~ ~

As Spencer regained consciousness, he found himself on his hands and knees staring into his own vomit. His breathing was deep and fast. Back rushed the awareness of where he was and what he was facing. Along with it came dizziness, and his head throbbed as though a claw had raked through his brain.

He staggered to his feet, looked up, and froze. Arnold was up a tree hanging from a branch by his belt. It had been pulled up over his belly by the weight of him. His arms and legs were flailing and by his screams and grimace, Spencer knew he was in excruciating pain. Beneath him, Billy was laughing hysterically.

"No," whispered Spencer, "Not again."

He snatched up his bag, gathered whatever energy he could muster and bolted toward the gates. He reached the street, turned left, and slowed to a stagger. He cast a look into the playground through the linked wire fence. Nobody was following him. Two older students had lifted Arnold to the ground and Billy and several other boys had surrounded him.

Several paces from the bus stop Spencer stopped and dropped his hands to his knees. He drew several deep breaths. He couldn't believe it had happened again. A feeling of hopelessness overwhelmed him.

A cool breeze brushed his face and as he filled his lungs with the fresh air, a peculiar sensation tugged at the inside of his head as if his thoughts were being shuffled in his mind. His attention was drawn to the other side of the street. He turned and stood up straight. Staring back at him was a tall, slender man, probably in his twenties, although Spencer couldn't be certain. He had short, spiky, blond hair and wore a black suit and shiny black shoes that made him look official and important.

Sitting next to him was a large, muscular dog like the racing dogs he had seen on television. It had a brown patch across its pointy face and it sat rigid like a statue. Its pearl black eyes fixed on his.

The stranger gestured with a nod and a smile. Calmness drifted through Spencer's mind. His breathing softened and without prompting, a picture of his brother dropped into his thoughts like a photograph had been forcibly placed there. He saw Oliver as clear as the stranger on the other side of the street. It was Spencer's favourite picture, taken at Christmas after Oliver opened his Manchester United football kit and quickly put it on. Like always, he looked happy.

Spencer hadn't intentionally thought of Oliver, but there he was, in his mind as sharp and focused as if he were standing in front of him.

The stranger smiled again and nodded.

"I can help you find him," said a calm voice. Spencer looked around, but there was nobody standing nearby. He hadn't noticed the stranger's lips move either, but somehow, Spencer knew it was he that had spoken to him.

As Spencer was trying to make sense of it all, a different, angry voice shouted from behind him. It wasn't in his mind. It rattled through his eardrums and shattered the image of Oliver in a split second.

"Hey, Freaky."

Spencer shot a look over his shoulder back along the path and saw Billy stomping furiously toward him.

"Oh no, not again," groaned Spencer quietly.

"What did you do to Arnold?" demanded Billy.

Spencer turned to face him. "You were there. I didn't touch him."

He didn't know how these things happened and he had no control over them, but he was sure no physical contact was ever made.

Billy took a step closer. His bulky, heaving chest a few inches from Spencer's and his face contorted with rage.

"Don't play games with me. I know you're a freak. I'm on to you, Quinn."

A small cluster of boys standing at the bus stop noticed them arguing and started synchronised clapping and chanting. "Fight, fight, fight. . ."

"Not so fast, Chunky," said a female voice.

Billy spun round.

Frankie stood in front of him, face to face.

Spencer let out a quiet sigh of relief. Frankie was shorter than Billy and had a light frame, but she was county Capoeira champion. Most of the school had seen her in action. She was fast and particularly good at the low sweeping kicks. There was no way Billy could win.

Billy stepped closer to her. "And what are you going to do about it?" he said.

Frankie simply smiled and raised her eyebrows, but said nothing.

Billy glanced over his shoulder at the boys behind him. They had stopped clapping and chanting and moved closer, keen to see what was going to happen next. A girl and a boy fighting was not to be missed.

Billy shot a piercing glare at Spencer. "I'll get you, Quinn," he said. He paused briefly and then deliberately shouldered past Frankie and marched back along the path.

Frankie brushed aside a strand of red hair that had fallen out of her ponytail. "Looks like I made it just in time," she said, smiling.

"Where were you? I waited for ages."

"Sorry. Mr. Crabtree kept me back to tell me it's been a

pleasure teaching me Biology and that I should choose it as one of my subjects for next year." Frankie rolled her green eyes.

A yellow bus pulled up alongside them and shuddered to a halt. Its doors snapped open and the group of boys rushed forward, pushing and shoving, each one desperate to get on first.

Frankie stared at Spencer with a frown. "Are you okay? You look terrible."

"Not really. They got me in the playground. And that thing happened again," he replied, glancing at her sideways.

"Oh no, I'm really sorry, Spence."

Spencer could tell by the look of concern on Frankie's face that she meant it. But before he could explain what had happened, the bus driver began roaring at them. "Are you getting on this bus or what? I ain't got all day you know."

Spencer and Frankie stepped onto the bus.

He followed Frankie up the aisle. A group of rowdy boys at the back were throwing paper balls at a girl sitting further down the bus. Frankie stopped at two empty seats near the middle and stood aside to let Spencer sit next to the window. He was glad to sit down. His body ached and his legs were still trembling.

He peered out of the window and looked up and down the street for a glimpse of the stranger, but he was nowhere to be seen.

"Did you see him, Fran?"

"See who?"

"That man standing across the street with the dog."

"No, I didn't. What about him?"

Spencer paused. "Oh, nothing," he said, but there was something familiar about him. The man had looked at him, nodded and smiled, like he knew Spencer. And why did Oliver drop into his thoughts? And the voice?

"So, what happened in the playground?" asked Frankie.

"I put Arnold in a tree and hung him on a branch by his belt," said Spencer, blurting it out like it was an everyday occurrence.

Frankie laughed.

"It's not funny, Fran. He could have been hurt," said Spencer, annoyed she hadn't taken it seriously. "I blanked out again and when I came around he was up a tree, screaming his head off."

"Sorry."

"Do you remember when Lanky wouldn't stop jabbing me with a pencil? You were there. You saw it happen. His mouth jammed open. It was like that with Arnold. An intense pain filled my head and everything went white." The anxiety welled up inside him. "What's wrong with me, Fran?"

There was a pause and then Frankie replied, "I told you before, I think you should tell someone about it. You should see a doctor or something."

Dread stirred in Spencer's stomach. "Are you kidding? I saw what happened to Oliver and they didn't believe me when he was kidnapped. One policeman even laughed in my face when I told him what happened." Spencer's face burned at the memory. "No way will I talk to doctors, or the police, or any of them again."

Frankie leaned closer and whispered, "Well, that was different, Spence. A monster coming into your room and dragging your brother through a hole in the air is not something you hear every day."

"What do you know? You weren't there. I know what I saw. Oliver was taken and I should have helped him. It's my fault he's gone."

"Shhh, calm down, I'm sorry, and it's not your fault," said Frankie, quickly glancing around the bus.

Despite his anger, Spencer knew she meant what she said. She was the only person who believed his story. She was the only person who acknowledged the truth about the strange things he could do. He could sense Frankie was more concerned than she was letting on, but the mere fact she was sitting beside him and not avoiding him was worth more than he could ever tell her.

Frankie continued. "But they pick on you to make you do those things. Now you look pale and sick. There could be something wrong, that's all."

"I'm not sick," replied Spencer. "It's something else. You've seen it. Don't you ever get the feeling that you're, you know… different?"

"We're all different, Spence," replied Frankie.

Spencer looked at her. "That's not what I mean," he said. "I just wish I could stop it."

He turned his gaze beyond the window and cast his mind back wistfully to his hometown and his old friends. Back to the place he lived for twelve years before that terrifying night when everything changed. Before the events that forced them to leave their family home and live with his grandmother, back to the time his father and Oliver lived at home. But it all seemed such a long time ago, a distant memory.

Slowly, the bus rattled its way through Little Mead, weaving through the traffic and shedding passengers every now and again.

It passed the majestic museum, the town hall and rumbled out to the edge of the town where it rolled past a grand gothic stately home shielded by two enormous iron gates that once greeted noblemen and ladies. Today however, the house was cloaked by vegetation and the gates were chained and padlocked, strangled by twisting vines and overgrown weeds that spilled through the gates onto the pavement.

A little way past the house, the bus slowed and ground to a halt at the end of Oak Lane. It let out a long loud hiss and the doors flipped open.

"Come on," said Frankie, jolting Spencer from his reverie.

Spencer stood up, slung his bag over his shoulder, laboured up the aisle behind Frankie and stepped off the bus.

They strolled along Oak Lane. On the right side, red brick Victorian houses sat behind picket fences and neatly trimmed gardens. On the left side, giant, gnarled oak trees grew out of an overgrown hedgerow. Beyond the hedgerow, green sweeping countryside soaked up the afternoon sunshine.

"Sorry, Fran, for flaring up at you like that," said Spencer.

"Forget it. I already have," replied Frankie and smiled. "Do you and your Mum have a vacation planned this summer?"

Spencer shook his head. "Not likely. Mum's been really depressed lately. It was never like this back home. I catch her staring at pictures of Oliver sometimes. It's a year since it happened and they still haven't found anything, but every day it's like she's waiting for news. I don't know what to do," he shrugged.

"Oh, Spence, I forgot. I'm really sorry."

Spencer had a rush of guilt. He never meant to make Frankie

feel bad. "It's okay." He looked to the ground and kicked a stone into the road.

They stopped next to a small white wooden gate. The paint at the bottom of the pickets was flaking off, revealing rotten wood beneath. Beyond the gate, leading up to a blue, wooden door and cutting through an overgrown weedy lawn, was a long, uneven narrow path edged with broken stone borders. The narrow house was sandwiched between number four and number eight. It stretched to three floors and shabby sash windows overlooked the garden.

Frankie turned to face Spencer. "If you want to, you can come over to my house tomorrow and hang out," she suggested. "Dad has gone to Manchester and he won't be back until tomorrow night. Mum and I are having a barbecue. Why don't you join us?"

Spencer looked thoughtfully up at the house. "Thanks, Fran, but Dad's coming over tomorrow, and Mum says I have to spend time with him. I haven't seen him in ages."

"Well, if you change your mind," Frankie said, turning. "Call me." She looked back down the road ahead of her. "I'd better get home or Mum will come looking for me. I'll call you on Sunday."

Spencer raised his arm and waved as she ran towards home. He watched her step into her garden three houses away and dart behind a wall of conifer trees.

He pushed the gate open and started up the crooked path toward the front door. He placed the key in the lock, turned it, and gave the door a gentle nudge with his right shoulder. The door swung open.

CHAPTER TWO

The Moonlit Dog

Spencer entered the gloomy hall and pushed the door shut behind him. Furniture polish filled his nostrils and the sound of rattling cutlery, clinking plates, and glasses echoed down the narrow hall from the kitchen.

"Oli…uh…Spencer, is that you?" called Spencer's mother.

Spencer hesitated. His heart sank. It wasn't the first time she got their names mixed up and he knew it wouldn't be the last.

"Yeah, Mum," he called back and dropped his school bag beneath the coat rack.

Spencer's mother entered the hallway with her light-blue shirt tucked into her jeans, and a towel slung over her shoulder.

"Hello, love, did you have a good day at school?"

"Uh, yeah…" Spencer lied. As he spoke, there was a thump on the floor upstairs.

Spencer's mother cast a fatigued look to the ceiling. "What is your Grandmother doing now?" she sighed.

Spencer shrugged. "Probably making more mess for you to clean up."

"I should go up and see if she's okay. I'll be with you in a minute, Spence," she said and rushed up the stairs.

Spencer stepped into the living room and stopped. The beige, patterned cushions on the sofa looked liked they had been inflated. The wooden coffee table sat in the middle of the room with the usual assortment of magazines stacked neatly on top. Even though the house was neat and warm, it didn't feel like home to Spencer. Everything in it was ancient and he felt disconnected from it somehow.

Looking around the room, anybody would have thought two boys lived there. Photographs of Oliver and Spencer adorned the shelves of the dark wooden bookcases placed either side of the fireplace. But that wasn't all. Spencer's mother kept many of Oliver's things. His coat hung on the coat rack in the hall. His school bag sat at the bottom of the stairs. And his Manchester United football kit was folded neatly in Spencer's sock drawer and none of it had moved since they were placed there almost a year ago.

Spencer walked towards the television in the corner of the room. He stopped in front of it and stared up at a photograph of Oliver. It was like looking into a mirror. The only difference was the smile, which had always won Oliver greater affection. But all that had gone now. The memories were slowly fading, like they were images from an old movie he once watched and he could only remember bits of it.

Bending down to switch on the television, Spencer stopped, turned and stared at the phone. It was going to ring, he thought. And then it did.

He darted towards it and picked up the receiver, but his mother had also answered it upstairs and was greeting the caller. Spencer recognised his father's voice instantly.

"Hi, Liz," said his father.

It was good to hear his voice, thought Spencer, but it sounded troubled.

"Why are you calling?" said Spencer's mother, sharply. "Please don't tell me you're not coming over this weekend."

She sounded angry and abrupt.

"Well, the problem is…" began Spencer's father, but he was interrupted.

"There's always a problem with you, John," snapped his mother. "You're not coming are you?"

"But…I can't."

Spencer opened his mouth to speak, but stopped himself. He wanted to say it was okay and that they shouldn't argue. He hated it.

"Why do you even bother?" said Spencer's mother. "Spencer needs to see you, especially this weekend. Don't you understand that? You know what he's been through."

"I can't, I'm…" but before his father could finish, Spencer heard a click and his mother had put the phone down.

The evening seemed to slow to a crawl after that, but then most evenings did these days. His grandmother periodically shuffled in and out of the kitchen carrying a tray of tea and biscuits and his mother stared sullenly at the television. Spencer wondered if she actually looked at the screen at all and imagined her drifting into her own misty void full of Oliver.

Spencer had tried several times to find the words to tell his mother about the things that were happening to him, but he couldn't do it. She was often in this vacant, troubled mode and already seemed to have more than enough to worry about.

He didn't want to burden her with more. She probably wouldn't believe him anyway.

It was almost ten o'clock when Spencer decided to go to bed. He pulled himself up from the sofa and started towards the door. Then he paused and looked back at the thin, lonely figure that was his mother. "Goodnight," he said.

She glanced in his direction and said, "Goodnight," with a weak smile and sadness in her expression.

Spencer climbed the stairs to his bedroom on the second floor and pushed the door open. In the centre of the room, against the wall, his bed sat covered in a red and white duvet. On a chest of drawers next to the door stood a photo of Spencer and Oliver, standing in a football stadium. It was Spencer's favourite photo. They looked happy.

Beneath the sloping ceiling, bookshelves were stuffed full of his favourite books. A window to his right overlooked his back garden, and beyond that, an overgrown garden and a crumbling wall smothered a large, dilapidated, stately house.

Spencer lay awake in the darkness for hours. His mind filled with thoughts of Oliver and where he might be. He recalled the horrific night when Oliver vanished, his haunting cries, the rushing wind and the dazzling white light, followed by the deathly silence. Oliver was gone.

Oliver's terror-filled face haunted his dreams. What took Oliver? Why didn't it take me? No answers came.

Spencer's thoughts settled and as he began to drift to the space where reality meets dreams, he heard something different. It echoed from the still black void of his mind.

A dog's bark.

He jolted and opened his eyes wide, but he couldn't see anything through the darkness.

There it was again. It wasn't vicious. It was just one bark and then it stopped, as if the dog was announcing itself. It wasn't unusual for a dog to be barking but it was late and it came from just outside his window.

Spencer pushed back his duvet, swung his legs out of bed, and his feet touched the cold, wooden floor. He stood, crept towards the window, and peered down into the garden.

From the gloom, staring up at him was a dog.

He gasped and moved back out of sight. It was the dog. He was certain of it. It had the same long snout; the same statuesque form, and he couldn't mistake the brown patch across its face.

Spencer edged towards the window again and leaned his head forwards. It was still there, sitting patiently in the middle of the lawn looking up at him with the moonlight licking its black, glossy coat. Then it stood, barked again, and turned. It padded towards the picket fence and out the garden gate.

He watched it hurry down the path along the back of the terraced houses. Then it stopped and disappeared through a hole in the wall that surrounded the garden of the old house.

Spencer reached out and placed his hand on the wall. It was solid and the night chill had settled on his skin. He couldn't be dreaming.

His gaze settled on a beam of light. Standing in the shadows beneath a porch at the side of the large, old house, was a tall figure holding a torch. The stranger was motionless, as if waiting for something or someone.

Spencer glimpsed the dog enter the doorway.

The stranger hesitated, looked up at Spencer, and then followed the dog into the house.

Spencer was dumbfounded. The cold air suddenly gripped him. He shivered, quickly climbed back into bed and wrapped his duvet tightly around him. He was sure the stranger was the same man he saw outside school. He had the same slim build and spiky haircut, but what did he want?

~ ~ ~

Spencer woke early the following morning with sunlight streaming through the window. Sleepy and yawning, he soon remembered today was the anniversary of Oliver's kidnapping and he knew how difficult the day would be for everyone.

He also remembered the events of last night. He swung his legs out of bed and rushed over to the window. He blinked and squinted past the dazzling sunlight, but there was no sign of the dog or the stranger and the old house looked like it always had done, abandoned and forgotten.

Feeling apprehensive, he got dressed, went downstairs and stopped at the kitchen door. His grandmother stood at the counter preparing breakfast. She looked over her shoulder and smiled at him briefly.

"Good morning, love," she said. "Sit down. You must eat some breakfast."

"Where's Mum?" asked Spencer.

"Oh…she popped out. She'll be back shortly," she replied, lifting two slices of toast from the toaster.

Spencer walked over to the dining table and sat down while

his grandmother waddled towards him carrying a plateful of toast.

"Gran?" he began.

"Yes, dear?"

"Do you know anything about the dilapidated old house?"

His grandmother halted abruptly and wobbled to prevent the toast from sliding off the plate. She looked at him, her expression turning to a grimace. "Stay away from that place. Do you hear me? Bad things happen in there, terrible things. Your mother already has too much to think about without you getting into any trouble."

Spencer drew himself upright and fidgeted in his seat. "What do you mean?" he said.

His grandmother placed the plate on the table and faced him. "It's not a place for children to be playing, that's all you need to know. Do you understand?" she said, glaring at him and pointing her crooked finger.

"Yes, of course," replied Spencer.

His grandmother wandered back to the counter shaking her head and mumbling to herself. She sounded agitated and he was sure he heard the words 'missing' and 'died', but he couldn't be certain. He decided not to question her further.

It was ten thirty when Spencer was scraping the left over burnt edges of his toast into the bin and the doorbell rang. His grandmother started towards the hall, but Spencer darted across the kitchen and cut her off. "It's okay, Gran. I'll get it," he said.

His grandmother turned and went back to washing dishes.

Spencer hurried along the hall and opened the front door. Frankie was standing on the doorstep dressed in jeans and a white T-shirt. "Hi, Spence," she said, smiling.

"What are you doing here? I thought you were going to call me tomorrow?"

"I was. But I spoke to your Mum earlier, on her way out, and she said your Dad's not coming, so I thought I would call around. I can call back tomorrow if you like?"

"No, come in. I'm glad you're here. There's something I want to tell you." He pulled the door open and Frankie stepped inside. "Let's go up to my room," he added, glancing towards the kitchen where his Grandmother was clattering plates.

He climbed the stairs and Frankie followed. When they reached his room, Spencer closed the door and he told her about the dog, the strange figure standing in the shadows, and how he saw the same man the day before outside the school.

"Why would a dog be barking at you outside your window in the middle of the night? Are you sure you weren't dreaming?"

"No, it was real. And I know it was the same dog. It had a brown mark across its face."

"But I don't get it. You see a man and a dog outside school. Then, in the middle of the night, you think you see them enter that creepy house and you think he was trying to get your attention? It doesn't make sense."

"I don't think anything, I know what I saw," said Spencer. But then he thought for a moment. When she put it like that, it did sound a little weird, so he decided not to tell her about the voice he heard in his head or the picture of Oliver he saw in his mind.

"I'm sure it was the same man. Just after I put Arnold in the tree, he was standing across the road, and then again last night at the old house. Isn't that more than a coincidence?" insisted Spencer.

A smile crept across Frankie's face as she walked over to the window. Spencer followed her. They gazed down at the old house. Tall crumbling chimney pots reached for the sky and its long windows were boarded up except for the very top windows in the loft. The garden was enclosed by a high, moss-covered stone wall that had seen better days.

"But why you, Spence?"

"I don't know. But I think he's been watching me for a while."

Frankie gasped and looked at Spencer as if she had figured it out. "Maybe you did something to him, or his children, or something like that."

"I don't think so. He looks too young to have kids and I think I'd remember if I did something to him," said Spencer shaking his head.

"Then maybe he just wants to help you…with…you know."

"What?"

"That thing you do," said Frankie.

"Why would he want to help me with that?"

Frankie shrugged. "I don't know, but I was thinking about it last night. What if you could control it? Have you ever tried to do it on your own?"

Spencer looked at her, bewildered. "What do you mean?"

"You know…make something happen, but control it and remember what you did."

"Are you crazy?" Spencer turned away and walked back to the bed. He sat down and rubbed his forehead, thinking of the pain it caused. "No way, I'm too scared. I'll probably set myself on fire or something dumb like that."

"Try it. I'll watch and make sure nothing happens to you," said Frankie with an eager tone in her voice.

"But I don't know how. It happens on its own. I don't ask it to happen."

"You must have some idea, some sort of feeling?"

"Well, sort of. I may think about what I would like to do to them before it happens, but I'm not sure."

"Look, you see this?" said Frankie pointing at a picture of Oliver on top of a bookshelf. "See if you can move it."

Spencer considered it for a moment. He couldn't see what harm it would do, apart from give him a severe headache. "Okay, but stand back, I don't want you to get hurt."

Frankie backed up and watched keenly from the door.

Spencer stared at the photo, demanding it to move with his thoughts. He squinted, he glared, and shuffled closer, but the photo didn't budge.

"Nothing's happening, Fran."

"You're not concentrating. Just relax. Maybe you're trying too hard. I know. Imagine it's a picture of Billy," said Frankie with a wicked grin.

That was easy, he thought. Spencer focused on it again. This time he saw Billy's angry face and large shoulders in the picture frame. He scowled at it and concentrated hard. All of a sudden the picture started wobbling, slowly at first. Then it rose into the air and started spinning, but before Spencer saw what happened next, the white light filled his mind followed by the darkness which quickly consumed all his thoughts.

The next thing he saw was Frankie's distressed face looming over him.

"Spencer, wake up. Wake up. Are you okay?"

He lifted his head and glanced around the room.

"Where is it?" he said, swallowing hard. The nausea crept up his throat and he swallowed again to push it back down.

"It's over there. It flew across the room and smashed against the wall," replied Frankie, nodding towards the corner of the room. "Thank God you're alright." She looked concerned. But as Spencer sat up and leaned back against his bed, her expression turned to awe.

"What?" he shrugged.

"You did it."

Spencer got to his feet shakily, and sat on the edge of his bed. "But I blanked out again," he said, rubbing his head. The pounding had settled into a numb ache as if someone had belted him on the head and he was now feeling the after effects.

"Yes, you did, but it was amazing. You have something special inside you, Spence, I'm sure of it," said Frankie, shaking her head in astonishment.

"Now you see why I can't tell anyone. I really am a freak."

"No, you're not, stop thinking like that," said Frankie as she stood up and walked over to the window. "It's amazing, Spence. I wonder if he knows what it is and that's why he's hanging around."

Spencer wondered if Frankie could be right, but then another thought struck him. "I wonder if he knew Oliver could do it too, and that's why he was kidnapped. Maybe he's the kidnapper and now he wants me."

Frankie shook her head. "I don't think he wants to kidnap you. He would've done it by now."

"So why is he hanging around in a damp, smelly house?"

"I don't know. Maybe he's just waiting there until he gets a chance to speak to you. It's a good spot to see you coming and going."

"It's a bit weird, though," said Spencer.

"Why is it weird? He's hardly going to come up to you in the middle of the street and say 'Hi, I see you have special powers, pleased to meet you, my name is blah, blah, blah'," said Frankie, tilting her head from side to side as she spoke. "We could go and check it out and see if he's in there? You know, confront him face to face."

"Do you think he'll still be in there?" said Spencer.

Frankie shrugged. "There's only one way to find out." She turned and looked down at the house and said, "Mum told me that it belongs to a couple of archaeologists. They bought it last year and were going to restore it, but I don't think they've been in there since then. Apparently there's a caretaker that looks after the place, but I've never seen him. If he's in there, he doesn't do a very good job."

"I see kids hanging around in the garden sometimes," said Spencer.

Frankie smiled. "Yeah, but they don't go inside. They're too scared."

"Of what?"

"They think it's haunted. Load of rubbish if you ask me."

"Are you sure you want to go in there? It could be dangerous," said Spencer.

"Yes, of course," Frankie replied rolling her eyes. "You're not wussing out on me are you?"

Spencer looked away and brushed his hand through his hair, "Of course not," he said.

"I'll tell you what. Let's meet after lunch, at one o'clock by the willow tree on the back path. I know an easy way into the gardens without climbing the wall. We'll go and take a look."

Spencer somehow knew the stranger wanted something from him and he had to find out what it was. "Okay," he said.

For the next hour they talked, but Spencer listened mostly to Frankie guessing who the man with the dog might be.

"Maybe he's a reporter after a story? It is, you know, a year."

"No, I don't think so. Reporters don't wear expensive black suits and hang out in ruined houses," replied Spencer. He'd met plenty of them to know that.

CHAPTER THREE

The Darkness

The clock on the kitchen wall read twelve fifty-five. Spencer devoured his cheese sandwich and leapt up from his chair.

"Going somewhere?" asked Spencer's mother.

Spencer stopped dead. He hadn't heard her come in. He looked into her sunken eyes. "I'm going to Frankie's," he said. He was sure his mother would notice the lie in his forced smile.

"Okay. Just don't be late back," she turned, dropped her bag to the floor and leaned forward onto the counter.

"Are you Okay, Mum?" said Spencer. "I don't have to go. I can stay here."

She stood up straight and turned to face him. "No, no, I'm fine," she replied, "I've been to church this morning and, well, you know."

"Why didn't you tell me you were going? I would have come with you."

"I didn't want to wake you. I wanted all of us to go as a family, but your father couldn't make it," she said and shrugged one shoulder. She continued, "I'm fine. You go. Frankie will be waiting."

Spencer stood for a moment and watched her walk into the

hallway before he turned and left through the back door.

A blanket of ominous, grey clouds threatened rain and obscured the sky, but it was a warm day nonetheless and a gentle breeze carried the smell of fresh cut grass.

He ran to the end of the garden, opened the gate and dashed left along the path. When he reached the willow tree, Frankie wasn't there. He waited fifteen minutes and it began to spit rain. He thought she might have changed her mind. He kicked the tree trunk several times and paced up and down the path. He was about to give up and go back inside when he heard Frankie call, "Spencer! Wait!"

She came running towards him. "I'm sorry. My dad came home and he was excited about his new job. I had to stay and listen to him," she said.

"His new job?"

Frankie waved her hand as if to brush the question aside. "I'll tell you about it later," she replied. "Let's go."

She ran ahead and hurried along the path following the seemingly endless stone wall that surrounded the garden.

"It's just up ahead," she said, pointing to a large hole in the wall big enough to crawl through. "It'll take us close to the side door."

Spencer watched Frankie get on her hands and knees and crawl though. He quickly followed and emerged in a shadowy clearing surrounded by overgrown bushes and huge oak trees. He stood up, brushed the dirt from his jeans and surveyed the drink cans, sweet wrappers, magazines and other litter scattered amongst the leafy cavity.

"Look there," said Frankie, pointing towards a narrow path

carving its way through the nettles and brambles.

"Okay, let's go," said Spencer.

He crept along the path, carefully pushing the thorny stalks aside and shuffling around nettles. The path ended abruptly and they found themselves standing at the edge of a large clearing at the side of the house. Spencer took a step back into the shadows and crouched down. The weather beaten building was much larger close up than it appeared from his bedroom window. Frankie was right, it was creepy.

With its enormous bay windows and grand arched doorways, it was probably once a fine looking manor, but it had been void of human occupancy and care for many years and it now stood derelict, robbed of its grandeur.

A large green door set beneath a porch groaned as it swung open. "Look," said Spencer, eagerly nodding towards it. "That's where the stranger went in."

"Why is it left open?" asked Frankie.

"I don't know, but it's exactly where the stranger was standing when I saw him from my window. Come on, let's get a closer look." He stood up and crept out of the bushes, but stopped suddenly as something crunched beneath his foot. He looked down, grimaced, glanced back at Frankie and put his finger to his lips. The gravel was concealed by moss, weeds and sprawling ivy, giving the appearance of an overgrown lawn.

Frankie nodded.

Together, they tiptoed across the clearing, past a weathered water fountain and stopped beneath the porch next to the door.

Spencer listened. Nearby bird tweets and the rustling of the undergrowth is all that he heard. He leaned closer to look inside, but the gap was too narrow. He reached out and pulled the door gently. It creaked and moaned as it slowly revealed a dark vestibule with a grimy black and white chequered floor.

"I thought we might need this," said Frankie, pulling a torch from inside her denim jacket and handing it to Spencer.

"Good idea." He took it from her, switched it on and pointed the light into the house. "It looks all clear," Spencer whispered. "Shall we go inside?"

"Okay, but let's be careful, everything's probably rotten," replied Frankie.

Spencer listened carefully for any sounds as they crept into the dank, musty hallway. The temperature dropped and his skin prickled. He pointed the torch at the tall decaying walls and high ceiling. Black mould curled the beige patterned wallpaper from the walls. Holes in the ceiling, where the plaster had fallen, revealed the weave of wooden strips beneath, and the stench of a dead animal filled the air. At the end of the hall, a narrow staircase ascended into darkness.

"Let's look in there," whispered Spencer, pointing the torch beam toward a wide doorway to their right.

They entered a cavernous room. The ceiling was high and ornate coving ran around the top of the walls. To their left, a grand fireplace with intricate floral carvings sat in the centre of the wall. Ivy had wormed its way into the cracks at the edges of the windows and grasped the walls like giant green hands.

"There's nothing in here," said Frankie, still standing in the doorway.

"Except that!" said Spencer, pointing the light beam at a dead rat caught in a trap in the corner of the room. Its black, plump body twisted where the trap had clamped it. "I wonder who set that, it looks fresh," he added as the stench pushed him back.

"Yuk! It's disgusting," Frankie whispered, putting her hand over her nose and mouth. "It must have been the caretaker. Who else would set traps?"

They left the room and went back into the hall.

Spencer nodded towards the staircase at the far end. "Let's go down there," he said.

They crept further into the gloom, stopping at the foot of the staircase, next to a closed door. Spencer reached out, turned the wooden handle, and pushed the door. It was locked. He turned to face the stairs.

"Stop," Frankie grabbed Spencer's arm. "The steps might collapse," she said.

"Okay, I'll be careful," said Spencer.

Frankie tugged on his arm again. "Are you sure you want to go up there? It doesn't look like anybody's been in here for years."

Spencer somehow knew the man was trying to contact him. He couldn't give up that easily. "Just a little further," he said. "If we don't see anything at the top, we'll go back."

He started up the steep, narrow staircase. It curved around to the right and each stair groaned with every cautious step. At the top, the darkness was dense.

Spencer stopped on the last step and listened. Nothing revealed itself in the eerie silence, although he had a strong sense that someone, or something, was watching him. He shone the torch left then right before climbing the last step into a narrow corridor. The beam of light didn't reach an end in either direction. The walls were covered in dark red velvet wallpaper that was peeling at the edges and in the corners. There were no windows or doors, just a dark hollow void in both directions.

Frankie climbed the last step and stood close to Spencer.

"I don't think he'll be up here," breathed Spencer. But just as he finished speaking, he snapped his head to the right and flicked the torch beam in the same direction. The light licked something black and shiny before it dashed from view.

"I saw that too. What the hell was it?" said Frankie, her voice abrupt.

"I'm not sure, but I think it may have been a dog." Spencer tried to make his voice sound more confident than he felt. There was a pause. Doubt crept into his mind. Maybe it's a trap, he thought. Nobody knew they were here. Had he made a big mistake? "No, let's go back, it's not safe," he said.

"Hang on a minute. If that was the dog, maybe it'll lead us to him. What's the matter, afraid of the dark?" said Frankie, her voice composed and confident.

"No," said Spencer. That's all he could think to say.

"Well, let's go then."

Spencer turned, peered into the emptiness and began creeping through the murk. Frankie followed. When they reached the end, there was no dog, only another corridor stretching to their left and right. Spencer shone the torch in both directions, but all he could see was a dark empty void.

"Which way did it go?" whispered Frankie from behind.

Spencer listened and glanced again, left then right.

"This way," he said, finally choosing a left turn.

As they crept through the dark, the floorboards groaned. They passed panelled doors with ornate metal doorknobs. The corridor stretched further than the light could reach and the words of his grandmother echoed in Spencer's mind. 'Bad things happen in there, terrible things', but he pushed them aside and continued on.

Then Spencer stopped abruptly. With his arm outstretched, he thrust the torch out in front of him. At fifteen paces, two glowing discs beamed back at him.

"Look," said Spencer.

Frankie gripped Spencer's arm. "What is it?"

Spencer's hand trembled as he searched the dark with the light beam. It struck a large black shape. Sitting patiently in front of them was a dog. The dog. It had the same brown patch across its face and the same glossy, black coat.

It stood for a moment and then silently padded around the next corner.

"Why did it leave?" asked Frankie.

Spencer hesitated for a moment. The dog did the same thing the night before, as if guiding him somehow. "I think it wants us to follow," he said.

He crept forwards and stopped where the dog had sat. He leaned around the corner and cast the beam down the corridor.

"Can you see it?" asked Frankie.

"Yeah. It's sitting at the end, waiting. C'mon, let's move closer," he said, his confidence growing.

As they inched forwards, the dog slipped silently out of sight again. Spencer and Frankie swapped glances and then hurried forward to glimpse it before it darted from view once more.

At every turn, the dog moved faster until they were running through a maze of dark, damp hallways. The floorboards whimpered endlessly. They passed countless doors, peeling walls, and the crumbling ceiling stretched into the murky void. Thick cobwebs brushed Spencer's face, but still, they went on, corridor after corridor, left then right, on and on. Where was it leading them? How were they going to get out?

Spencer halted so unexpectedly that Frankie ran into the back of him. The dog had stopped up ahead and was glaring back at them with its illuminated eyes.

Grasping the torch in his shaky right hand, Spencer pointed it eagerly and waited for its next move. A moment later, the dog turned and slowly vanished around the next corner.

"What's it doing now?" said Frankie, exasperated.

Spencer didn't answer. Together they crept along the hallway until they reached the corner. Spencer stood with his back against the wall, leaned forward and peeked around, but the light beam did not find the dog.

"It's vanished," said Spencer stepping out from the corner. He frantically waved the torch left to right as he peered through the gloom. "It's just a door. There's nothing there except a boring door."

Frankie came and stood behind him. "What do you mean it's vanished?"

"It's gone. It's not there."

"It can't just vanish. Dogs can't open doors."

"Especially locked ones," said Spencer. He was sure he heard Frankie giggle but it was no time for jokes.

"Well, open it," said Frankie.

Spencer hesitated but then stepped forward. He reached for the handle and turned it. The hinges squealed as the door swung open.

He gasped.

A figure of a boy was standing inside the room. But then it distorted and wobbled. It was his own reflection looking back at him. For a brief moment, his heart lifted and he thought he had found Oliver.

"There's something in there, Fran. Look," he said, directing the torch light. He took two cautious steps inside the room, and seeing no one, ventured deeper. It was a small, dark room. Standing in the centre was a black frame as big as a door and inside the frame was what looked like a giant mirror. Where the glass should have been, was a sheet of blue glowing liquid, moving and distorting like the surface of the ocean. Spencer shone the torch at it and shards of light bounced back and danced on the walls and ceiling.

He took a closer look. The frame had smooth rounded edges and curved corners, which gave it a hi-tech appearance. It was an odd looking thing to have inside an old house, he thought. At the top of the frame, in the middle, was a 'T' symbol set inside a circular shaped plaque.

"I wonder what it is." said Frankie stepping around it.

Spencer shook his head in disbelief. It didn't look dangerous. He reached into his pocket, took out a coin, and tossed it at the liquid wall. It vanished.

Frankie's mouth fell open. "Where did it go?" She walked around the frame. "It didn't come out the back."

They exchanged glances.

Spencer fought the urge to reach out and touch the strange liquid wall, but it was too great. He lifted his right hand and plunged it into the watery surface. His hand seemed to melt and swirl like ink in water. He waited for pain, but there was none. Frankie let out a gasp and Spencer quickly pulled his hand back, fearful that he might never see it again.

"Wow!" he breathed, flexing his fingers making sure they still worked.

"Are you crazy?" said Frankie.

"Calm down. Its fine," said Spencer, still gaping at his hand in amazement.

Frankie moved closer and stared at his hand. "What did it feel like?"

"Cold and sort of silky." Spencer's gaze left his hand and settled on the liquid wall. "I reckon we were meant to see this," he said looking at it in bewilderment. "I'm having a look."

Frankie thrust her arm in front of Spencer. "Don't be ridiculous! You can't put your head in there."

"Why not? My hand is fine, look," said Spencer waving it in front of Frankie's face.

"No," she insisted, brushing his hand away. "You're not sticking your head in there. I won't let you."

"What do you think is going to happen?"

Frankie looked at him and then at the wall. "I don't know. I just don't think it's a good idea. What if…well, you know…"

"I drown? Or lose my head?"

"Yeah."

"Look," he said and stuck his hand in the wall again and

pulled it out, repeating it several times. "My hand is fine. C'mon, we're wasting time. You can hold my other hand if it makes you feel better. Then, if you think I'm in trouble, you can pull me back."

Frankie looked at the liquid wall and then back at Spencer. "Okay, but any sign of trouble and you're out of there," she said and gripped his right hand.

Spencer turned to face the silent, rolling wall of liquid. He stepped as close to it as he could without touching it. A moment of doubt crossed his mind, but he dismissed it.

"Are you ready?" asked Spencer, glancing around at Frankie who had become agitated. "Don't worry, it'll be fine," he assured her.

"I'm ready," she said, but the nervousness in her voice didn't sound like she was ready at all.

Spencer closed his eyes, took a deep breath, and moved his face forward. Cold nipped at the tip of his nose, and then his whole face as though ice cubes were melting on his skin. His whole body quivered as he fought the impulse to pull away. He opened his eyes to see a tunnel of swirling mist rush past him. He tumbled uncontrollably through the air, but he could still feel Frankie's grip. As quickly as the spinning began, everything stopped, the mist cleared, and he saw it. But sooner than his brain could digest it, Frankie tugged on his arm and he was yanked backwards. The misty tunnel rolled again and before he knew it, he was back in the dark room with Frankie's shrill voice filling his ears.

"Oh my God! Are you all right?" she shouted, which didn't help Spencer get over the dizzy, sick feeling that had got hold of him. "Your head, it...disappeared! Your body was just standing there and, oh God! Spencer, it was awful!"

Her hand touched his face and he couldn't help jerking away. "Are you alright? That was horrible."

Spencer scrunched his face to ensure it was still intact. He staggered to the wall and propped himself against it while trying to organise his thoughts and regain his bearings.

"Spence, are you okay?" repeated Frankie. "Speak to me."

He met her gaze, but could only manage a nod.

"What did you see?"

Spencer took a deep breath, but the muscles in his jaw were stiff and he found it difficult to speak. "A room – there's a room in there," he mumbled.

"A room…but how?"

"I don't know. That's what I saw. There isn't much light, it was hard to see."

"Did you see the dog?"

"You pulled me back before I got a chance to look around," he said, pushing himself away from the wall. He staggered before turning to face the liquid monolith. "It must be some kind of doorway. The dog led us here, I'm sure of it. I think we need to go through."

"Please tell me you're joking! You have no idea what's in there," snapped Frankie, tilting her head towards the watery frame.

"I didn't see anybody in there. We can't go back through the corridors. So unless we go through there, we're dead."

Those words silenced them both. Spencer was sure the dog led them here deliberately. If that was the case, the stranger would be close by and Spencer could find out what he knew and why he was following him.

Frankie reached out her hand and poked the liquid wall with her finger, before pulling it back quickly and examining it. She looked at Spencer and then back at her finger and took a deep, surrendering breath. "Okay, but once you're in, don't go anywhere without me," she insisted.

"You know I wouldn't do that," said Spencer. He went and stood in front of the frame once again. He composed himself as if he was about to dive into a swimming pool for the first time. "You keep hold of the torch and as soon as I go through, you follow."

Frankie took it and nodded slowly.

Spencer stared at the undulating wall. What if they couldn't get back? Where did the room beyond lead to? He smiled at Frankie to disguise his concerns. He took a last deep breath, closed his eyes, and stepped forward.

CHAPTER FOUR

A Cold Embrace

Spencer gulped the cold air. His movements were laboured and his heart thudded. He opened his eyes and everything around him burst to life. Mist churned chaotically. Air rushed passed him like somebody had opened a door to a storm. His stomach heaved as he was shunted one way, then another, like he was sliding around on the back seat of a speeding car. His arms flailed in search for something to grasp, but there was nothing.

All at once, everything stopped. His surroundings rushed into focus and he stumbled onto a hard smooth floor… alone. The darkness consumed him and he could hear a deep continuous hum like he was in the basement of a large factory. He glanced down and found himself standing in a circle of dim, white light embedded in the floor. There was no sign of the old house, Frankie, or the dog for that matter, just a small, black, circular room a little larger than his bedroom.

Spencer turned slowly. The ceiling was low enough that he could reach up and touch it. The smooth, black walls went all the way round and there wasn't a door or window in sight. Behind him was a frame with a liquid panel that looked identical to the one he had stepped through a few moments ago. As he stood examining the undulating surface, a swirling mass of colour began seeping from the edges of the frame, coiling like coloured paint mixed in water. He stepped back and watched Frankie's screwed up face materialise. That was followed by a foot, a leg, and then her whole body stumbled out until she was standing in front of him, dazed and perplexed.

"Oh wow! That looked so weird," said Spencer.

Frankie wobbled.

Spencer reached out and grabbed her arm.

"Where am I?" she said. "Am I alive?"

"Of course you're alive," replied Spencer. "But I don't know where we are."

"Is the dog here?"

"No."

"I knew it. We shouldn't have gone through that thing. Now what?" she said, rubbing her stomach.

"If we go back," said Spencer nodding at the frame, "we'll end up back in the old house. There must be more to this place," he added as he walked over and placed his hands on the cold wall. Then, as if someone had flicked a switch, the circle of light in the floor went out leaving them in total darkness.

Frankie squeaked in alarm.

"What did you do?" said Spencer, spinning on his heels to face her, but she had been swallowed by the darkness.

"I didn't touch a thing," said Frankie.

Before Spencer had time to move, they were bathed in a dim red light set in the ceiling and a whirring sound started from the liquid wall. Thin metal plates slid from the edges of the frame and covered the liquid panel.

A calm female voice filled the room. "Portdoor is deactivated.

Please stand away from the wall. Portdoor is deactivated. Please stand away from the wall."

Both Frankie and Spencer looked around, but they couldn't determine where the voice was coming from. A heavier mechanical sound surrounded them as the walls began to revolve slowly, while the floor remained still.

Frankie came and stood next to Spencer. "What's happening?" she said.

"I don't know," Spencer replied as he watched a gap in the wall open up. Freezing air swept into the room. The gap grew wider and when it was as wide as a door, the wall stopped revolving. Spencer's jaw dropped at the sight before him.

"What is that?" whispered Frankie, as she grabbed Spencer's arm.

In front of them was a vast room. It was the biggest room Spencer had ever seen. Bigger than the gym at school and bigger than the cathedral he visited in York a couple of summers ago. It was gigantic and reminded Spencer of an airport terminal.

"Please leave the Portdoor chamber," said the female voice.

"Portdoor chamber? What is she talking about?" whispered Frankie.

"I don't know," said Spencer as a plume of breath rolled from his mouth.

"Please leave the Portdoor chamber," repeated the voice.

Shivering, Spencer and Frankie edged cautiously into the cold, gigantic domed room. The curved ceiling must have been eight stories high and white metal girders as thick as tree trunks supported it. The most peculiar thing of all was the entire room was covered in a white frost and for a moment Spencer thought it was raining. He looked up and saw dripping stalactites clinging to the girders.

As they crept slowly into the hall, he noticed more black doors lining the curved wall. They looked like elevator doors in a hotel lobby, but there were too many to count at first glance. He saw that each door had a number and two small lights on the wall above it, one green and the other red.

Children of varying ages came and went from the chambers and dashed off in all directions. Some were adorned in red and grey overalls, while others were dressed in regular clothes, like Spencer and Frankie.

"What is this place?" Frankie said with wonder.

"I don't know that either," said Spencer.

"Look at the kids, Spence. Do you notice something odd?"

Spencer looked at them, but they seemed like normal kids to him. "What about them?"

"There are so many twins."

Frankie was right. They weren't all twins, but more than half were identical pairs.

"I wonder if Oliver is here?" said Frankie.

"I was thinking the same thing," Spencer replied, surveying the gigantic room, now scrutinising each person his eyes settled upon. Then he gripped Frankie's wrist. "Look," he said, nodding towards the back of the room.

"What?"

"It's him. The stranger."

Sure enough, the blond man was standing on the other side of the hall, staring at Spencer and smiling just as he had done outside his school yesterday. But there was no sign of the dog.

"Go and speak to him," said Frankie, nudging Spencer with her shoulder. "Go on, it's what we came here for."

Frankie was right. With a nervous sigh, Spencer turned and started towards him, but then stopped dead as a large, red-cheeked woman wearing a white padded coat and gloves to match marched towards him.

"Come along you two. We don't have all day. Make your way to the greeting desk, please."

Spencer stopped and turned to look at Frankie.

He turned back to the large woman and said, "But…"

The large woman interrupted. "There's no time for questions, hurry along," she demanded, outstretching her arms and scooping them towards the desk. Spencer glanced back across the hall towards the stranger, but he had gone.

As Spencer walked towards the desk, he noticed the uniformed children had strange metallic objects dangling from their belt and peculiar electronic devices of which he had never seen before were moulded to their right forearms.

As they approached the desk, he noticed two white numbers printed on the front of it. A five and an eight with a dash between them, but they were only just visible through the frost.

Behind the desk sat a blonde woman beaming a friendly smile. "Welcome to TIG, the Tezla Institute for the Gifted. Can I have your name please?" she said quickly, as if she had said it a thousand times before.

Spencer was confused. Why was she asking his name? He was sure there must be some kind of mistake.

"Come along, young man. You must have a name, everybody has a name," said the woman. Spencer regarded her warily. She was wearing a navy blue uniform with a large identity badge pinned to her lapel. Printed on it was the 'T' symbol Spencer had seen on the black frame back in the chamber.

Beneath the large 'T', the badge simply read:

MARY STEINBURGH
Registrar Assistant

"Um…what is this place?" asked Spencer, perplexed.

"You'll find out soon enough. All I need is your name, please," insisted Mary.

He looked around at Frankie. She raised her eyebrows and nodded towards Mary.

"Spencer Quinn."

Mary looked at him as if he had just sprouted an extra nose. Spencer noticed the woman sat at the next desk also stopped what she was doing and glanced over.

"Did I say something wrong?"

Mary shook her head. "No," she said. "Put your right hand on the scanner," she added, patting a glass disc just large enough for a hand to rest on it. Spencer hesitated and then placed his hand on the glass panel. A light strip darted along the glass and Spencer quickly jerked his hand away.

Mary smiled. "It's not going to hurt you. It's just scanning your hand for identification. You'll have to do it again please," she said, gesturing towards the scanner.

Frankie twisted her mouth to disguise a smile and looked away.

Spencer placed his hand back on the glass panel and held it

there. This time it scanned successfully.

"All done," said Mary. "Now that didn't hurt did it?" She slowly turned her head towards Frankie while keeping her eyes fixed on Spencer for as long as her head would allow. "And you?" she said, eventually shifting her eyes to Frankie.

"Frankie Rawlinson," she replied politely.

"Frankie…Rawlinson…Rawlinson," repeated Mary as her gaze shifted to the flat, glass screen monitor in front of her. She delicately tapped the glass keyboard with the pads of her fingertips so as not to break her long, purple nails. "Your name doesn't appear to be here. How do you spell your surname?" she asked.

"R – A – W – L – I – N – S – O – N," said Frankie.

"One moment please," said Mary, her fingers dancing lightly across the glass keyboard, barley touching the surface where the letters appeared in luminous blue. Then she shook her head. "No, it's not here. You'll have to wear a visitor's badge." She touched a button on her keyboard and two identity tags, the size of credit cards, were dispensed from a slot next to the scanning machine. "Take those," she said nodding to the cards sitting in the tray. Spencer picked them up and handed one to Frankie.

Frankie's badge simply had 'VISITOR' printed on it while Spencer's had his name, the word 'SEEPER', in bold, capital letters and a photograph of his head and shoulders taken only moments ago. In the centre sat a microchip smaller than his little fingernail.

"Now make your way to the waiting area and someone will be along to see you shortly," said Mary, pointing towards the far side of the hall.

Spencer was convinced there must be some kind of mistake. The blond man had practically invited him. All he wanted to do was talk to him. "But you don't understand…" began Spencer.

Mary interrupted. "Look, please go and wait over there. Someone will be along in a moment and they will explain everything to you," she said and then bellowed, "Next!"

Behind them, a boy, carrying a fat backpack, approached the desk and nudged Spencer to one side. He was about the same age as Spencer, with short, neatly trimmed blond hair and unusually bright blue eyes.

"Name," said Mary, now sounding somewhere between bored and irritated.

"Karl Dud," said the boy in an American accent. He turned to look at Spencer. "Hi," he added and smiled, revealing wire braces around his teeth.

"Hello," replied Spencer.

"So much ice - looks like I missed all the action," said Karl, looking up at the domed ceiling.

"Umm, I guess so," said Spencer, but he had no idea what the boy was talking about.

"First time here, huh?" asked Karl.

"Uh…yes."

Karl looked back at him with a frown as though he was about to ask another question when Mary cut in.

"Look, please go to the waiting area, it's a busy time you know," she said, fanning her hand at Spencer and Frankie.

Spencer's face burned and Karl raised his eyebrows and smiled. He walked away from the desk towards the waiting area. What kind of place is this? And where had the stranger disappeared too?

"Come along, this way," shouted the large women waving her arms like she was guiding a car into a parking space.

Spencer and Frankie walked faster, which is all they seemed to do here. Everybody seemed to be in such a hurry.

The waiting area was a small white room at the edge of the hall. Rows of children sat upon red, moulded, plastic seats, each one fixed to the floor by a single metal pole. Some of the children appeared nervous and fidgety, while others were excited as they watched the uniformed kids emerge from the chambers around the edge of the hall. Spencer noticed one boy near the front perusing a magazine titled:

THE PARANORMAL OBSERVER

On the front of it, in bold black letters was 'Realm Key Moved' and beneath it a picture of what looked like a Rubik's cube, but it was much bigger, silver, and had strange symbols on each of the small squares.

He heard many languages being spoken. Some were speaking French, which he recognised from school, and others were speaking German. He glanced towards the back of the room and noticed many twins sat among them.

"Over there," said Frankie, nodding towards four empty seats in the front row. They walked over and sat down.

Spencer looked around in wonder. What had they walked into? There were more kids than adults but they didn't appear to be in any distress, in fact, quite the opposite. He then noticed Karl shuffling towards them, dragging his backpack along the floor behind him and then he dropped into the seat next to Spencer.

"What's your name?" asked Karl.

"Spencer Quinn. And this is Frankie."

Frankie smiled and nodded.

The moment Spencer said his name the other kids sitting around him began whispering. He couldn't help notice the boy reading the Paranormal Observer started flicking through the pages quickly and then showed his friend a page from it.

"It's you," said Karl disbelievingly.

"What do you mean?" said Spencer stunned. He turned to look at Frankie who was equally puzzled by Karl's remark.

"I read about you and your..." began Karl, but then stopped.

"About my what?"

"Uh...nothing," said Karl and then went silent and began looking around the room.

"What's that he's reading?" said Spencer nodding at the boy with the magazine.

Karl looked at the boy. "It's a news magazine for people like us. You can't get it outside. It's for our eyes only."

"People like us?"

Karl looked stunned. "You'll see. Don't worry about it. You're in safe hands here," he said.

Spencer assumed he must have read an article around the time Oliver was taken. It was in every national paper in the country, but he wasn't sure if it had made international news or even the Paranormal Observer.

"What is this place?" said Spencer.

"It's TIG. Tezla Institute for the Gifted," replied Karl in a loud voice. "It's the best institute there is for people like us."

"You said it again…'people like us'?"

Karl frowned. "Are you kidding me?" he said.

Spencer noticed Karl was getting agitated, but he had to find out what was going on.

"You really don't know anything do you?" said Karl.

Both Frankie and Spencer shook their heads in unison.

"Didn't you get a visit from an inspector?"

Spencer shook his head again. But then he wondered if the blond stranger was an inspector.

Karl looked puzzled.

"A Tezla official should have come to your house. They came to mine and spoke to my parents. He told 'em everything. Who I would be assigned to, what I would be doing, everything. My brother's been coming here for two years," explained Karl.

"Well, they may have not been able to find me. I've moved around a bit. My parents have split up and I live with my mum at my grandma's house."

"Ah, sorry to hear that," said Karl, shifting awkwardly in his seat.

Spencer broke the uncomfortable silence. "So, your mum and dad, they know you're here?"

"Of course! Why wouldn't they?"

Spencer looked out towards the hall. "So what goes on here?"

"I'm in the Shrieker's dorm, look," said Karl, thrusting his ID badge up to Spencer's face. "It's better if someone else explains it all to you. You must be here for a reason and I'm sure you'll find out soon enough."

"What are we waiting for?"

"We're waiting for someone to come and escort us to our dorms. They'll be here soon," explained Karl.

"Dorms?"

"Yeah. Jeez man, you really need to catch up. Most of us live here during coaching sessions. We don't have to, but the nearest Portdoor to my house is hours away so mom and dad thought it best if I stayed here," explained Karl.

Before Spencer could respond, he noticed three people enter the room through a metallic door to his left. A tall woman led them. She had long, wavy black hair and wore a dark suit and rectangular rimmed glasses. A girl with frizzy black hair wearing a long white coat, and who appeared to be around the same age as Spencer stood behind the woman. As they came closer, he noticed her ID badge pinned to her breast pocket:

HAZEL JONES
Seeper Assistant

Spencer could only wonder what that meant. But when Spencer laid eyes on the third person, he nudged Frankie in the ribs. "It's him, look," he whispered.

"Ouch! Who?"

"The stranger," said Spencer as quickly and quietly as he could.

Slowly, the room fell silent, like somebody was turning down the volume until all that could be heard was shuffling and the occasional sniff and whisper.

Karl leaned over and whispered in Spencer's ear, "The woman in front is the Principal. She's French, but she speaks good English. My brother said she's much better than the crazy dude that was here last year. He was German—strict as hell."

All three of them came and stood at the front of the room. The Principal looked directly at Spencer and said, "Bonjour Monsieur. Spencer Quinn?" In a soft, gentle French accent.

The sniffing and shuffling evaporated and everyone settled. There was an air of expectancy.

Spencer stood up slowly. "Yes?" he said.

As soon as he spoke, the shuffling and whispering behind him erupted again. He was half expecting to be dragged away as if he was some sort of criminal, although he couldn't imagine what he had done wrong.

"Could you please follow me?" the Principal said.

Spencer didn't answer immediately. "Are you sure it's me you want? What have I done?"

The Principal smiled. "Yes, I'm sure it's you we want. You have done nothing wrong. If you follow us into the next room, I will explain everything to you and you may re-join your friends shortly," she replied.

Spencer looked down at Frankie. He didn't want to leave her with strangers. So he asked, "Can my friend come too?"

The Principal shook her head. "S'il vous plait, it will only take a moment or two and then you can return here. There is nothing to worry about, I can assure you."

He thought for a moment and stepped towards them. If they knew anything about Oliver, he had to find out what it was. He knew Frankie could take care of herself, and he didn't think either of them was in danger.

The Principal turned and moved towards the metal door. Hazel also smiled and gestured for him to go before her. Spencer threw a fleeting look over his shoulder at Frankie. Her lips were scrunched and she was frowning. Karl had his thumb raised and his expression was excited. Then he mouthed the words, 'I'll take care of her', but Spencer thought it would most likely be the other way around.

He went through the door into a dark corridor and turned left into a small, white room. It was completely bare except for two silver chairs, one on either side of a small metal table.

The Principal walked towards the chair nearest the door. "Please, take a seat."

Spencer kept them all in his field of view as he edged around the table and sat. The Principal sat opposite him, rested her arms on the table and clasped her hands together. Hazel and the blond man stood by the door and observed in silence.

Spencer wondered why the man hadn't said anything to him. His legs shook nervously, just like they did when Oliver disappeared and the police questioned him over and over again.

"Let me do the introductions before I begin," said the Principal. "My name is Angeline Pastuer, I am the Principal of this fine Institute and these are my colleagues. Drake, head of Seepers, and Hazel, Drake's assistant."

Spencer looked at them and forced a smile, but remained silent. Hazel smiled back and nodded, but Drake didn't flinch. He remained stone-faced and not at all amicable.

Spencer opened his mouth to speak, but the Principal raised her hand and silenced him.

"I imagine you have many questions to ask, but I will explain everything first," she began, pulling her chair closer to the table.

"You are in Tezla, an academy for very special and gifted people. Every cadet at the academy has a special ability. It is the job of Tezla to help them nurture and control that gift."

"But what has that got to do with me?" said Spencer.

The principal paused, looked at Spencer thoughtfully and then continued. "Okay, let me explain in a different way. We know you, Spencer. And we know what happened to your brother."

Spencer leapt to his feet and knocked his chair backwards, sending it clattering to the floor. "How do you know me? How do you know about Oliver? What's going on here?"

The principal remained seated and calm. "Please sit down, Spencer," she said, gently waving her hand in the air as if she was patting an invisible animal in front of her.

"No. You tell me right now or…or…" said Spencer, his voice shaking.

"Or what?"

There was an awkward pause and silence.

Was that a threat, he wondered? He didn't think so, they were being too friendly. In fact, the principal's voice was calming and reassuring.

"Please, sit down and I will continue. I realise this must be a great shock to you," she said.

Spencer hesitated. He had overreacted. His breathing shuddered as he took a deep breath, picked up the chair, and sat back down.

"We know all about you because it's Tezla's policy to detect and record every, let's say, unusual event around the world and store them in our ethereal library. But that's only a fraction of what we do here. What's more important right now is this. You are gifted, Spencer. We have been watching you for a long time. The blackouts you are experiencing, they're not an illness. Like all cadets here, you have telekinetic powers that have incredible potential and we can help you grow and use them for good things."

Angeline paused. She looked at Spencer and smiled, as though she was gauging his reaction to this news. Spencer was dumbfounded and totally speechless.

"You have broken the rules. Of course you were unaware that you were doing so, but you have been exposing your power."

"Exposing?" said Spencer.

"Yes. Your power has been leaking out. When you get angry or excited, you have a power surge. You do not control it, or channel it. You simply blow a fuse – poof," said Angeline and gestured a cloud of smoke with both hands.

"You, Spencer, are an identical twin and that makes you a Seeper. Most of the cadets here are Retrievers and do not possess the power an identical twin can conjure."

Spencer began listening more intently. The enormity of the situation was difficult to grasp, but some things were starting to make sense to him now. Like how he put Arnold in a tree and the other weird things that happened around him when he was angry or stressed.

Angeline continued. "As I explained, over recent weeks, Drake has been trying to contact you. We needed to draw you in before anything fatal happened to you."

As Spencer listened, his mind quivered like an insect was crawling over his brain and he found it difficult to concentrate. It was the same feeling he had outside the school when he saw Drake.

"Normally we educate the parents and make them aware of their child's ability and potential. But this can, on occasion, be traumatic for the parents and take some convincing. Sometimes the parents already know and it's simple. In your case, however, things are very different. Our initial due diligence indicates that your mother is not emotionally strong enough to handle this information. Secondly, under normal conditions, when a twin is severed from a sibling, the remaining twin usually emancipates all power. It leaks out and is lost quite quickly, but in your case this has not happened. Even though Oliver is no longer with you, you still retain your power."

Angeline's voice started to sound distant. Tiredness gripped him and his eyelids drooped. He noticed Drake was looking at him through narrowed eyes, but he quickly looked away, as if he had been caught staring.

"Are you feeling okay, Spencer?" asked Angeline.

"Yes, I'm fine," he replied, as the tiredness faded and his alertness returned.

"Before I go on, is there anything you would like to ask me?" she said, leaning back in her chair.

The one question that had burned his lips for the past year shot out of his mouth like a caged animal being released. "Where is Oliver?"

The principal glanced around at Drake and Hazel. "We can't be certain, but we believe we know who took him," she said.

The words hit him hard. His chest shuddered as he took a deep breath and suddenly, there was a flicker of hope, the finest of threads to latch on to, something he hadn't felt for a year.

He sat up rigid and placed both hands on the table. "What do you mean you believe you know who took him? Is he alive?" The words tumbled out as if he couldn't say them quickly enough.

Angeline shook her head. "We know very little. The tyrant that took him is called Arrawn. He has been kidnapping twins from all over the world. We cannot be sure, but we believe he is harvesting them and extracting their power. For what reason, we do not know. We know you were with Oliver the night he was taken, but we do not know why Arrawn left you behind. We hoped you could help us understand that." Angeline fell silent and stared at Spencer expectantly.

The impact of the information was still reeling inside his head. Could Oliver still be alive after all this time? Then the vivid images of that fateful night began to unfurl in Spencer's mind like it had happened only yesterday.

"I remember lying in my bed, half asleep. My eyes were closed. I had my back to Oliver," began Spencer. A lump formed in his throat and his voice cracked as he spoke. "I wanted to look. I really did. Oliver was calling my name over and over, but at first I thought he was kidding. He always joked around. Only after he started screaming and calling for Dad did I realise something was really wrong."

He swallowed hard and blinked back the tears that began stinging his eyes.

"Dad was banging on the door, screaming for someone to

let him in. Then I opened my eyes and turned to face Oliver. The light blinded me and all I could see were Oli's huge eyes and he was really scared. He was crying and his arms were reaching out. I jumped out of bed and tried to grab his hands, but I couldn't reach 'em. I was too late. I tried, I really did. Then he was gone. He just disappeared through a hole in the air. It was my fault. I should've listened sooner. Then it wouldn't have happened."

Spencer cried. He tried to control it, but he couldn't stop himself. It was the first time he had shown real emotion in front of another person. It just came out of him like he had been bottling it up and the cork had popped.

Hazel turned away and looked at Drake.

Angeline reached across the table and put her hand on Spencer's shoulder. "It's okay. It wasn't your fault, Spencer. Listen, we can come back to this later if that's what you would like."

"No," said Spencer, quickly wiping the tears from his cheeks with his sleeve. "Where is Arrawn and why is he doing this?" he asked quickly before she decided to end the conversation. He wanted to know everything.

Angeline paused briefly before answering. "Like I said we don't know why. But he resides deep inside a realm called Asgard. We know little about it. We are exploring, but it takes time."

"Realm? What's that?"

"That is too big a question for me to explain here. If you join us, Drake will explain realms to you."

Spencer looked at her with unease. He couldn't understand what was happening to him. One minute he was at home eating breakfast in his kitchen, now he was listening to a French women talk about realms and telekinetic power. He wondered what was expected of him. He was only twelve years old.

"There is one thing we are sure of Spencer. We must rid Asgard of this tyrant. He has turned it into an evil place, full of ill will and death. Entire races have been destroyed and the remaining inhabitants live in fear and hide in the shadows of the mountains."

"What do you want from me?" said Spencer.

"We would like you to join us, Spencer. We can help you. You still retain your power after Oliver has gone. This, we believe, is something special and may help us conquer Arrawn. Of course, you will not be alone. You will be amongst your own kind, Seepers. But the choice is yours. However, if you decide not to join us, it could prove fatal for you."

"Fatal?"

"Oui. The power will intensify and unless you gain control, it will eventually overwhelm you and may even kill you. There is another option. We can do a small procedure that will rid you of that power, if that is what you want."

Spencer took a deep, shuddering breath and slumped back in his chair. Was she just saying that to get him to join Tezla? He knew the 'power seepage' as she called it, was getting worse. Each time it happened he felt weaker and sicker, so that bit was true.

Angeline interrupted his thoughts. "You cannot change what you are Spencer, only what you can do. Greater things, darker forces are at work here. Join us and learn how to become a Seeper and we will conquer this together." Angeline paused, leant across the table and then said, in a gentle, whispering voice.

"But you must do what you feel is right in your heart," and sat back in her chair.

Spencer looked at all three of them in turn. They stared back at him as if expecting an answer there and then.

"You don't have to decide now. I will leave you with those thoughts, Spencer. I urge you to stay with us for the day and attend the orientation speech and the tour. You will learn much more about us and then you can make an informed decision. I will let Hazel guide you back to your friends and hopefully, I will see you again soon. Take care, Spencer," she said and stood up, turned, and walked out of the room, followed by Drake.

"Follow me please," said Hazel in a shy, gentle voice.

Spencer took very little notice of her and didn't speak another word, but simply ambled along behind her with new questions spinning through his mind. What was the procedure she mentioned? Could Oliver still be alive? He knew one thing for sure. He was going to find out.

CHAPTER FIVE

Orientation

Spencer spun to look at Hazel. "Where's Frankie? What have you done with her? I promised her I wouldn't leave her alone. She'll be worried where I am."

Hazel's whole body jolted at Spencer's outburst. "Please, calm down. If you follow me, I'll take you to her," she said in a light, but confident voice.

Could he trust her? What if she was lying? Spencer couldn't be sure.

She turned and led Spencer through the metallic door into the short, dark corridor. Spencer had taken little notice of it the first time he was here. But now he saw that it was dark, except for a white light that shone through a small window at the opposite end. Hazel closed the door. A mechanical click told Spencer the door had locked and a dim red light illuminated the corridor.

"Don't be alarmed by the locked door," she said. "It's only a security measure."

Security against what, Spencer wondered. He was now trapped and even if he wanted to get out he couldn't. He stood in the dark corridor alone and began to question whether he had made a big mistake.

Hazel strode on. "Please, follow me," she instructed.

They walked to the far end and stopped in front of another door. Hazel pushed it open allowing white light to flood in. She held the door open and waited for Spencer to step through into a long arched glass corridor. It reminded him of being at Sea World where the tunnel went under the water, except there was no water or fish here. He could see outside. The corridor appeared to be at some height and spanned a void to a vast metal and glass tubular construction. He glanced up and down, but the top and bottom of the building was cloaked in a white mist, as if the building sat in the clouds.

Spencer peered through the glass as he walked. He saw more corridors criss-crossing the void, some above and some below him. Glass elevators slid silently up and down the walls, stopping periodically at different levels. He had never seen anything like it.

At the end of the corridor they turned left. Spencer noticed a white door on his right with a sign above it that read:

SHRIEKERS

Then he remembered it was printed on Karl's ID badge. Spencer had no idea what it meant, but something told him he was going to find out soon enough.

He trailed behind Hazel, taking in the facility, feeling lost and alone. Then, as he gazed through the glass wall at the stirring mist, something large and solid crashed into him, sending him tumbling to the floor. He looked up and saw a boy of some bulk glaring down at him.

"Hey, watch where you're going you idiot," yelled the boy.

Two other boys stood behind him and laughed. Spencer sensed familiarity. Was this how his life was meant to be? Always attracting the worst of human kind like some kind of thug magnet.

Slowly, a small crowd began to gather. They looked down at him, pointed and scuttled off giggling.

"I'm sorry," said Spencer, picking himself up off the floor, but the boy that had knocked him over was already walking away. It seemed wherever he went, he was picked on. Was he going to be bullied here too?

Hazel came scurrying to his aid. "Are you alright?" she said with an air of concern.

"Yes, I'm fine," replied Spencer looking back along the corridor. "Who was that?"

"Colin Dud. He's the academy ecto champion."

Spencer's mind omitted the last part of what Hazel had said and honed in on the surname 'Dud'. "Karl's brother?" he said enquiringly.

"Yeah, that's right," replied Hazel. "He'll probably be another ecto champion too if he's anything like his brother."

Spencer gave Hazel a quizzical look. "Ecto what?"

"Every year the academy awards a prize to the cadet who deposits the greatest amount of ectoplasm in one year," said Hazel. "Colin has won it for the last two years in a row."

Spencer was about to ask what ectoplasm was when a bing-bong sound echoed down the corridor. The same synthetic voice Spencer heard in the Portdoor chamber spoke again.

"Please move along," she said. There was a pause and then

she spoke again. "Keep to the left at all times."

The crowd had already dispersed and Spencer continued along the corridor next to Hazel. "What happens in there?" he asked, nodding at another door to his right with a sign above that read:

ECTOLOGY

"It's the ectoplasm research and teaching laboratory," said Hazel. "If you attend, you'll soon learn what lies behind these doors," she added.

They soon approached another door:

LECTURE THEATRE

A woman with a harsh face that looked as though a frown had been stamped on it held the door open. Hazel rushed towards her. "Thank you, Elissa," she said, relieving the woman of door duty. Elissa raised an eyebrow, harrumphed, and then turned abruptly and walked into the theatre.

"Frankie is in here. Please go in and find her. I'll meet you later," said Hazel, stepping to one side to let people past while she held the door.

Spencer stepped inside. It was a large room, but nowhere near as large as the entrance hall. Blue seats escalated to the curved back wall. Two large flat screens hung on a wall facing numerous seats. One of the screens read:

WELCOME TO T.I.G.
TEZLA INSTITUTE FOR THE GIFTED

Spencer recognised Angeline standing on the small half-circle stage in front of a wooden pedestal. She was thoughtfully staring at a glass sheet in front of her.

Several other official looking men and women sat on red chairs along the wall beneath the screens, facing the cadets. An old man with grey, wild hair that stuck out in all directions sat on the end seat closest to the door. He wore a long white coat, half moon spectacles, and he had his head buried in a large thick book that looked as though it was far too heavy for him. Next to the old man was the woman Hazel referred to as Elissa. She sat upright and rigid with her arms folded and her legs crossed. She was tapping her foot like she was waiting impatiently for something to happen.

Spencer glanced around the room and spotted Frankie waving her arms. He was relieved to see her. She was near the back and was pointing to an empty seat next to her. Spencer scrambled up the shallow steps and dropped into the seat next to Frankie.

"You promised me you wouldn't leave me alone, Spencer Quinn. I was really worried," she scowled.

"Sorry, Fran, I had to find out what was going on."

"Are you crazy? You don't know these people, anything could have happened."

Spencer told Frankie all about what Angeline had said to him. He told her all about Arrawn and he also told her about Oliver. She seemed to calm down after that.

"Is he still alive?"

Spencer shrugged. "They say they don't know."

"Looks like they've been planning on getting you in here for a while," said Frankie. "What are you going to do?"

"I want to get a good look at this place," he replied. "I want to find out more about Arrawn and where Oliver is being held."

He wished he could tell Frankie about his potentially fatal outcome if he didn't attend Tezla, but he remembered her reaction when he told her that he had used his power on Arnold. She insisted that he should tell someone and get some help. He was sure that she would insist that he tell someone about his potential demise, too, and decided to keep it to himself.

"How are we going to get out of here?" whispered Frankie.

Spencer hadn't thought about that. In fact, he had quite forgotten about his life on the outside. They had been gone a few hours and he wondered if his mother might begin to worry about him, but he doubted that. Her head was usually full of Oliver and she probably wouldn't notice he was gone until it was getting late.

"I don't know," he replied. But secretly, he was becoming more curious about this place and he was in no hurry to go home.

The constant chattering that filled the room slowly faded to silence. Angeline had her hand in the air and she was smiling at the expectant faces staring back at her.

"Bonjour," she said in a composed voice. "I am Principal Angeline Pastuer. I would like your attention momentarily while I give out some announcements." She looked down at the glass screen in front of her and paused, then looked up, smiled, and continued. "Mr. Twitch, our new head of technologies, has informed me that the basement and the ancient Portdoor are out of bounds for reasons I can not disclose here."

The frizzy haired old man lifted his head, muttered something under his breath, then buried his head back into his book and continued reading.

"It appears we have some interesting new recruits amongst us," her eyes settling on Spencer. He shifted uneasily.

"We have trained many of the finest Seepers and Retrievers here at Tezla, and this season will be no exception. The mature cadets are aware of the troubles we face. It's going to be a testing year for us all. Tezla will be pushed to its very limits. I am of course referring to the mounting threat in Asgard. Arrawn grows stronger with each passing day. The utmost vigilance is required. We must stand firm," she banged her fist on the pedestal, "and collectively, we must do our utmost to prevail."

The hair on Spencer's neck stood on end. There was a long pause. Everybody was motionless and quiet, in awe at Angeline's words.

"We have recruited the finest staff to assist and train you in Retriever and Seeper traditions. There have been some advances in various departments, as Mr. Twitch will display in the weeks to come. Of course, Miss Nerts is our newest recruit."

Elissa nodded very slowly, almost bowing.

"She will be ensuring our Ectology department is up to date with current ectoplasm advances. And of course, let's not forget Drake, head of Seepers. As most of you know, he has been with us for many years and due to advances in Portdoor exploration, he will be guiding some of you to new, unexplored realms."

"What's she talking about?" whispered Frankie.

Spencer didn't respond. He was more interested in watching Drake, who appeared not to be listening to Angeline at all, but was staring acutely at a small device in the palm of his hand.

Angeline continued. "So, let me welcome all new cadets to the academy, and, as always, I encourage all mature cadets to support them. Finally, we have time for a few questions."

Several hands shot in the air.

"Colin," said Angeline pointing at a boy near the front.

"Is there an ecto-prize up for grabs this year, Miss?" asked the boy.

"Oui, of that I am certain. It has always been a tradition since Professor Tezla opened the academy. See Mr. Fingus for more information. He keeps track of all ectoplasm deposits and of course, you can track all deposits on the electronic board in the entrance hall."

Mr. Fingus stood and nodded feebly in acknowledgment. He was small and wiry with thinning hair and he hunched over like an old man, but Spencer didn't think his face looked old at all.

A small whooping noise came from the boy that asked the question. It was Karl's brother.

"Going for a new record are we Colin?" asked Angeline, light-heartedly.

"Yes, Miss, I'll do my best."

"Good to hear it boy. Now then, are there any more questions?"

More hands shot up.

"You," said Angeline pointing to a boy halfway up the room to Spencer's right.

"Can you tell us anything about the new shape-shifter programme?"

"Oui. Adding to the many categories of ghouls we already study, the ghoul research department has finished researching shape-shifters for the time being. There will be a new schedule beginning in a couple of weeks. It will extend the day a little, but we will have additional breaks to compensate." She glanced around the room. "Next."

"Here, Miss," said a boy waving his arm enthusiastically. Spencer recognised Karl. The boy he met in the waiting room earlier and brother of the thug that knocked him over. "When do we get to see the ghouls, Miss?" he asked.

"You'll be given a guided tour right after this session," replied Angeline, dismissing the question as if it wasn't very important.

Frankie leaned closer to Spencer and whispered, "Why do they keep talking about ghouls?"

"I don't know. Angeline never mentioned anything about ghouls to me."

As Angeline finished speaking, the door to the theatre burst open. Everybody's head turned to see who it was. A short, pot bellied, bald man walked in. He was wearing a silver body suit that looked like silk and revealed every dip and bulge. Three others, clearly much younger than the man also wearing silver body suits, followed him. They strode over and stood next to the stage.

"What's with the fashion statement?" Frankie whispered.

Spencer laughed through his nose, desperately trying not to make a sound.

"It appears we have run out of time," said Angeline. "Would any of the staff like to say a word before we finish?" She turned to look at the occupied row of chairs behind her, but none of them shifted.

"Okay, finally, I would like to thank you all for your time and patience, and I hope you have a productive time at the Academy this season. Carefully and quietly, could all mature cadets leave the theatre now? All new cadets remain seated and I will hand you over to Albert and his assistants. Merci."

The teachers all stood up and followed her out through the door, leaving Albert and his assistants standing alone on the stage.

CHAPTER SIX

The Shape-Shifter

Chatter and excitement erupted from the cadets as the last staff member left the theatre. They were followed by the bulk of cadets that filled the room and they seemed to be all mature cadets. Spencer noticed a small group of boys taunting Albert as they jostled past him, patting their heads and rubbing their stomachs, pointing and laughing at him, but Albert completely ignored them. When the bustle settled, there were around thirty newly recruited cadets remaining.

"Quiet please," shouted Albert, but he had a small weak voice, which held very little authority and everybody took his or her own time to settle. When silence finally arrived, Albert strolled up to the lectern and began to speak.

"My name is Albert Sternpike and it's my job to supervise the holding pens here at Tezla," he said.

Spencer thought Albert looked a little nervous as he spoke. It was clear he wasn't used to speaking to crowds, but he sensed Albert was a kind person and was tolerant of the cadets joking around.

"In a moment, we'll be giving you a guided tour of the academy, but before we do that, I need to split you into four groups. When I say so, I want group one to stand over there with Joseline," he said, pointing to one of his assistants. She was a short girl with long blonde hair tied back in a ponytail. "Group two with Marcus." He was a tall lanky boy with short brown hair. "Group three with Andrew." A short, plump boy who looked no older than the cadets themselves. "And group four is with me," he said finally.

He pointed at each cadet in turn and said a number between one and four. Frankie was assigned to group one. When he pointed at Spencer, he said four. Spencer wondered how Frankie would react, considering what happened the last time they were split up. To his surprise, she seemed to accept it quite well.

"I'll see you at the end of the tour," said Frankie. She spun on her heels and went and stood with her group. Joseline addressed them. "Please follow me. Stay with the group at all times, do not wander off," she said firmly. She walked to the door and held it open to allow her group to file out. Spencer noticed Frankie had paired up with another girl and before she stepped out, she looked fleetingly over her shoulder to give Spencer a smile.

Andrew's group left next, quickly followed by Marcus's.

Albert began waving his arms in a scooping motion. "Gather around and listen. You heard Joseline tell the others. Do not wander off. Make a friend and make sure you can see that person at all times."

Spencer inspected the eight remaining cadets and they all seemed paired, except one. Karl Dud's face lit up the second he spotted Spencer.

"Hey, man," said Karl. "Isn't it awesome? We're in the same group."

"Yeah," said Spencer trying to sound enthusiastic, but he found it difficult to keep up with Karl who moved and spoke a hundred times faster than everyone else. Spencer felt exhausted just thinking about it.

"So what did the principal have to say?" Karl stared at Spencer with his eyebrows half way up his forehead and waited for a response.

"Not much really," Spencer replied, not wanting to go into the details of what Angeline had told him. He wasn't even sure if he was allowed to talk about it. "You're Colin's brother, right?" he asked, changing the subject quickly.

"Yeah, but keep your voice down. I try not to tell too many people," he said quietly. "Since he's been ecto champion he thinks he owns the joint. He's such a jerk."

Albert went and stood in front of the door. "Please follow me closely," he said, waving over his shoulder as he led the cadets out of the theatre and along the corridor. Spencer and Karl hurried along at the back of the group.

"I bumped into Colin earlier," said Spencer, "quite literally."

"I bet he had his buddies with him?"

"Yeah, he did. He knocked me to the floor, right there." Spencer nodded to the spot where he had fallen.

"Yep. That sounds like Colin."

"If he's like that, why do they let him in here?" asked Spencer.

"Because he's good. When my brother was young, Mom knew he was different. He kept doing stuff, you know, knocking stuff over without touching it. When he started moving furniture around and we found the car in the neighbour's pond, it really freaked Mom and Dad out, but it was pretty impressive stuff. Then Tezla turned up," explained Karl.

"That's sort of what happened to me," said Spencer, relieved that he wasn't simply lured in and that there were others like him.

"Yeah, but you're a twin, right?"

"Well, yeah."

"Twins are different. They have more powers and can usually do more than one thing. They're sort of special. And if your family has a history of twins, you could be really special."

Spencer shook his head. "My father wasn't, but my grandfather was a twin. I don't think there's anymore down the line."

"They reckon if twins go all the way back to the start of time, they're most likely linked to the powerful ancients," Karl said.

"Have they found any twins like that?"

"No, I don't think so, but the academy is not that old. A lot of powers are dormant and the kids don't even know they've got 'em."

"So what about you? How'd they find out you were special?"

"Well, when Mom found out about Colin she kept an eye on me and she could just tell," said Karl, "but I'm not as good as him, of course!" he said, rolling his eyes.

"Come on you two, keep up!" hollered Albert from the front.

"So what can you do?"

Karl smiled mischievously. "Do you want to see?" he said, enthusiastically.

Spencer hesitated, a little unsure of what to expect. "Uh. Yeah," he finally answered.

Karl stopped walking. "Here goes…" he said. "Now you see me…"

He shut his eyes. From his head down to his toes, his body split apart into a million tiny particles and then vanished within a blink of an eye.

Spencer stepped back. "Karl?" he gasped, reaching out his hand to feel the space where Karl had been standing a moment ago.

"I'm here."

Karl tapped him on the shoulder.

Spencer spun on his heels. "Wow, how did you do that?"

"It's called popping," laughed Karl. "I can't go very far, but it's all I'm good at. I'm hoping Tezla will teach me to control it and use it in different ways."

"That's pretty impressive. Does it hurt?" Spencer asked, still shocked at what he had witnessed.

"Nah," laughed Karl.

Albert shouted again. "You two, please keep up. We don't have all day."

They both started walking again.

"So what's Drake like?" asked Karl. "My brother says he's creepy. A major weirdo and keeps to himself most of the time. Did you see him in the theatre? Something's not right."

"What do you mean?"

"He never spoke to anyone. He wasn't even listening to the principal and then he rushed out at the end," Karl explained. "What do you think made him rush out like that?"

Spencer shrugged. "I only met him briefly. The principal did all the talking. Drake didn't say a word, he just stared at me."

"He was probably tapping you."

"Tapping me? What's that?"

"It's the ability to mind read. Some of the guys here can do it, but not everyone. I bet Drake can do it," Karl said in a serious tone. "Sometimes, if they're really good at it, they can change your thoughts, move them around or tear them out like pages from a book. I doubt his powers are that strong though. It's a rare ability. If you show you have tapping potential, you get to focus on it in your second season."

"Can people really read minds?" Spencer asked. He had only seen that sort of thing in movies. He never thought people could really do it. Then he remembered the feeling he had when Angeline was talking to him and when he was standing outside school and Oliver popped into his head. Maybe Drake was tapping him then. Spencer quivered at the thought.

"Of course. Jeez, man, you've got a lot to learn," said Karl. "You'd better watch Drake. He's always doing experiments and stuff. Cadets have been injured in the field. He sends them into situations before knowing what's out there."

"That can't be true," said Spencer, alarmed.

"That's what I heard from Colin."

They walked a little further in silence before Spencer asked the next question.

"What does Drake actually do here?"

"He looks after Seepers, your kind."

Angeline had called him a Seeper and he had it printed on his badge, but he still wasn't sure what a Seeper was.

"So…what's a Seeper, exactly?" said Spencer.

Spencer heard Karl sigh as if he was the dumbest person on the planet.

"Basically a Seeper can travel out of this realm into others. That's different worlds to you and me, and they—uh, you—have cool powers too. Retrievers, that's me, can only stay in this realm and have dumb boring powers. If we go outside of this realm, we'll shrivel and die. Pretty lame if you ask me. It's something to do with the intensity of the power inside you. The stronger the power, the more protection you have from the effects of travelling through the veils."

"What are the veils?"

"The veils are the spaces between realms. Travelling through them can be pretty tough on your body."

Spencer was dumbstruck. Did these things really exist? "By the way, your power isn't dumb or boring. I think it's pretty cool," he said.

Karl smiled. "Thanks, man."

Albert had led them back into the huge lobby and stopped in front of a Portdoor entrance. Unlike the other Portdoors, it had no lights or numbers.

"We've already seen these, sir," said a Chinese girl standing next to her twin sister.

Albert turned and raised his eyebrows. "Not this Portdoor," he replied as he reached out and placed his finger in a hole in the wall. As the door slid open, Spencer and Karl shuffled to the front of the group. Spencer stared in astonishment through red, horizontal light beams that shielded the doorway. "What is that?" he whispered.

"It's an ancient Portdoor," replied Karl, equally in awe.

In front of Spencer was a room, a little smaller than his bedroom back home. Several spotlights shone down on a gigantic, oval stone frame raised on a plinth, bathing it in eerie blue light. The frame was much taller than Spencer and the top of it stopped inches from the chamber ceiling. Its width stretched from wall to wall. Spencer imagined several people could easily step through it at once. Unfamiliar symbols that reminded Spencer of Chinese writing were etched in the stone all around the face of the frame. The whole thing looked out of place and seeing it cast an ominous silence among the group.

"This is where it all began—the original ancient Portdoor," said Albert, with a sense of pride in his voice. He pointed at the red light beams across the doorway. "The barrier is here because it's currently off limits. If you touch the beam, you'll get a nasty shock, so please stand back." Albert gestured with his arms and then continued. "This is the Portdoor Dr. Tezla first discovered and he built the academy around it."

Spencer saw smooth, worn steps just beyond the barrier leading up to the main frame. A knee height pedestal with a square hole in the top that looked as though it should contain a square object stood beside the steps.

"The device is currently inactive, but when it was first discovered, Professor Tezla used it to travel to various realms, including Asgard."

Spencer stared at the Portdoor in wonder. Could Oliver truly be through there? If they knew he was there and this led them to him, why didn't they just go and get him out?

"Isn't that where Arrawn is?" Spencer accidentally blurted

out.

"Yes, very good. What's your name, son?" said Albert.

"Spencer, sir. Spencer Quinn."

Albert eyed him curiously. "Ah, yes. Well, very good, Spencer. At least somebody has been listening," he said as he placed his finger back in the hole. The door closed. "Now we're going to make our way into the pens," he said. "Please follow me."

"Come on," said Karl. "This is the good bit."

Spencer turned and followed.

Albert led them out of the lobby and back into the corridor. Up ahead, the group had stopped in front of a large door. There was a sign above it that read:

HOLDING PENS
Personnel Only

Spencer stood on tiptoe and peered over a shoulder to see what Albert was doing. He had his forefinger in another hole that was circled with a red flashing light. Then the ring pulsed green.

"Ah, here we go," said Albert. The door slid open, revealing a small, brightly lit room beyond. Albert stepped aside and waved the group forwards before following them in and closing the door behind him. As the door closed, another one opened on the opposite side of the cramped room. Another square, dim room came into view as the door slid out of sight. Shiny metal lockers lined the walls. In the middle of the floor were long, silver benches with moulded seats to accommodate bottoms perfectly.

The room was lit by a thin, blue, florescent strip circling the top of the wall.

Spencer could hear a deep guttural hum coming from beyond the walls, like they were inside the belly of a giant machine.

"Please form a line at the hatch and receive your uniform. These will protect you should you come into contact with any ectoplasm residue," said Albert.

"Ectoplasm residue? What's that?" Spencer asked Karl while shuffling along behind him.

"Haven't you read your Seeper induction manual?" Karl asked. Then a sudden realisation draped across his face. "Oh, I forgot. You didn't get one did you? That means you didn't get the book, 'Ectoplasm Sources and Uses' either."

Spencer shook his head.

"Okay, no problem," Karl said. "We'll pick them up in the ethereal library."

The line shortened quickly. The hatch was a circular hole in the wall. The lady sitting on the other side of the hole wore big glasses with thick lenses that magnified her eyes, making them look as big as golf balls. She scanned Spencer's ID badge, and then handed him a pair of neatly folded silver overalls, just like the pair Albert was now wearing.

"Drop them in the bin at the end of the tour," said the woman, pushing the words out of her mouth as they scraped the back of her throat.

The overalls were as soft and flexible as silk, but he was sure it was some other material he had never seen before. They had the Tezla 'T' badge printed on the left breast pocket. Spencer climbed in, pulling the particularly fine zipper up to his neck. They were a perfect fit and so light that he hardly noticed he was wearing them.

"When you have your uniforms on, please come and stand behind the white line," shouted Albert stepping up to a gigantic metal door with a red light above it.

A sign on the door read:

PERSONNEL ONLY
Proceed with extreme caution

"Once we go beyond this door, you must stay behind the railings at all times and do not bang on the glass enclosures."

Karl nudged Spencer. "This is going to be so cool," he said.

"What's in there?" Spencer asked.

"Ghouls. Lots of them."

"I don't get it. Why do they have ghouls here?"

"Listen, man. It's complicated. I'm sure Albert will explain as we go along," Karl said, pulling up his zip.

When everybody was behind the white line, Albert inserted his forefinger into another hole in the door. A moment later, the door let out a hiss and a click and the light above it turned green. It sank back into the room beyond and gradually slid to the right.

"Some of the ghouls are shy," said Albert. "But they can also be very dangerous, so you must listen carefully and do as I say at all times."

The group's nerves silenced them, like they were about to go into an exam. Spencer felt uneasy. What were they going to look like? Why were they here? He looked over at Karl, who seemed to be jiggling involuntary.

Albert let the students step past him. Gasps and whispers rippled through the group. Everybody shuffled along and scrambled to get a look, including Spencer.

They entered a long, narrow room. The large door hissed as it closed behind them. Spencer stopped walking to look around in awe and astonishment.

A menacing aura filled the room. It was the same feeling when walking home in the dark, sensing something may be lurking nearby, waiting to pounce.

Spencer looked down with apprehension. He was standing on a perforated metal walkway and he could see another floor below. He gripped the handrail and looked up. Steel tubes the size of tree trunks and red, green, and blue wires as thick as fingers trailed across the ceiling. Vast glass chambers elevated along both sides of the walkway glowed a luminous green.

Albert weaved through the group and stood next to the first chamber on the left which boasted a substantial metal frame supporting thick glass walls. A green mist tumbled and churned inside.

Albert gestured the group. "Can everyone please move closer and stand between the two red lines," he said and waited for everyone to settle before he began.

"When Dr. Tezla discovered the first ancient Portdoor and ventured into the realms, he quickly discovered that the populous of these realms were a conduit for a substantial reservoir of power. It's an energy source so immense that we're still struggling to understand where it comes from. But one thing we do know for sure, the power inside each of you has the same composition, and therefore, potentially the same origin.

"However, being comparatively dumb and void of this energy, most humans are oblivious to the existence of other realms and the forms that exist within them. They just don't see or feel it, and therefore don't believe it. Except people like you, of course, with heightened senses and abilities," Albert looked at the group and smiled.

"We capture and hold many ghouls from various realms for study. We also provide a service to the UN and in return we get a portion of funding. The veils between realms are getting weak, full of holes, and ghouls often leak into our realm so we capture them and bring them back here. It can be a messy job, but somebody's got to do it. The main reason we keep them here is to train Seepers and Retrievers in the defence against ghoul attacks. Seepers go into realms and will encounter all sorts of nasty specimens." Albert paused and turned to face the chamber.

"The glass chamber you see here is an example of a holding pen or an enclosure, much like you might see at a zoo. However, inside this enclosure is a Soul Stalker. Named as such because it has the ability to appear in spirit or solid form. Soul Stalkers come from a place called Growan, a green, misty realm. They're one of the most violent of all ghouls and they rarely materialise unless they need to."

Spencer stepped up to the enclosure and peered in. The floor was covered in white sand and stone and there were two large padded cubes a little larger than a microwave oven, one red and the other blue.

He couldn't see a Soul Stalker, but his skin prickled and somehow, he knew something was in there, watching and waiting.

The group began to mumble impatiently.

"It's empty," said Karl, frowning at Albert.

Albert didn't look at Karl. "It only looks empty," he said. "Let me show you." He walked around to the side of the enclosure and stood in front of a console. Spencer watched Albert type something into the keyboard projected onto a glass sheet, and then he looked gleefully into the enclosure as if he knew what was about to happen. "Pay attention," warned Albert.

The group went silent and peered into the enclosure expectantly. All of a sudden, green and blue strands of electricity danced erratically around the enclosure along with the muted sounds of crackling.

Spencer was spellbound. Every hair on his body prickled to attention when he saw it. A heavy green cloud slowly materialised and stirred angrily through the air, darting instantaneously from one side of the chamber to the other, leaving a trailing blur in its wake. The creature changed shape as quickly as it moved and at one point Spencer was sure he could see a large, mutated head bearing a set of horns and fangs the size of fingers.

Like a bat from a cave, the blue box hurtled through the air and slammed against the glass with a loud thud. Spencer instinctively shrieked and ducked, as did the rest of the group.

The box settled on the sandy floor and everybody started talking excitedly.

"How cool was that?" said Karl.

Slowly, the green mist dissolved and then vanished.

"That was just a taste of what a Soul Stalker is capable of," said Albert. "If encountered, they can do a lot of damage and are capable of possessing and controlling humans."

After the excitement had passed, the group broke apart and small groups crept along the walkway, eager to see the contents of the next enclosure. Albert followed close behind, explaining what they would see next. "Here we have a Shape Shifter. It looks very boring don't you think?" he said in a theatrical tone. "But don't let that fool you."

Spencer stepped up to the glass. The chamber was darker and more menacing than the Soul Stalker enclosure. It was like a creepy, dank forest. Several black, rotting trees leant against the glass and a pool of black, rancid water played host to several moss covered logs in the middle of the floor. Any colour or life that may have existed in the enclosure was sucked out by a dim, cold light. At first there didn't appear to be anything there, but then Spencer saw it; a dense black cloud appeared, cloaking a solid figure beneath.

"What's that?" said Karl. "It looks like the last one."

Albert explained. "These critters can take on any form. They can peer into your minds and use an image from your thoughts, so be careful what you think about. They come from the realm of Silva, a depressing place mostly covered in rotting forest."

"Can you make it change shape?" asked Karl excitedly.

"It's not that simple. We can't provoke it like the Soul Stalker. It'll change when it pleases," replied Albert.

The cloud began to drift menacingly around the walls of the chamber, reaching out with wispy tentacles, feeling its way. Spencer heard and felt a heavy vibration as if it was stomping around the enclosure. After circling, it stopped in front of him.

He stared at it, transfixed. His mind suddenly jolted as if two large hands had grasped it. Sorrowful, crying voices rushed through his head like a howling wind, but he couldn't make out any words, just wailing cries. He tried to step away from the glass, but found his feet rooted. The pressure on the sides of his head and shoulders grew. A sense of foreboding crept through his mind and then he had an overwhelming feeling of despair.

The black cloud slowly began to change shape. It twisted and coiled until finally, a pale, dead looking Drake materialised in front of him. He hung limp, his mouth wide open as if he were laughing, his wild eyes staring intently at Spencer.

"Move away," bellowed Albert, "Quickly, move away." He rushed over and stood between the enclosure and Spencer. There was a sudden release and Spencer stumbled back against the handrail. The ghoul burst apart and transformed back into the dense black cloud before rolling away to the rear of the chamber.

"Are you alright, son?" asked Albert.

He was completely aware of what had happened and there was no pain. "Yes, I think so," he said. "A little dazed, that's all."

"Try and stand upright."

Spencer stepped away from the railing. "Why did it turn into Drake? It was horrible. I couldn't move at all," he said.

Albert didn't answer straight away. He turned to the other cadets and said, "You can all move along now," and waved at them. He turned back to Spencer and smiled at him. "They can be brutal at times. I suspect it was drawing from you. I did warn you," he said. "Come, let's move along."

CHAPTER SEVEN

The Locked Door

The cadets observed one enclosure then another. Even though Albert had instructed them not to do it, the cadets were absorbed in tapping on the glass in a futile attempt to taunt each ghoul and get a response. They weren't taking any notice of what Albert was saying.

Karl came and stood next to Spencer. "What happened back there?" he said.

Spencer shook his head, still feeling a little dizzy. "I'm not sure. The Shape Shifter got inside my head and I couldn't move."

"It sure looked freaky. Why did it change into Drake? Were you thinking about him?"

"No. Well, I don't think so," said Spencer. Then he realised he should have known what he was thinking about, but he couldn't remember.

By now all the other cadets had spread out along the walkway and Albert was trying to explain, in his loudest voice, that the next enclosure was occupied by a Haunter and that it was captured in the Drog realm. "These ghouls are commonplace," he said. "They can be troublesome at times, but they rarely cause physical harm to humans. However, some do possess mild Soul

Stalker qualities."

The dizziness had passed and Spencer went and stood next to Albert. He started discussing the contents of the enclosure with a few cadets. Spencer peered inside. It was bathed in red light. The floor was covered in rocks and what appeared to be bubbling lava pools oozing jets of steam or smoke.

The Haunter was a mean, brawly ghoul. It looked like an ugly man with no legs, just a pointy wisp of mist where his legs should have been. It simply floated a foot in the air. It had a powerful upper torso, a bald head, and a grimace that would scare the bravest of men. It drifted around the enclosure as if looking for a fight, but it ignored the boys that were trying to provoke it, as if they were insignificant and it had dealt with much bigger things in its time.

As Spencer moved away from the chamber, he passed a walkway branching to his left. It led to a large red metal door with a small window the size of a book. Printed on the door, in bold, red letters was:

DANGER!
KEEP OUT

Spencer wondered what could be behind the door to warrant such a sign. He looked around to see if anybody was watching him. Albert was talking to the group about the Chiller ghoul in the next frost covered chamber and Karl was tapping on the glass trying desperately to get its attention, but he wasn't having any luck.

What harm would it do to peer in the window, Spencer

thought? He crept up the walkway toward the door, but he only managed three steps before Albert bellowed at him. "Stop right there."

Spencer stopped and spun around.

"Where do you think you're going?" said Albert marching up to Spencer and grabbing his arm with a surprisingly firm grip.

"I was only looking, Sir" said Spencer, desperately trying to think of something to say that didn't make him sound guilty or stupid.

"Get back in line and stay away from that door."

Everybody stared at Spencer and his face burned. He didn't understand why it made Albert get so mad. He rejoined the group and stood next to Karl.

"Can't you keep out of trouble for five minutes?" said Karl.

"I only wanted to see what was behind the door," whispered Spencer.

Karl quickly glanced around and leaned in close to Spencer. "Colin told me about that. Nobody knows, but whatever is behind there must be important. They keep it well guarded and top secret," he said.

"Why?"

"Don't know. But I bet we could find out," said Karl, sounding like he was up for a challenge.

Albert began calling. "Can you all make your way over here please?"

Spencer and Karl followed the rest of the group along the walkway, past the Chiller enclosure to the end. It took a few minutes for everyone to gather and settle down and for Albert to begin lecturing again.

“Behind me, in the next room, is the Shrieker enclosure. We have to keep it separated due to its ability to kill with its sound. Therefore, to enter you must wear a pair of these,” he said, holding up two small, silver objects no bigger than the tip of his finger. “Earplugs. Just pop one into each ear, small end first, then tap the side and they’ll activate. It has a small receiver inside each one so I can still speak to you. Now step forward, one by one, and take a pair.” He began handing them out to each student.

“Once we get inside, do not, under any circumstances, remove them from your ears. Is that clear?” Everybody nodded and muttered acknowledgement. Spencer could tell Albert was deadly serious because he gave the group a long lasting stare that could have said, ‘if you do, you’re dead’.

“Put them in your ears now. I’m going to open the door.”

Spencer watched Karl push an earplug into one ear and then in the other. He gawped in amazement as a tiny, antenna like arm popped out of the centre of each earpiece, unfolded and fanned around the ear to cover it entirely. Spencer smiled in astonishment and did the same. Once the earplugs had fanned out, he was amazed at how it blocked out all noise from getting through. The only sound he could hear was his own amplified breathing and swallowing.

Albert placed his finger in the hole and the door slid open. The group filtered through the doorway and waited on the other side for Albert to close the door behind them.

This room was much smaller than the last. It had two glass chambers, one on either side of the walkway, each one very similar to the previous chambers.

The first on the left was illuminated by a red light and the floor was covered in sand with a pile of rocks in the far corner. From behind the rocks came a most peculiar looking creature. It looked like a giant green potato with long bony arms, pathetic flimsy wings, and a worm-like tail. It was roughly the same height as Spencer and it used its two long arms to walk and manoeuvre. Spencer doubted whether it could actually fly. Its tatty, leathery wings were frayed on the edges and were very small. It had an enormous mouth with a thick bottom lip that stuck out and stretched from one side of its head around to the other.

Albert's voice came through the earplugs. "This creature is a Gobbler, part of the Shrieker family. It exists as a physical entity and can be found in many realms. This particularly disgusting creature was captured in Asgard by two senior Seepers from Drake's team."

Spencer looked straight at Albert when he mentioned Asgard. So they've actually been there, he thought. Angeline didn't mention that.

Albert continued. "The Gobbler could eat a small child whole and spit out its bones before he knew what had happened. It can emit a scream that would liquefy your bowels and make your ears bleed if you were to hear it. It can't fly, but research suggests the wing like limbs are antenna, sensing movement and sound vibrations."

Spencer stepped closer to get a better view. The creature turned and lunged at the group, flapped its pathetic wings and opened its cavernous mouth, letting out a wail that could barely be heard through the earplugs. Spencer imagined the sound could be fatal without earplugs. Stringy, yellow drool dangled from short, spiky black teeth and stretched between swollen gums. Spencer shuddered with the thought of meeting the creature face-to-face and backed away from the glass.

He turned to observe the opposite chamber. A white mist gently swirled around the base of the softly lit enclosure. A tall, slender female ghoul appeared with pearly white hair that came down to her waist. She floated and gracefully swirled around the chamber. Spencer thought she looked beautiful, but very sad.

"She's a Siren. Don't be fooled by the striking beauty," said Albert standing behind Spencer. "She uses her looks, along with the most enchanting songs you're ever likely to hear, to lure her victims. She renders them helpless, but what happens after that, nobody has ever lived to tell."

Spencer turned to ask Albert a question. He wanted to know where the Siren was captured, but Albert had walked away and was having trouble prising the cadets away from the Gobbler enclosure. The cadets were making faces mimicking the Gobbler's scream, which made it scream even more. After much attempted scolding, Albert managed to gather them around the exit.

Above the door another sign read:

SPIRIT REALM
SILENCE PLEASE

The moment Spencer stepped through, a serene atmosphere settled the group into a daze like state. It was like stepping into a church; just as large, but circular and void of any enclosures or walkways. A bright strip high up on the ceiling filled the room with light. Spencer recognised the strip instantly. It was like the hole Oliver had vanished through, except this one had bands of radiant light hanging from it, curling and waving as if in a gentle breeze. Glowing orbs dropped in and out of the bright light and calmly drifted amongst the curtains of radiance, like they were soaking up the rays.

"To take off your ear plugs. Tap the centre gently and they will fold away. Then pop them out and drop them in the basket next to the door," Albert said.

Everybody did exactly that and then gathered in a group. Albert gestured at the ceiling. "This is an example of a split, or a hole in the realm walls that was never closed. You'll learn about realms in your respective classes. However, this is the only split that we have found open and we're unsure how it got here. We believe it's a hole into a spirit realm. It wasn't left open intentionally, we're sure of that. Something or someone punctured their way through and left in a hurry. We have not ventured inside as no portals have been detected."

It occurred to Spencer that the whole room was a chamber itself, but it had no barriers like the others and clearly didn't need them. He looked across the room and noticed Joseline's group hadn't left. Even more curiously, Joseline was talking to Frankie, but he couldn't make out what she was saying.

Albert had stopped talking and had also become distracted by what was going on. "Wait here, I'll go and see what's happening," he said in a concerned tone. He strode across the room and spoke to Joseline while Spencer watched inquisitively.

Then Albert came striding back, smiling.

Before Spencer could open his mouth, Karl spoke. "What's

going on over there, sir?" he asked boldly.

"A spirit came down into the room, but was confused. Frankie spoke to it and calmed it down and now it has returned." Albert shrugged and turned to look at Spencer. "She's your friend isn't she?"

"Yeah," replied Spencer.

"Well, she appears to have a way with them."

Spencer stared across the room and saw Frankie looking back at him. She threw him a big smile and a small excited wave. Spencer lifted his hand and waved back slowly as she left the room through a large door on the opposite side. She did have a way with animals and perhaps she had the same ability with spirits, thought Spencer.

"That's the end of our tour," announced Albert. "You can all leave through that exit over there," he said pointing to the door that Frankie had left through.

Spencer and Karl left the spirit enclosure and emerged into a large, bright room brimming with excited cadets. Spencer overheard several of them exaggerating his Soul Stalker incident to their friends.

"Mist started pouring out of his eyes and his ears," said one boy while motioning the mist with his hands.

"Quinn was floating in the air and he started to mutate," said another.

Karl looked at Spencer and rolled his eyes, "ignore them," he said and patted Spencer on the shoulder.

Spencer looked around the room. His gaze met with Frankie's. Her face lit up when she saw him and she rushed to greet him.

"I'm going to mingle," Karl said, and he disappeared into the crowd.

"Hi, Spencer," said Frankie with a beaming smile. "That was amazing. Did you see what happened?"

"No, I..." began Spencer, but Frankie interrupted him.

"A spirit came down into the chamber, but it was lost and looked frightened. I started talking to it and that seemed to calm it down. Joseline says I seem to have a real way with these creatures and she said she wants me to help out in the enclosures."

"Fran, that's brilliant," replied Spencer, sounding enthusiastic.

"You know what this means, don't you?" continued Frankie. "It means I get to come here every day, like you. Joseline says she'll help me and train me. Isn't it exciting?" Frankie's face beamed with joy and she couldn't stop clapping and jumping up and down. Spencer had never seen her so happy.

He didn't want to take away Frankie's moment of glory, but he had to tell her about the Soul Stalker. "I had a weird experience," he said.

Frankie's smile quickly faded. "What do you mean?"

Spencer told her all about the incident. "It was really creepy," he added.

Frankie frowned. "Why did it change into Drake?"

Spencer shrugged. "I don't know."

Albert bellowed at the top of his voice from the other side of the room. "Can everybody please pay attention?"

The room fell silent and Spencer spun around to look at him.

"Those of you staying in the academy can now go to the cadet common room and you will be guided to your dormitories. Those of you not staying should make your way to the entrance hall. If any of you have any questions, you can find my office on the second floor next to the ethereal library."

As Albert finished hollering, everybody began talking again.

"Hello, Spencer," said a voice behind him.

Spencer turned to see Hazel. "Oh hi, Hazel," he replied, followed by an awkward silence.

"If you two follow me, I'll escort you to the entrance hall."

"Uh, okay, but what happens now?"

"You're not staying at the academy, so it's time to go home," said Hazel.

A twinge of disappointment dashed through his mind. He looked at Frankie and noticed that she too looked unhappy. Nevertheless, they followed Hazel through a door, which led them into the lecture theatre. She seemed distant and didn't speak. Spencer hadn't known her long, but he sensed there was something troubling her. He attempted to spark a conversation.

"So, is the old house part of the academy?"

Hazel shook her head. "The house is just a disguise for the Portdoor. We have them located all over the world, in lots of different places, but of course, not all are old houses. Some are in tunnels underground, others are in buildings that the public think are important, like the house next door to the Prime Minister. The dog is simply a guide. It will always guide a Tezla cadet, but should anybody else enter the house, they'll never see the dog or find the Portdoor. The corridor maze changes every day and only the dog can guide you to the Portdoor," explained

Hazel.

"What about Frankie? She's not a cadet," said Spencer.

"She came through with you and we occasionally make exceptions. By all accounts, I think you'll find she'll become a useful asset to the academy," said Hazel and smiled.

They arrived in the entrance hall. It was almost empty apart from two cadets exiting a Portdoor chamber and a woman who sat at a desk talking to somebody through her mouthpiece.

"Where is everyone?" asked Frankie.

"They're probably in the dinner hall on floor three. It usually gets quiet around this time," replied Hazel. She stepped up to the woman behind the desk and said, "Spencer Quinn and Frankie Rawlinson to leave through Portdoor six to location E45N12."

The woman didn't look at Hazel immediately, but spoke to the person in her mouthpiece first. "Sorry Sandy," she said. "Couple of kids here need a lift, give me a minute." The woman speed typed on to the glass. "Portdoor six is now open. May I have your ID badges, please? You will be issued with new ones when you arrive next time," she said, and then went back to her conversation while holding out her hand. They were discussing an article she had read in the Paranormal Observer about a ghoul that had possessed a boy who had then tried to leave Tezla through a Portdoor and almost killed himself.

Spencer and Frankie handed her their badges and then turned and followed Hazel to Portdoor six.

"Will we see you tomorrow?" asked Hazel in a flat tone. Spencer and Frankie exchanged glances.

"Yes, of course," said Spencer.

Hazel forced a smile and said, "Very well, you had better go before she closes the Portdoor. I'll see you tomorrow. Bye." She turned and walked away.

Frankie and Spencer stepped inside the small chamber. The wall began to revolve as Hazel walked away.

"Do you think there's something wrong with her?" asked Frankie.

"I wondered that," Spencer replied. "Something seems to be bothering her." But Hazel's problems didn't occupy his thoughts for long. He had lost track of time and wondered if his mother was worried.

He turned to face the Portdoor. The metal shield covering it had retracted, revealing the glistening wall of liquid. "I'll go first, Fran." He stepped around her. He shuddered knowing what was about to happen and then stepped into the Portdoor.

The familiar nausea and the falling was the same, but it seemed much quicker this time. Before he knew it, he was standing in the room on the first floor of the old house. Straight ahead of him was an open door and he could see the top of the stairs.

Frankie quickly appeared behind him. "Going through that thing gives me the creeps," she said.

"It's going to take some getting used to, that's for sure," replied Spencer in a tone that suggested he wasn't happy to be there.

"What's wrong, Spence?"

"Oh nothing," he replied, trying not to sound too depressed. But there was something wrong. He was going back to his house, back to his life, which seemed vacant and depressing in comparison to the academy. He knew it wasn't his mother's fault. If only he could fix her. He knew that bringing Oliver home safe and sound would solve the problem, but he wasn't sure that was ever going to happen. Telling her what he now knew would probably send her over the edge, and him into a straight jacket. There was no way she would believe him so he decided not to mention Tezla or Oliver to her at all.

"Come on, let's get out of here before the caretaker shows up," Spencer said and he began descending the stairs.

They crept through the dark hallway, and stepped out of the house into the long shadows of the early evening sunshine. The light shift made Spencer squint, but the cool breeze on his face was refreshing. He could hear children playing in the distance and the sound of a lawn mower close by.

They ran across the gravel yard and through the bushes as quickly as they could. When Spencer emerged from the hole in the wall and stood up, he was rooted to the spot. Standing in front of him with two of his cronies was Billy Hood.

CHAPTER EIGHT

Seepers

Spencer swallowed hard. Arnold and Brandan stood behind Billy's menacing frame, flanked at each shoulder. Spencer had seen Brandan, like so many boys, hanging onto Billy's shirt tail, but hadn't yet had the misfortune of meeting his fists.

Arnold looked at Spencer dubiously and edged further behind Billy as if trying to avoid Spencer's gaze.

"Look who it is, boys," said Billy with a lopsided grin. "We've been looking for you. What you did to Arnold. Thought you was going to get away with it did you?"

"Billy, just go. Leave us alone," pleaded Spencer, not wanting a repeat of the playground incident.

"Us? Whad'ya mean, us?" said Billy, and just as he said it, Frankie emerged from the hole. "Well looky here, the perfect couple. What have you two been doing in the bushes, hey?"

Frankie got to her feet and stood next to Spencer. "Oh. I thought I heard voices. Why don't you just get lost, Hood," she said.

Billy and his cronies burst out laughing.

"What's so funny?" said Frankie.

Billy pointed at her. "You," he said. "You're not going to

pull that action Barbie scam again, there's three of us here now."

"No, you're right. I'm not." Frankie looked at Arnold and smiled. "How's your...you know..." she said and simply nodded. "Spencer, do your thing."

They all stopped laughing and looked at each other.

Spencer shot her a look.

Arnold squeaked and Brandan shuffled closer to Billy. Nobody spoke for a few seconds while they all waited for the next move. Spencer wondered if Frankie really meant it, but then it dawned on him what she was trying to do and decided to play along. "O.K," he said, nodding. "Which one?"

"Hmm," said Frankie, placing her hands on her hips. "You could try giving them some elephant ears," she said.

Spencer restrained a laugh.

"Billy, I don't think this is a good idea," said Arnold, tugging at Billy's shirt.

"Stop whining," Billy said, stepping closer to Spencer. "Go on then – do it. Let's see that hocus pocus."

"Billy, don't push him. You know he'll do it," said Arnold, taking a step back.

Billy just raised his hand, demanding silence.

"Okay that's it, I'm out of here," said Arnold stepping further back before turning to run as fast as he could. Brandan shot a look at Arnold and then back at Spencer. Without uttering a single word, he bolted too.

Billy's face turned from a smug grin to purple rage. "Get back here you wimps," he hollered.

"Look Spence," smiled Frankie. "You just have to give one of them big fat elephant ears now."

Billy started backing away, his fists clenched and his face deep red. "I'll—I'll get you two," he said turning and following Arnold and Brendan.

Spencer was relieved to see them go. "Good idea, Fran," he said.

"Yeah, that was close. We'd better get going, it's getting late."

They both walked along the dusty path and stepped into Spencer's back garden. He looked down at his watch. "Fran, it's just gone six."

"Darn it. Mum's going to kill me for missing dinner," said Frankie, glancing nervously along the terraced houses. "I'd better go."

"Me too. I'll call for you tomorrow. Early," said Spencer.

He watched Frankie dash along the row of houses, ducking beneath the neighbour's kitchen window as she passed, until she came to her house and went inside. He turned, pushed the back door open and stepped into the kitchen.

He was greeted by loud voices coming from the living room.

"I've told you why I couldn't make it. You have to stop this, Mary," said a voice Spencer recognised instantly.

Spencer's mother sniffed. "It's just been so difficult, lately. I wanted the three of us to be here, for Spencer's sake."

"I know, I know. But you can't continue like this. Spencer must see it and feel it. We have to move on, it's been a year. He's not coming back."

There was silence. Spencer imagined his mother giving his father a stare that said 'I can't believe you just said that.'

Spencer hated all the shouting and arguments they had had

since Oliver vanished. He wanted to turn on his heels and go straight back to the academy.

He crept through the kitchen, into the hallway, past the living room door, but paused at the bottom of the stairs.

"I'm sorry, I didn't mean to say that," said Spencer's father, his voice gentle and sincere. There was no response. "Well. Okay. I'll leave now and come back when Spencer is home."

Spencer quietly climbed the stairs. He reached his bedroom door and stopped. The front door slammed shut.

Collapsing onto his bed, he stared at the ceiling and pushed his parents from his thoughts. He began thinking about the academy and the amazing things he had seen there. He tried to imagine what the realms might be like, particularly Asgard. He thought deeply about becoming a Seeper and what it would mean for him. But mostly, he thought about Oliver and whether he could still be alive.

~ ~ ~

The following morning, Spencer woke from a dreamless sleep. He lifted his head, gazed across the room, and focused on his clock that read eight fifty-five.

He listened for any movement in the house. He could hear the faded mutterings from his grandmother, and the radio drifting up from the kitchen. He was excited by the prospect of going back to Tezla and scrambled out of bed. He washed, stumbled into his clothes, and hurried down the stairs, passing his grandmother as she hobbled into the bathroom.

He stepped into the kitchen to see his mother busy cleaning.

The radio was playing a tune and the sun brightened the room. If a stranger walked into the house at this moment, they would think his life was perfect, but Spencer knew it was far from it.

"Morning, love. I've poured you some cereal," said his mother.

Spencer looked at the bowl on the kitchen table and said, "Thanks, mum." He dragged the chair along the floor from beneath the table and sat in it.

"There's tea in the pot if you want it. Gran is still in bed," said his mother as she frantically wiped the counter as if it could never be clean enough.

"I just saw her go into the bathroom," Spencer said, pouring milk into his bowl. He began spooning cereal into his mouth while watching his mother clean. He wondered what his father was doing here yesterday and why his mother hadn't told him he was coming.

"Have you spoken to Dad, recently?"

Spencer's mother stopped cleaning for a second and then continued. "He wants to see you next week," she said.

"Oh, okay," he replied. "Do you know when he's coming over?"

"He's very busy, but he's going to let me know what day is best."

Spencer considered further whether he should tell her about Tezla and Asgard and all the things that had happened, but she had been through enough. Angeline was right. She wasn't ready.

"What are your plans today, Spencer?"

Spencer swallowed a mouthful of cereal and then lied, "Uh—I'm going to hang out at Frankie's."

There was a pause. "Well, Okay, but please be sure you're back before dark." She stopped cleaning and put the cloths and squirt bottles away beneath the sink. "I'm going to the shops. Do you want anything?"

Spencer shook his head no.

"Okay, I'll see you later, then," she rubbed her hands together and walked into the hallway.

Before Spencer could say goodbye, his attention was suddenly drawn to the radio. The music had ended and a woman newsreader was talking.

'Two boys from Stockly-Upon-Heath went missing last night. The twins were taken from their beds during the night and their whereabouts are currently unknown. The parents are being questioned at this time and police have begun a search of the area. We'll have more on this situation later, but now, here's John with the weather.'

It was a short report, slipped between a political incident at Downing Street and the weather. But Spencer knew instantly what had happened and where the twins had gone. As he sat pondering the news, he was startled by a knock on the back door.

He stood up, walked to the door and turned the handle. The door swung open.

"Hi, Frankie, come in," he said spinning on his heels.

Frankie stepped inside. "Good morning to you too."

"Sorry. I was listening to the radio. Have you heard the news this morning?"

"No."

Spencer told her about the news report. "It's him again, I know it is," he said.

"What can we do?" said Frankie.

"Not a lot, but if it is him, I'm sure Tezla will know about it. Which reminds me, we ought to be going," he said. "I'll leave a note for Mum, to remind her where I am. She forgets a lot these days."

He found a pen in a top drawer among a pile of bills and a nest of grocery receipts, then pulled out a torn white envelope and wrote:

Staying at Frankie's for lunch. Be back later.
S.

He placed it on the dining room table where he was sure his mother would see it, switched off the radio, and left.

They made their way along the path and scurried through the hole into the garden, but stopped where the bushes met the gravel.

"Look, the back door is open again," said Spencer.

"Let's just run for it," said Frankie.

Spencer surveyed the garden for any sign of the caretaker. "Okay, I think it's all clear," he said and started across the gravel yard toward the porch. They stopped in front of the heavy door. Spencer peered inside before dashing through the dark hallway to the bottom of the stairs.

"Quick, hurry," Frankie whispered, nudging Spencer in the back. He scrambled up the stairs, turned right at the top, and walked to the end of the corridor and stopped. He looked left then right, squinting through the gloom, but saw nothing but empty blackness.

"This way," said Spencer, and hurried left. They ran through the maze of corridors like they had done the day before, but this time, the route seemed different, as if the corridors had rearranged themselves somehow. But some things hadn't changed, like the dank smell hanging in the air, the cobwebs brushing across his face like tiny fingers stroking his skin, and the endless closed doors on both sides.

It wasn't long before they had turned a corner and stood in front of a closed door. Spencer stepped forward, turned the handle, and pushed it open. In the centre of the room was the Portdoor, active and ready to swallow them.

"You go first this time," said Spencer. He stood aside while Frankie entered the liquid wall, then quickly followed. Before he knew it, they were standing in the familiar dark chamber.

The walls rotated to reveal the gigantic vestibule. The frost had gone, but the hall was busy with cadets. Hazel stood alone at the chamber entrance, waiting, it seemed, to greet them.

"Oh, hello, Hazel," said Spencer. He wasn't sure what to expect today, but he hadn't expected Hazel to be waiting for them.

"Hi. I've come to check you in," she replied. "Frankie, Albert told me to tell you to meet him in his office, on the second floor, next to the library."

"Okay," said Frankie, smiling.

Hazel turned and walked toward the reception desk where Mary and the other receptionists sat. "This is Spencer Quinn and Fran…" began Hazel, but she was interrupted. Mary had raised her hand.

"Yes, I know who they are," she said.

Hazel looked a little embarrassed.

Mary stared at the screen in front of her and said, "The basement have informed me that your official security tags will not arrive until Thursday morning."

"The basement?" replied Spencer, puzzled.

"She means the biotech lab where they make all the equipment. We call it the basement because that's where the lab is," explained Hazel.

Mary handed Spencer and Frankie a thin, glass tag the size of a credit card with computer chips inside. "In the meantime," she said, "you will need to carry these with you at all times. It'll give you level two security access and will allow the central computer to track you around the academy." She looked at them and smiled falsely. "Have a nice day."

Frankie turned to Spencer. "Will I see you later?"

Hazel intervened. "Once the Seepers have met with Drake, we will send them to the dinner hall on the third floor for lunch at around twelve-thirty."

There was an awkward pause.

"I guess I'll see you there then," said Frankie. She smiled and dashed across the hall toward two doors in the far corner.

Hazel led Spencer through the entrance hall into the glass corridor. She kept a step ahead with her head lowered and she didn't speak a word. But he wasn't sure what to say either. He was hopeless at starting conversations, especially with girls. Then it occurred to him. The perfect opener; maybe she would know something about the twins on the news.

"Did you hear the news this morning?" he said, filling the uncomfortable silence.

"Yes, Angeline and the council are looking into it. Everybody suspects it was Arrawn, but nothing's been confirmed," Hazel replied, and then she went quiet again. They walked to the end of the corridor and turned left toward the theatre. He tried desperately to think of something else to say, but Hazel didn't make it easy for him.

"How did Drake become head of Seepers?" he asked.

"He's been fascinated with ghouls for as long as I can remember. He always told me that ghouls existed and then he started hunting them—and he would find them too. I didn't believe him at first so one day I went with him. It was a job for the D.D.G. They hired him. A Soul Stalker had seeped into our realm and was creating havoc at a museum in London. Drake was sent to plasmerise it."

"You mean you and he are…" began Spencer.

"Yes, we're brother and sister. I know, I'm mixed race and he's not. We were adopted."

"Oh, I see." The blood gathered in Spencer's cheeks, but he didn't think Hazel had noticed. "Who are the D.D.G?" he asked, quickly changing the subject.

"They're a secret government agency used for the Destruction and Defence against ghouls. They work with us in certain circumstances, but they're not as advanced as the academy. Their primary function is to exterminate ghouls that seep into our world. Drake wasn't satisfied with just destroying them. He wanted to know more about them, where they came from, and how they got into our world. Tezla heard about him and lured him in, just like they have with you."

Hazel paused and Spencer noticed a distinct change of tone, like she was sad about something, but she continued.

"The D.D.G. only operate in our realm, they don't venture to other realms like Tezla. When Drake discovered realm cubes existed, it became an obsession for him," she said as they passed the theatre door and continued to the end of the corridor. But before Spencer could ask Hazel about the cubes, she had already placed her finger in a hole, and a door had slid open revealing a small chamber beyond.

Hazel stepped inside. "Come," she beckoned.

Spencer followed. The door closed behind him while another opened on the opposite side to expose a large dimly lit room. Spencer paused for a second and his eyes widened. Three gigantic screens loomed down from a curved wall at the back of the room, each one the size of a small cinema screen. Below them, a vast console was covered in buttons and lights. The room reminded Spencer of the pictures he had seen of NASA Control.

Hazel walked further into the room and beckoned Spencer to follow. "Please take a seat over there," she said, pointing toward a row of seats at the back of the room. Spencer turned, and saw other cadets already seated. He smiled, nodded, and then sat in a seat on the end of the front row. It was like he was starting school all over again.

Hazel went and stood next to a tall black chair in front of the console. It began to swivel. Drake spun into view, his expression stern. He stood up, stepped forward and silently inspected them, like a military officer inspecting his squad. He scowled at Hazel.

"This lecture started five minutes ago. Where have you been?"

"Sorry, Drake. They had to be signed in," Hazel replied, turning her back to the students.

Drake turned back to the cadets. Spencer caught Drake staring at him, but he quickly looked away when Spencer noticed him doing it.

"Seepers," began Drake. "What are you?" He paused. His voice had a smooth, but commanding tone.

At last, Spencer thought.

"To understand the true nature of a Seeper, we need to go back to the time when it all began." Drake walked back and forth in front of them. "Thousands of years ago, the world we call Earth was a very different place. It was a fledgling realm struggling for existence amongst many realms."

While Drake spoke, Hazel stood to one side and waited patiently.

Drake continued. "All realms exist in their own time and space, separated by a fine transparent veil. Like our own realm, many of them teemed with life, while others were hollow, dark, and uninhabitable. These realms were once joined by deliberate perforations known as Portdoors."

Drake paused again and placed his hands behind his back while he paced. "Back then, within the realms, there were few evils and a lot of good and they were all governed by ancient Seepers. They were the peace keepers of their time. They were few, but very powerful. They were born from the very first identical souls that came into being at exactly the same moment in time. They grew as one but existed as a pair. They lived long and were gifted with supreme powers. Over time, the ancients administered and maintained the balance of good and evil in all realms, but with so many to care for, their job became too great."

Along the front row to Spencer's left, one of the Chinese twins thrust her arm into the air. Drake stopped pacing and turned to face them. "Please don't interrupt while I'm speaking. You will have time for questions later," he said sharply. The girl looked embarrassed and lowered her arm.

Drake continued. "One role of the ancient Seepers was to control access to Portdoors using realm cubes. There are eight cubes. Each one is a combination key that has the power to open, close, and change the destination of all Portdoors. When all eight keys are combined, they have unimaginable power."

As he listened to Drake, something occurred to Spencer: did this mean that he and the other twins at the academy were in some way related to ancient Seepers? He remembered what Karl had said, 'Seepers were the only cadets that could travel to other realms'.

Drake went on. "But something happened. The details are unknown, but over time, evil began to conquer good, eventually dominating some realms. The ancient Seepers began isolating the decaying realms by locking the Portdoors, preventing the evil from bleeding through. Evil retaliated and began amassing great armies of tainted souls and the vilest of creatures, until evil became very powerful. But it always kept good dangling by a thread and if it began to gather strength, evil would simply trim it back. But it would never destroy good entirely for it would destroy itself in doing so. Evil could not exist without good."

"Eventually, evil began to posses Seepers, turning them into Soul-Reapers. The Reapers spread far and wide like a plague, destroying any new souls that could become a Seeper. The time came when the ancient Seepers decided to protect all remaining good realms and surviving Seepers. They seeped into all good realms, taking the cube keys with them, and locked the Portdoors behind them. Once they had finished their quest, they hid the keys in the deepest oceans, on top of the highest mountains and buried them in the innermost caverns, thus eradicating the further spread of evil. This single decision isolated all realms, leaving them to develop independently, to determine their own destiny without Seeper authority. From that time, the ancient Seepers were never seen or heard from again."

"Now, thousands of years later, the ancient Seepers and the cube keys have long been forgotten by most. Portdoors have decayed. Realms have diminished. Many becoming predominantly evil, but others have flourished. In our very own realm in the year we call nineteen thirty-three, two human twins, Lazerus and Isaac Tezla, found the ancient Portdoor you see in the entrance hall. They were fiercely determined explorers and it was Lazerus that established this institution to further their research."

Drake's eyes shifted from person to person as if gauging their reaction. Nobody moved or spoke a word. Spencer was captivated. To any normal mortal, it would seem far-fetched and unbelievable, a story from a book perhaps. But Spencer had powers, he had seen Arrawn take his brother, and he had seen the weird creatures that came from the realms locked up in the pens. He knew it was all very real.

"Any questions?" Drake asked.

Several arms shot up, including Spencer's.

"Yes, Yi?" said Drake, pointing to the Chinese girl who raised her arm previously.

"How do you know all of this?"

Drake smiled. "When Lazerus discovered the Portdoor, he discovered many ancient scribes. At first they couldn't be deciphered, but over time, we have learned how to translate them. The translations are stored in the Etheral Library if you wish to study them."

"What happened to Isaac and Lazerus?" said a boy behind Spencer.

"We know that there was a dispute between the brothers during the development of the academy, at which time Isaac vanished. He doesn't appear in the records beyond that time. Lazerus went on to finish Tezla and died here at a very old age. Lazerus' tomb is marked by a stone in the floor, at the centre of the entrance hall." Drake raised his eyebrows, prompting more questions.

More arms shot up.

"Spencer?"

"What are the other realms like?"

"We've only explored a handful of them and they're all very different. Some are early in development while others are old and teeming with life. Many are filled with evil and others are good and peaceful and want to be left alone. But we will learn more about them in future sessions."

"Are you going to teach us to use our powers?" asked another boy.

"No, that's the job of Mr. Saunders. You'll be meeting him shortly. Well, time is pressing. If you want to learn more about the realms prior to our next session, visit the library. It has records of all of the events that have happened through time, but now we must move on. I will hand you over to Hazel who is going to run through some basic introductions," Drake said, smiling. He then turned his back and returned to his chair.

Spencer wondered what Drake meant by 'all events'. Did he literally mean everything? He wondered if Arrawn and Oliver would be included in those recorded events.

Hazel strode to the side of the room and disappeared into a small cupboard. She emerged carrying several small black shoulder bags. "These are your holdalls," she said as she handed them out. "They will hold all the utilities you'll need for your training. Inside, you will find a tablet. They are wirelessly programmed daily, updated with your personal details, your timetable, and important news and events. Oh and email, of course. Also on the tablet, you'll find a couple of essential reads, including your Seeper handbook—The Power Within, which will answer many questions you might have. You will also find 'A practical guide to Ghouls and Ectoplasm' which I recommend you read thoroughly."

The holdall reminded Spencer of his school bag back home, but this one was black and made of tough leather. It had the academy 'T' emblazoned on the front flap and it was lighter than he expected. He lifted the flap and peered inside, as did all the cadets. Sitting neatly in its own little compartment was a silver device, which he assumed was his tablet. Spencer also noticed the latest copy of the Paranormal Observer in another pocket, which he was keen to read.

He closed his holdall and watched Hazel go back into the cupboard and return with another batch of holdalls. "Your next Seeper session will be here on Friday morning. Please bring your tablets to every session, they will be updated with session notes and any research you are required to do for subsequent sessions."

While Hazel went through some basic evacuation procedures in the event of an emergency, which took some time and was very dull, Spencer looked over the room. His gaze danced across the console and the hundreds of buttons and flashing lights that adorned it. Then he noticed two Portdoors to his right and wondered why Drake would need separate Portdoors from those in the entrance hall.

"That concludes this session," said Hazel. "You may now make your way up to the dining hall."

CHAPTER NINE

The Missing file

The dining hall was a simple, large room with white walls, bright lights embedded in the ceiling, and no windows. Four rows of silver tables and chairs stretched from the doorway to the far end of the hall and a small queue had formed down the left wall.

The hall was by no means full, unlike the dinner hall at Littlemead High, which was always jammed full of kids squabbling for a chair.

As Spencer walked over to join the queue, he spotted Frankie sitting at a table with another girl with long dark hair. She was the same girl Frankie had paired with during orientation. In an attempt to draw her attention, Spencer covertly waved his hand. "Frankie," he called out, but she didn't hear him.

He felt a tap on his shoulder. "Hey, Spence," said a familiar voice.

Spencer spun around. Karl stood smiling in front of him.

"Hello, Karl," Spencer replied, wondering how Karl managed to be so energetic all the time.

"I've been looking out for you all morning," Karl said. "I found out what was behind that door in the holding pens. I asked Colin last night."

"What did he say?"

Karl leant forward and whispered. "First he told me he didn't know, but then I threatened him with blackmail. I know stuff about him. Anyway, he reckons they have a cube in there, but they don't want anyone to know about it."

"You mean an ancient realm cube?"

"Yeah. Keep your voice down, man. I'm not supposed to know about it."

Spencer shrugged. "Why do they want to keep it a secret?" he said, shuffling along in the queue.

"Because it's a realm cube. If someone like Arrawn finds out it's in there, he'll try and take it. But Colin says it's sealed and the security is solid. Nobody could get in except for the few people who have access."

"Drake said they were used by the ancients for controlling Portdoors or something."

"Yeah, it's something like that. It's Seeper stuff. Listen, I have a free hour before Ectology, you've probably got the same. Do you want to go up top?"

"Up top?" said Spencer.

"Yeah—top floor. The Ethereal Library. Oh, of course, you haven't been up there yet, have you?"

Spencer shook his head.

"It's awesome, man. If you want to find out more about realm cubes, it's all there. You just have to look for it."

"Okay. Let me check my timetable," said Spencer pulling out his tablet. It was slimmer than a mobile phone and no bigger than a large calculator. He flipped open the lid revealing a small screen on the inside. He turned it one way then another. "How do you switch this thing on?" he asked, turning it over in his hand.

"Here," said Karl, reaching over and pointing at a touch pad on the base of the device. "Put your thumb on that."

Spencer placed his thumb on the pad. The tablet beeped to life. The screen lit up in a soft aquamarine blue and the same female voice he heard in the Portdoor chambers welcomed him. "Welcome, Spencer Quinn," said the voice out of a tiny speaker.

"Cool huh?" said Karl.

"Yeah," said Spencer, dumbstruck.

Then the tiny voice spoke again. "Please say your name." Spencer looked at Karl for guidance. Why was she asking his name? She knew his name.

"Go on. She wants to record your voice pattern, that's all. You won't have to do it again. When you want a record of something, you speak instead of using a keyboard," said Karl.

Spencer lifted the device to his mouth. "Spencer Quinn," he said, feeling self-conscious.

"Please repeat."

Spencer looked at Karl quizzically and shrugged. "Spencer Quinn," he repeated.

"Thank you," said the tiny voice and the screen filled with several glowing icons.

"Touch that," Karl said, pointing at a clock icon. Spencer touched the picture and a timetable rolled out across the screen. "Yes, I do have Ectology this afternoon."

"Cool, we'll go together."

"So, what's so awesome about this library?" Spencer asked

as he folded his tablet and slid it back into his holdall.

"It's the biggest library I've ever seen. You can research any realm, ghoul, or event that has ever happened!"

"You mean every event that ever took place?"

"Yup. You know, you really should read your manual, dude."

Spencer was startled when a fat lady at the kiosk shouted at him.

"You want some lunch or what?"

"Oh, sorry, yes please," Spencer replied, picking up a silver tray. It had moulded compartments in which the women slopped mashed potatoes onto one side and sausages and beans on the other.

He was keen to sit with Frankie and hear about her day, and tell her about the cubes. He glanced around the hall and saw Frankie heading for the exit, "Frankie," called Spencer.

She spun around to face him. "Oh hi, Spence. I'm going to the library. Do you want to come?"

"Yep, we'll be there," Karl interrupted.

Frankie looked at him and frowned. "I guess I'll see you up there then." She sighed, dropped her shoulders, and strode away.

Spencer sat in the seat where Frankie had been sitting and Karl sat next to him. He hadn't realised how hungry he was. They scooped the food into their mouths as quickly as they could and remained silent until they had finished, which didn't take long.

"Shall we go?" said Karl, leaping up from his chair before Spencer could respond.

They placed their trays on the trolley next to the door, left the hall, and made their way to the top floor via the elevator. They stepped out and followed the sign that read:

ETHEREAL LIBRARY

Many doors lined the white panelled walls. The first door on the right was closed and half glazed with frosted glass with letters that were illuminated blue and read:

MISS E NERTS
HEAD OF ECTOLOGY

Then the letters faded and new ones appeared:

OUT TO LUNCH
BE BACK IN 30:43

The numbers were counting down.

"We've got her for Ectology," said Karl nodding toward the closed door.

"What's she like?"

"Nobody knows…she's new. I read about her in the Tezla news that was sent to our tablets. I bet she's strict. Her photo looked tough and she's got a constant frown baked into her head," replied Karl.

They passed four more doors, all of them with a different name and department. The sixth door was open, but Spencer could still read the sign. It read:

DRAKE JONES
HEAD OF SEEPERS

He looked into the room as he passed. Drake and Hazel were standing face to face. Drake was jabbing the air with his finger. They were arguing, but Spencer couldn't hear what they were saying. He noticed Hazel was crying. Then, as if he had sensed him looking, Drake turned and glared at Spencer with narrowed eyes. Spencer quickly looked away and continued walking. After four paces, he glanced back over his shoulder. The door slammed shut.

"Did you see that?" whispered Spencer.

"See what?"

"Drake and Hazel were arguing and Hazel was crying."

"They've been doing that a lot lately," Karl said, dismissing it as if it was nothing.

They reached the end of the corridor. Albert's office was on their right and looked empty. Two enormous oak doors were directly ahead. They were unlike any other doors in the academy. Detailed carvings of distorted figures and haunted faces were etched around the frame. The handles were large, round black metal hoops that needed to be turned for the doors to open.

"Why are these doors different from the others?" asked Spencer in awe.

"The library tower was the first wing to be built. It's on top of the ancient Portdoor and is said to be where Isaac did all his research," Karl said, reaching out to turn the handle. He pushed the door and it swung open.

The library was a circular room. He had the same feeling he had when he walked into St Paul's cathedral in London on a school trip, like he had stepped back in time. Unlike the cathedral, the floor here was dark wood that creaked when they stepped on it. In the centre of the room, a black metal staircase occupied a large hole in the ceiling and looked as though it belonged in a museum. Small, round, ornate wooden tables, each with four equally ornate chairs filled the majority of floor space. Dark wooden shelves covered every inch of the wall crammed full of books of all sizes. Some were evidently new, while others were old and tatty with spines dangling by a thread.

Two signs hung above Spencer's head.

The first read:

GROUND FLOOR – INTRUSIONS

The second sign indicated the books were organised in date order. The first line on the sign read '1980 – 1990' and had an arrow pointing to the left and beneath it was '1991 – 2000', with an arrow pointing to the right.

"I'm going up a floor to weapons and contraptions," said Karl. "You coming?" he asked. But just as Spencer was about to answer, he spotted Frankie sitting alone, reading.

"No, I'm going to hang around down here for a while."

"Okay, I guess I'll see you later," Karl said and rushed up the staircase.

Spencer went over stood next to Frankie. "Hi, Fran," he said. He thought she looked important in her new uniform. "Nice outfit."

"Thanks. I look like I'm wrapped in tin foil." she said and rolled her eyes.

Spencer dropped into the seat next to her. "What are you

reading?"

"Well," she began and looked down at the book in front of her and back at Spencer. "I hope you don't mind. I was looking for a record of Arrawn." Frankie raised her eyebrows, "And Oliver." She stared at Spencer as if she had done something behind his back.

"That's weird. I was thinking of doing the exact same thing," Spencer said, in an attempt to make her less anxious.

Frankie relaxed and began to talk about it more enthusiastically. "Something's not right here, Spence," she said. "I quickly checked through the missing persons section, but I couldn't find anything. Then I came over here to look through intrusions for last year.

"Karl said they've records of all intrusion events. It should be here."

"It should be, but the whole July volume is gone. I'm looking through August, but there's no mention of it," said Frankie as she leafed through the pages. "August the first has the most intrusions – listen to this."

Frankie began reading from the pages.

"Location, Germany - Cologne, sector 11/H, time, 22.11. Hans-Flybibler Outchten, age 62, Soul Stalker encounter, level 3 attack, ref 27567." She paused and leafed through a few more pages.

"And this one, Location, England - London, Sector 22/S, time 21.43. David Smith, age 12, encountered a Soul Stalker, damage to environment, no harm to human, level 4 intrusion, ref 27568," she said and closed the book. "Your event isn't here."

"But why would they remove it? Maybe somebody's

borrowed the volume it's in," suggested Spencer curiously.

"No, you can't borrow books from here. You won't get past the door if you're carrying one out. They have alarms on the doors and all the books are tagged," she said nodding at the doors. "If you want information from here, you can instruct the computer to send it to your tablet. But the July log must have been officially removed from the library. Maybe there's something in it that they don't want us to see."

"But what could that be?" said Spencer. He glanced around and noticed a flat screen monitor on a table nearby. "What are those things over there?" he asked.

"Touch screens. They have all these records stored digitally," she said, looking around at all the books on the shelves. "You can use the screens instead of the books if you want to."

"Have you tried it?"

"No."

Spencer got up and walked over to the monitor. 'Welcome to Tezla Ethereal Library Intranet' was printed across the screen in bold white letters on a dark blue background. The academy's emblem was a lighter, faded blue and stretched across the whole screen behind the letters.

"How does it work?" asked Spencer.

"It's like your tablet," Frankie replied, and she touched a small image of the library door which had 'Enter' printed beneath it. The screen cleared and was quickly filled with several options:

- Search by reference number
- Search by date

- Search by name

Spencer prodded the screen on 'Search by date'. The screen prompted Spencer to select a millennium. Then it prompted for a century, a decade, then a number between zero and nine representing the year in the decade, and finally the month. Spencer touched July. The screen flashed a message that read:

Please wait – Searching

It only took a few seconds and the screen presented him with another message:

File is currently unavailable

Frankie gasped. "See, I told you," she whispered.

"I don't understand why they would go to the trouble of removing it," said Spencer.

"There must be something in it they don't want people to see. Something must have happened that night, Spencer. Think back and try to remember."

"I've told you everything. Angeline asked me the same thing."

A frown fell across Frankie's face. "But how did Arrawn get into your room?" she asked.

Spencer realised he had never questioned that before. "He must have used one of the Portdoors," he said. "But wait. When Angeline took me into that small room, I remember she said that Portdoors are static, they don't move around. And you can only go from one door to the next."

"So how did he get into your room?" repeated Frankie.

They stared at each other silently.

"Yesterday, Hazel mentioned something about Drake becoming obsessed with realm cubes," Spencer began. "Then today, Drake mentioned them in his speech. He said the ancient Seepers used the cubes to get around. Karl reckons they have one here, locked behind the door in the pens."

"What are they?"

"I'm not sure exactly, but they were used a long time ago by the ancient Seepers. They're some sort of key that changes a Portdoors' destination."

"Let's go up a floor. There's bound to be something on them up there. Look at the sign — Weapons and Contraptions," said Frankie, and started up the staircase. Spencer followed.

The room was very similar to the one below except it had a gigantic glass, dome roof.

"Over here," Frankie said, pulling Spencer's sleeve. "Look, ancient devices. Realm cubes must be here somewhere," she said, running her finger along a row of old leather bound books while muttering the titles. "'The Doppler Ray', '101 Ancient Ghoul Hunting Devices'."

She continued across the bookshelf and back, until she came to a shelf near the bottom.

"Here," she said, yanking a large tatty book from the shelf. "'Mysteries of the Ancient Realm Keys' should tell us something," she said, dropping the book on the nearest table. She flipped it open and stroked her hand slowly down the contents page.

"It says there are eight keys," Frankie read. "Each key is

made up of sixty-four smaller cubes, forming one large cube. On the face of each small cube is a symbol. Each slice of the large cube can twist, thus rearranging the smaller cubes, creating an almost unlimited combination. When placed on a pedestal next to a Portdoor, it will change the destination of that Portdoor based on the chosen combination."

"That doesn't tell us much," said Spencer.

"Sounds like a Rubik's cube," said Frankie. "Listen to this," she added excitedly. "Sometime in history, it is believed that something went wrong. The cubes became more powerful than the Seepers had ever intended. Soul Reapers stole them and started using them without the need for a Portdoor."

Spencer remembered what Drake had said in his session 'something went wrong.'

Frankie looked up and stared at Spencer with a look of disbelief on her face.

"What?" said Spencer.

"That's it. Arrawn must have a cube and he knows how to use it like the Reapers did. That's how he moves about and that's how he got into your room."

At that moment, Spencer spotted Karl walking toward them. Frankie snapped the book shut and placed it back on the shelf.

"Are you guys okay?" Karl asked. "You look like you've just seen a ghoul!" He chuckled. Neither Frankie nor Spencer laughed. "Okay, bad joke. We had better get going, Spence. We shouldn't be late for our first Ectology session," he added.

The three of them left the library together. Spencer and Frankie concealed what they had been discussing and rode the elevator to the ground floor in silence.

"I'll see you later, Fran," said Spencer. Frankie acknowledged with a nod and left them at the elevator doors.

CHAPTER TEN

Ectoplasm

As Spencer walked toward the lab, Miss Nerts was standing in the doorway, her eyes narrowed as she pointed rigidly into the room. "You're late," she snapped. "Find a seat and sit in it."

Spencer did exactly as she instructed. He entered the packed room and looked around. It was small. Single desks filled the floor space, much like a traditional classroom. Along the front wall, glass phials full of a green, glowing substance sat neatly in little racks inside a row of metal cabinets.

Spencer found empty seats in the front row. He could only assume everybody wanted to be as far away from her as possible.

Miss Nerts walked over to the front of the room, peered over her glasses, and addressed the class. "You are here to learn the science and uses of ectoplasm," she began. She spoke slowly. Her voice was unusually deep and gravely for a woman. Her presence demanded silence and not a single utterance came unless she requested it.

"Ectoplasm is the lifeblood of all realm dwellers. Every microscopic particle is pure delectable energy. It should not be fooled with. It should not be poked or prodded, and it demands respect from all who yield its power."

She paced the floor while sweeping a long slow gaze across the room with her sunken eyes.

"Spencer Quinn," she bellowed.

Spencer shuddered as she spoke his name. He considered leaping out of his seat to stand to attention.

"You were late to the session today, therefore you can answer the first question," she said. "Tell me. From what was the first ectoplasm extracted?" She stood glaring down at him and waited for the answer.

Several hands shot into the air. Spencer and Karl exchanged looks. Karl's mouth moved silently, trying to tell him the answer. His eyebrows were raised and his eyes rolled from left to right, but Spencer hadn't a clue what he was trying to say.

"I don't know, Miss," Spencer said.

Nerts eyes narrowed more. She took little notice of the other cadets with their hands in the air.

"Such a simple question, Quinn. Is it too difficult for you? Very well, let's try a different one shall we? What is the name of the scientist who did the first extraction?"

Once again, several hands thrust into the air. Karl nodded his head with an urgent glare, but Spencer had no idea who the scientist was. He hadn't had time to read all the books like the others.

Sniggering filled the seats behind him.

"I don't know that either," he said rather pathetically.

Miss Nerts shook her head in disappointment. "They are simple questions, Quinn."

She continued to ignore the other cadets, intent instead on

ridiculing Spencer in front of the whole class. The sniggering turned into laughter and Spencer wished he could curl up and crawl under his seat.

"Quiet," bellowed Nerts. Everybody was instantly silent. "The first ectoplasm was extracted from a shape shifter in 1936 by Dr Lazerus Tezla. Every cadet in this academy should know that," she barked, "including you, Quinn," she pointed at his face, her finger inches from his nose.

Nerts made her point very clear and turned her attention to the rest of the class. Only the occasional menacing glare shot his way after that. The session got hands-on as it progressed. Miss Nerts handed out glass phials full of ectoplasm for closer examination. Spencer held his phial up to the light to inspect it more closely. He tipped it one way, then another, but the ectoplasm didn't move with gravity, it simply swirled and coiled of its own accord.

Without warning, there was a sudden pop followed by smashing glass at the back of the room. Everybody gasped and looked around in unison. A boy had dropped his phial and the misty ectoplasm was creeping across the desk as if it were alive.

"You clot!" screamed Nerts.

The ectoplasm cloud was growing and sprouting misty tentacles. It reached out and latched onto the boys arm, coiling around it like a snake climbing a branch. He leapt up and started screaming, frantically waving his arm in the air. But before anybody could do anything, the ectoplasm slipped up his shirtsleeve.

The boy's face froze rigid with fear. His eyes darted one way then another. He began to twitch like he was being poked with a sharp object.

Nerts grabbed what looked like a tiny silver vacuum cleaner from the wall. She pulled a round nozzle from the front of the device and extended the flexible metal tube up the boy's sleeve. She quickly flipped a switch on the handle and the device hummed into action. Instantly the ectoplasm was sucked from the boy's shirt and filled a phial attached to the back of the device.

Nerts stood over the boy and glared down at him with a half satisfied smile. "You were lucky boy. Ectoplasm retains its original characteristics and can easily possess a living creature if not handled correctly. You must treat it with respect."

The remainder of the session passed without further insult or incident. Miss Nerts gathered up all the phials and placed them carefully back into the racks. When it came to an end, Spencer left, feeling downhearted. Why did she pick on him like that?

He met Frankie in the entrance hall and they made their way home—through the Portdoor and out through the old house. As they walked up the path and past the willow tree, he told her about the attack.

"Why did she do that?" asked Frankie.

Spencer simply shrugged, "I don't know."

"Hey, I asked Albert about the realm cubes," said Frankie, sounding as though she was trying to cheer him up.

Spencer lifted his head. "What did he say?"

"Not much really. He just looked at me and smiled. But if what Karl's brother says is right and they have a cube behind that door, I reckon I could get him to show us. He's a bit of a softie when you get to know him."

"He'll never do that. It'll be more than his job's worth."

Frankie didn't reply. They walked into Spencer's back garden and up to the back door.

"I guess I'll see you tomorrow," said Frankie.

"Same time?"

"Yeah, okay. See you," replied Frankie and darted along the back gardens toward her house.

Spencer glanced down at his watch, it was only five thirty. He was early. He pulled his holdall up onto his shoulder and stepped into the house. The smell of cooked chicken lingered in the air and he could hear the television in the lounge. Without stopping, he walked straight through the kitchen, along the hallway, and up the stairs to his room. He dropped his holdall onto the floor and flopped onto his bed, exhausted.

~ ~ ~

The next two days in the academy passed without incident, unless you included getting lost several times, the challenge of sidling through the old house each day, and the utterances from the other children as Spencer walked by.

Spencer and Frankie arrived Thursday morning to a bustling entrance hall. Spencer had looked forward training day. Finally he was going to learn how to control his power. He strolled over to the desk and glanced up at the enormous electronic score board on the wall. Colin was the number one ectoplasm retriever, but his closest rival, Tom Inman, was behind by only fifteen ecto units. It was proving to be a close contest.

"Name?" said a small lady sat behind the desk. It wasn't Mary. This lady was called Helen.

"Spencer Quinn," he said quickly.

"Ah yes. Your identity tag has arrived. Please take it and put it around your neck," she handed Spencer a small piece of glass dangling from a fine metal thread as smooth and flimsy as silk. He examined it closely and curiously. It was a little larger than his thumbnail and very thin. Inside the glass was a tiny single computer chip with several metal strands branching from it like spider's legs. He hung it around his neck and tucked it inside his shirt.

"The tag is fire proof, ecto proof, water proof, and all kinds of damage proof. The only thing it doesn't resist is stupidity so don't lose it," she said sternly. She then turned to Frankie, smiled forcibly, and raised her eyebrows.

Frankie stepped forward. "Frankie Rawlinson."

Helen typed at her keyboard, paused briefly, and then handed Frankie a tag also. She glared at them alternately.

"You will no longer need to check in and out, the system will keep track of you, but you must be wearing your tags. If you're not, you will be identified as illegal intruders. Do you understand?"

Spencer and Frankie nodded together.

"The tag is also a basic communications device. The edge of the tag is lined with Illumos, and the central computer can activate it through a signal. Illumos is an intelligent liquid substance that glows various colours when activated with a small electronic charge. Red for an emergency, flashing amber if you're late for a session, and so on. It's all detailed in your manual so please read it," she instructed.

A muffled beeping emitted from Spencer's holdall. He reached in, pulled out his tablet, and flipped it open. He placed his thumb on the pad and was greeted with a message on the screen, which read:

You're next session will start in two minutes and thirty-four seconds.

Training: Mr Saunders: Third Floor: Room Three.

You will be two minutes and twenty-five seconds late.

"How does it know that?" Spencer asked.

"The computer knows where you are now, and where you should be," said Helen. "You had better run, or you'll be even more late."

"Okay, see you later, Fran." Spencer dashed across the hall. He darted into an elevator and made his way up to the third floor. Room three was at the end of the corridor. As he approached the door, it beeped once and slid open of its own accord as if the door was expecting him.

Panting heavily, Spencer stepped into a crowded room of around twenty boys and girls, chatting excitedly, all dressed in the familiar silver suits. The room was a replica of the small room leading into the holding pens, but here, a large, metal table stood in the middle of the floor. Lockers lined the far wall, and there was a heavy metal door to the right.

"Hi, Spence. Over here," shouted Karl. He turned to his right and saw Karl striding toward him.

"Hi."

"Man, you're cutting it a bit fine aren't you? Listen. You have to go to the kiosk and collect your kit," instructed Karl plucking at his suit. "Quick, go," he added pointing to a hole in the wall. The same woman he saw in the holding pens was glaring at him through her thick lens spectacles. She swivelled in her chair, lifted a silver case from a shelf behind her, and dropped it onto the counter. Then she reached below the counter and placed a neatly folded silver suit on top of the case.

"Swipe," she ordered abruptly and nodded at a tiny slot in the desk. "Your ID tag—put it in the slot, boy," she insisted.

Spencer did as he was told.

"Have a nice day," she said lazily and pushed the case at Spencer. He lifted it thinking it was going to be heavy, but it wasn't heavy at all. He walked over to the table and gently placed the case down. On the top of the case, in the centre, was a green flashing button.

Karl came and stood next to him.

Spencer stared at the case inquisitively. "What's in it?"

"This," said Karl, holding up his right arm and beaming with pride. Attached to his forearm was a gleaming metal device. Spencer had seen them on the cadets who came and went through the Portdoors. It was covered in buttons, lights, and a small screen. A short nozzle protruded from the front and two round empty slots sat on each side of his arm.

"Wow. What is that?" asked Spencer, gobsmacked.

"It's a Plasmeriser. It's basically a ghoul gun. They're the academy's prize possession. Designed and developed here in the basement. They're very proud of this technology," said Karl. He leaned closer to Spencer and whispered. "Colin told me the realm pirates have tried to steal the blueprints." He held up his arm and admired the Plasmeriser. "And you can see why."

Spencer looked at him puzzled, "Pirates?"

Karl shook his head. "Never mind."

"Why do I need a ghoul gun?" Spencer asked. "I thought we were going to learn to use our powers."

"We are. You'll see. Just open it and put it on," replied Karl nodding at the case.

Spencer pressed the green flashing button on the lid. It clicked three times, hissed softly, and popped open. Inside, lying snug in soft white moulded padding, was a gleaming Plasmeriser. It looked like something out of a James Bond movie, Spencer thought.

"It's called the EP-V3, Plasmeriser. It's so cool," Karl said, sounding like he had received the best Christmas gift ever. "That's your utility belt," he added, pointing to something folded neatly in the lid of the case.

Spencer lifted the Plasmeriser out of its snug padding. It was much lighter than it looked. He held it out in front of him, turning it one way then another.

"It's mostly made of titanium," Karl said enthusiastically. "The titanium is mixed with some other metals to make it suitable for ectoplasm retrieval. The ingredients are kept a secret, but the colder it gets, the stronger it gets, which is perfect when catching ghouls."

Spencer stared at it in awe. "It's amazing."

"Roll up your sleeve and slip it on," insisted Karl.

Spencer did as Karl suggested and guided his hand through the arm grip on the base of the device. It instantly moulded itself to his forearm, but it was light and apart from the initial cool sensation of metal on skin, he hardly noticed it was there.

"Wow! How does it do that?"

Karl smiled. "It's covered in sensors and adjusts itself to fit."

"No wonder the pirates want it," said Spencer. He slipped on his silver body suit and wrapped the belt around his waist. As soon as he joined the buckle and catch, it clicked and tightened automatically. He picked up his case and holdall and walked over to the lockers. They were all numbered and had a tiny red flashing light on the handle, except one. Number six-zero-eight had a green static light.

Karl tilted his head toward it. "That's yours," he said.

Spencer pulled it open and placed the case and his holdall inside. When he closed the door a faint click assured him it was locked.

As Spencer was limbering up, getting used to the suit and a Plasmersier on his arm, a short muscular man with a shaved head emerged from the heavy metal door. Silence filled the room.

"Listen up. My name is Tom Saunders. You can call me, Sir," he said in a military tone.

Mr Saunders looked like a fitness instructor. His skin-tight black t-shirt revealed bulging muscles. He was wearing navy blue jogging pants and white trainers. His bottom jaw was angular and jutted out.

Karl nudged Spencer in the ribs and whispered. "He's supposed to be a really good trainer. He's won loads of awards and he used to work for the government, secret service, apparently."

"How do you know this stuff?"

"I read my books."

Saunders raised his voice again. "Can you all make your way through this door please," he shouted and stepped back to let the cadets filter past in single file. They all squeezed into a small dark chamber and stood shoulder to shoulder. Spencer stood in the middle of the group next to Karl and watched Saunders close one door, snake his way through the group to the opposite wall, and open another.

A wave of gasps and excitement rippled through the cadets as each one stepped into an enormous domed room. It was easily big enough for a game of football, Spencer thought. The ceiling was high and the walls and doors were covered in what looked like the dull side of silver tin foil. A viewing chamber housing several rows of blue seats was up on the wall to his left.

"Come and stand here," called Saunders pointing to the floor space in front of him.

Everybody shuffled into place and only when they settled did Saunders begin speaking again.

"Welcome to your first training session. Today I'm going to be assisted by a mature cadet who will be helping me demonstrate how to use a Plasmeriser." As he finished speaking, a door opened to the side and Colin Dud, wearing a smug grin, strolled into the room and stood behind Saunders.

"Oh no!" muttered Karl. "It's my brother."

"Okay, quiet down please," shouted Saunders. "Today I'm going to begin by teaching you the ground rules of focusing and channelling your power through your Plasmeriser. But first, can anybody tell me the difference between a Seeper and a

Retriever?"

Many arms went up, including Karl's.

"Yes, Karl."

"The difference between a Seeper and a Retriever is that a Seeper can travel to other realms, but a Retriever can't," he said eagerly.

"Well, yes, that is one difference. Very good, Karl."

A broad smile crept cross Karl's face.

"Can anybody tell me why?"

Nobody knew the answer to that question, but Mr. Saunders was ready to explain. "If a Retriever attempts to enter another realm, he will expire within minutes. A Seeper has protection, but it's limited. When a Seeper travels to another realm, provided he eats or drinks something from that realm, he or she will be fine. If no water or food is taken within a couple of hours, he too, will die. We are still unsure why this happens, and why it only works with Seepers. However, they are simple rules. Learn them. They could save your life one day," Saunders looked at the group with wide eyes and raised eyebrows, as if he had made a very important point.

Spencer noticed Colin was sneering at him. Spencer quickly looked away.

"You should all have one of these," said Saunders, holding up his enormous arm, dwarfing the Plasmeriser attached to it.

Spencer nudged Karl. "Colin's staring at me," he whispered.

"Ignore him. He's a jerk. He's psyching you out."

Saunders then asked everybody to do something very peculiar. "Stroke your Plasmersier gently, like this." He ran his fingers along the smooth metallic surface. Spencer and Karl exchanged confused glances.

"Treat it with respect. This unit is your one and only defence against the enemy when you're in the field. Neglect it and you're realm dust."

A low mumble echoed around the group.

Saunders continued. "Now listen very carefully. This is important. To be able use your Plasmeriser, you need to connect with it. You need to feed it your thoughts and feelings. Think of it as an extension of your body. It is part of you, and you are part of it. The small screen will provide you with feedback. It functions as a map and radar, feeding you environmental information. It can inform you of your vitals, like heart rate, etc. and if you're in a team, it will show vitals and location information of your team members. All of this data is relayed back to our central computer here in the basement for analysis and tracking."

"The two slots down both sides of your arm house ecto-phials. I'm sure Nerts has told you all about ectoplasm and some of you may not need to use them. The phials housed here are made from toughened glass and reinforced with metal strands so they're very strong. Well, that's the basics of the Plasmeriser." He stepped aside, leaving Colin standing alone.

"Colin is now going to demonstrate how to catch a ghoul using his Plasmeriser. I want you all to move back against the wall and stand very still."

The cadets shuffled back against the wall, but Spencer remained at the front of the group and Karl stood next to him for optimal viewing.

Saunders marched over to the three metal cases that sat on

the floor by the door. He flipped open the lid of the first and lifted out a Plasmeriser, which was much bigger than Spencer's and Karl's, and handed it to Colin.

"Wow, awesome. He's got the new EP-V4," whispered Karl, awe struck. "It's supposed to be a prototype. It's got loads more features and power than these." He stuck out his arm.

The second case contained the same as the first, which Mr Saunders claimed for himself. The third case contained several glass phials. Saunders lifted one out, walked over to the group and held it up for all to see. The group surged forward for a closer look.

"I'm sure Nerts has told you all about this so I won't go on about it here. This is essence of ghoul," said Saunders holding the phial at arm's length.

The group muttered and whispered among themselves, then Spencer noticed Karl's arm shoot up in the air.

"Yes, Karl?"

"What ghoul did that come from sir?" he asked avidly. Spencer saw Colin roll his eyes.

"I really don't know and I don't care. It doesn't matter. All ghouls are made of this stuff, and ironically, it's this stuff that powers your Plasmeriser and dissipates the ghouls, as Colin will now demonstrate."

Saunders handed the glass phial to Colin, who carefully loaded it into one of the slots in the side of his Plasmeriser and then slid an empty phial from his belt and inserted it into the remaining empty slot.

Spencer watched keenly.

Everybody went quiet and shuffled into position to get the

best possible view.

Colin turned and paced to the edge of a white circle marked on the floor. Saunders put on a small headset and microphone behind a console, then waited.

Even though they were silent, excitement and energy oozed from the students.

No words were exchanged. Colin's signal came as a thumbs-up.

A low mechanical whirr emanated from the ceiling. A small hole peeled open high in the centre of the dome. The hairs on Spencer's arms stood on end as the temperature fell. The lights dimmed and then began to shimmer with soft turquoise light as if reflected from water.

"Release a Haunter," ordered Saunders into his microphone. His voice echoed eerily around the room.

Colin was standing feet apart as if he was about to have a sword fight, his Plasmeriser arm outstretched and raised.

There was a chilling silence; a moment where Spencer thought the world had stopped. From the hole in the ceiling, something dropped and began swooping effortlessly around the room, gliding like a bird hunting its prey, but this was no bird. It was a ghoul. As it swooped over them they could see its long white hair draped over its rotting skull and a shredded poncho that hung off its bony shoulders and trailed behind him. The creature had no legs, just a torso, arms, and a head.

It remained inside the circle like there was an invisible barrier keeping it there. Colin kept the ghoul in constant view, sidestepping as it swooped closer and away again. His movements were confident and effortless, like a footballer controlling a ball.

The ghoul stilled. It turned to face Colin and let out a haunting cry, charging him with jaws open wide. At that moment, a stream of ectoplasm burst from Colin's Plasmeriser, bathing the room in an eerie green glow. It engulfed the ghoul, snaring it in a frenzied ball of energy.

Electricity crackled in the air, Spencer could feel it prickling his skin.

For a split second, the ghoul stopped and glowered at Colin, like a bull preparing to charge. It did. Colin twitched his arm. He was focused. He didn't take a single step, but stood firm, his face as static as stone. As the ghoul charged towards him, it quickly coiled into a stream, like it was being sucked into a small hole. Then it vanished into Colin's Plasmeriser. It was as quick and abrupt as it was spectacular.

For a moment the room was silent as the lights came up, but then everybody cheered and burst with excitement.

"Wow," Spencer said, completely staggered.

"Wow," Karl repeated.

Both of them stared as if there was still something there to look at. "I've never seen him do that before," said Karl, slowly. Spencer sensed Karl had a newfound respect for his brother.

"Perfect!" shouted Saunders while clapping slowly. "That is why Colin is number one Retriever," he added proudly.

Colin ejected the phial from his Plasmersier, which made a faint hissing sound as it detached. Then he held it up, as if he had won a trophy.

Spencer turned to Karl whose mouth was still wide open. For once, he had nothing to say.

"Close your mouth Karl," said Spencer, jokingly.

"But, man, did you see that?"

Before Spencer could reply, Saunders came and stood in front of the group and said, "Okay. Who's next?"

Karl quickly leapt into the air and his arm was up in a flash. It was one of four arms to go up, but Spencer was sure Karl's was the first and probably the reason why Saunders plucked him from the group. Karl stepped out of the group and went and stood between Saunders and Colin.

Colin was shaking his head, clearly embarrassed by Karl's eagerness.

"Here, take this," instructed Saunders, handing Karl a canister full of ectoplasm. Karl handled it gently, with both hands, like it was a precious jewel and gazed at it while he waited for the next instruction.

"Go on, insert it into the left slot of your Plasmeriser and put this in the right slot," he added as he handed Karl an empty canister.

Karl did as he was told. He looked inquisitively at Mr. Saunders after each action for confirmation that he had done it correctly, which Saunders reciprocated with a nod.

"Now listen very carefully," Saunders said slowly, followed by his trademark stare. "I'm going to release the same type of ghoul as I did for Colin. It cannot harm you. This is why we use this particular Haunter. But if things do go wrong, don't panic, just stand very still and we'll handle it." Saunders stopped talking and waited for Karl's reaction, but he said nothing.

Saunders continued, "This next bit is very important. I want you all to listen carefully."

The occasional sniff and cough is all that could be heard.

"The confrontation between you and the ghoul is like a duel. You will need to focus. Feel its presence. Sustain eye to eye contact and connect with the Haunter, but most importantly, watch for, and identify the two primary moments. This will require your full concentration. The first moment will happen when it stops, turns, and taunts you mentally. You'll feel it tug at the strands of your mind. When it feels a weakness, it will attack you. Your skill and judgment is crucial here and you need to be in control. You need to feign weakness, like you're opening a door, but reveal it very slowly—draw it in like a fish to a hook. The attack will happen in a split second. It could materialise as a charge or perhaps some other ability the ghoul has. This Haunter is predictable, it will charge. Between attack initialisation, and potential human contact, is the sweet spot. There is enough time for you to react and slam the door in its face. That's when you grab it." Saunders stopped and stared. "Do you understand?"

Karl nodded slowly.

"Once the Haunter initialises attack, dig deep son," he said, thumping his stomach and staring down at Karl. "The ectoplasm in your Plasmersier will do most of the work so you don't need to channel your power as much as others would. Once the Haunter is in your grasp, hold it steady and then feed it your Plasmeriser. You must remain focused. Do not stray. Do not let anything come between you and it. You saw how Colin held it, and waited for the second primary moment. This is the moment the ghoul gives up and attempts an escape. But beware. There is a slice of time where the ghoul could flip out of your grasp. So, once you feel its weakness, clench your fist tight. The Plasmeriser will sense it and draw the ghoul in. If you miss one primary moment, it'll result in a fly-through or even a possession. One hundred percent concentration is essential. Nothing less."

Karl nodded again.

Spencer watched as Karl walked to the edge of the circle and waited. He didn't look as confident as Colin. He looked small and fragile and he kept glancing back at the group with a mixture of concern and excitement on his face.

"Karl, are you ready?" asked Saunders. Karl hesitated for a moment, glanced over his shoulder, and then raised his right thumb.

The lights dimmed and the hole in the ceiling opened once again. Everyone fell silent.

Swiftly, the same type of ghoul dropped from the ceiling and began circling. Immediately, Karl stumbled, trying to keep his eyes fixed on the ghoul. He turned awkwardly, looking over his shoulders as the ghoul circled him.

It took longer this time. It was as if the ghoul was sizing him up, searching for a weak spot. But even Spencer could see Karl lacked confidence. Colin had his face in his hands and was shaking his head.

The first primary moment came.

"Now Karl, now!" instructed Saunders. Karl flexed his arm and the ectoplasm burst from his Plasmeriser and trapped the ghoul, like Colin had done.

"Well done, now hold it steady," said Saunders.

Karl then made his first big mistake. He glanced over his shoulder and smiled complacently at the onlookers, with pride and confidence on his face. As he did so, he missed the second primary moment. The ghoul flipped out of the plasma stream and charged at him with such speed and force, Karl didn't stand a chance.

Spencer stepped away from the group and pointed. "Look out!" he shouted.

Karl turned back, but it was too late.

Everybody gasped in horror.

The ghoul passed straight through Karl's body and sent him crashing to the floor.

CHAPTER ELEVEN

First Draw

Karl lay trembling on the floor. Spencer rushed toward him, but was blocked by Saunders's bulky arm. "Stay where you are," he demanded.

The ghoul was still circling the room, swooping more belligerently now.

Colin loaded his Plasmeriser and easily captured it, while Saunders assisted a quivering Karl off the floor and over to the group.

"Are you okay?" asked Spencer.

"I really screwed up," replied Karl through chattering teeth.

"It was your first time, don't worry about it," said Spencer attempting to make him feel better, but it was clear that Karl had made a terrible mistake.

By now, everybody had surrounded Karl and was eager to know what it felt like to have a ghoul fly through him.

"It was horrible. It was like jumping into icy water. He was evil. I saw dead women and children and lots of blood. He did some terrible things," muttered Karl, his voice shuddering.

Spencer looked over at Colin who was smirking as though he enjoyed seeing his brother fail.

Saunders backed away from the group. "That's a good example of how not to focus," he bellowed. "Karl will be fine, but it'll take an hour or so for the shaking to wear off. In the meantime, who's next?"

The group seemed to shrink and retract from his question, including Spencer. Nobody wanted to follow Karl after what had just happened. When nobody said anything, a nagging voice in Spencer's mind told him he ought to volunteer. He had waited so long to learn about the power blazing inside of him and this was the perfect opportunity. But having seen Karl attempt it, he didn't want the same thing to happen to him.

"If nobody volunteers, I'll choose somebody myself," said Saunders. Then he looked at Spencer. "Quinn, are you trying to hide from me?" he said.

Spencer shook his head.

If it looked like he was hiding, he hadn't meant to.

Saunders pointed to the floor in front of him. "Get over here," he said.

Spencer stepped around to the front of the group.

"You saw what happened to Karl. Don't let the same thing happen to you. Do you understand?"

"But sir…" began Spencer.

Saunders interrupted him. "Put this into the right slot of your Plasmeriser," he said firmly.

Spencer took the empty phial and inserted it. Saunders handed him a second phial full of ectoplasm. "Put this into the left slot."

Spencer's fingers trembled as the phial clicked into place. He wasn't sure he could do any better than Karl. All he knew for sure was that he couldn't do any worse.

Saunders stood in front of him and checked that the phials were inserted correctly. "Follow me to the edge of the circle."

Spencer did as he was told, but fear griped him and he paused.

Saunders leaned over and looked him straight in the eye. "You can do this, Spencer. Forget them," he said quietly, nodding toward the group. "Cast them out of your thoughts and focus on the task at hand."

Spencer nodded slowly.

"You've felt the burn in the pit of your stomach and the searing pain in your head. Now, you have to prevent that from happening again. Channel it. The moment you feel it, visualise a fireball burning fiercely in the pit of your stomach. Don't run from it. Don't be scared. Grasp it with your minds hand. Then gently guide it up through your chest toward your right shoulder, hold it there and wait. When the Haunter reveals the first primary moment, guide the fireball down your arm and release it. Just let it go. You saw what happened to Karl. He lost his concentration. If you remain focused, you will be fine, trust me.

Spencer nodded.

"Okay, let's do this. Give me the thumbs up when you're ready to go."

After the speech Spencer felt a little more confident. The vision of Arnold up the tree and all the other times his power had pushed him to his knees flashed through his mind. It always ended with somebody getting hurt, but now, all he had to do was control it. He took a deep breath, looked down at the floor, cleared his mind, and then raised his thumb.

Saunders mumbled into his microphone and the ceiling peeled opened. Before Spencer could change his mind, the ghoul was swooping around him like a hawk circling its prey. Up close, the ghoul looked evil. Bits of flesh clung to its skull, its teeth were black and one of its eyeballs was missing. Loose skin flapped on the bones of its arms and Spencer could feel the ghoul probing his insides, rooting for his soul, searching for a target, something to grasp onto.

Spencer glared at it, not letting it out of his sight for a second. He raised his right arm and clenched his fist. He remembered how Colin moved, side stepping, using the whole circle. His heart pounded. His stomach twisted and burned. In his mind's eye, he imagined grasping a blazing fireball in his hand. The burn moved through his body as he guided the fireball toward his chest and then moved it to his right shoulder, just as Saunders had instructed. He was focused, cocooned, and alone.

Then it happened.

The first primary moment came. The ghoul stopped swooping and turned to face Spencer. He quickly released the blazing fireball in his mind's eye and the burn rushed down his arm. A blast of ectoplasm exploded from the tip of the Plasmeriser. It was powerful. The force of it shunted Spencer back a step, but he remained in control. He stood his ground, stared fervently at the thriving ball ten paces from his face, and waited for the second moment.

Muffled voices from behind him seeped into his thoughts, but he quickly pushed them out. His right arm began to tremble and he gripped it with his left hand, propping it up.

Then the second primary moment came. The creature

stopped thriving and grasped at its only chance for survival. But Spencer was too swift for it. He twisted his wrist. The tug of the Plasmeriser pulled the ghoul toward him at a terrifying rate, sucking it into the tube like a turbo charged vacuum cleaner.

The burning sensation faded. The room fell silent. Spencer gulped for air, like he had been submerged underwater. A rapturous applause erupted through the silence. The group whooped and cheered as if Spencer had won an Olympic gold medal.

Liberation ran through him, like he had released a lifetime of stress and anxiety. He stood for a moment registering what had just happened, breathing softly while staring into the space where the ghoul had been. It was the first time he'd felt like this. The first time his power was under his control. He looked down at the green glow in the tube that was empty before the duel, and then noticed the second tube was also full. No ectoplasm had been used. He turned and faced Saunders, stunned.

"What is it son?"

Spencer looked down at the two, full ecto canisters and then back at Saunders silently.

"Well I'll be a son of a Seeper," said Saunders. He held up Spencer's arm and stared at the two phials like they were liquid gold.

"Why isn't it empty?" asked Spencer.

"Looks like you don't need it, son. You have all the power you need inside of you. You don't need to power the Plasmeriser. Wow! Powerful stuff. I've seen a half phial and small traces left behind, but this beats the lot." Saunders smiled and looked down at Spencer like a proud father.

"But why? Why don't I need it?" Spencer was a little alarmed that he could catch a ghoul without the use of any ectoplasm.

"It means the power inside you is pure and strong, Spencer. Very strong." The other students were beginning to crowd around them. "Why don't we talk about this later."

Spencer nodded, a smile growing on his face.

"That was awesome. You did it, Spence and you kept a full phial," said Karl. "That's beyond awesome."

Everybody congratulated him. He had never felt this kind of pride before. For a few moments all his worries vanished and he had forgotten about his mother and Oliver. Nobody could take this moment away from him, or so it seemed.

There was one person who clearly wanted to. Colin marched toward him. "Think you're clever do you?" he whispered.

Spencer paused for a moment before handing him the canisters full of ectoplasm, "Uh, no. I don't," he replied, confused.

"Well, keep that up and I'll see to it that your life as a Seeper is short lived," he snapped, snatching the canisters from Spencer before walking away.

"Looks like you've got somebody worried," Karl muttered.

"Worried about what?"

"He wants to win the ecto-cup. It'll be the third time in a row if he does, which is a record for this academy. Nobody's achieved that before, but it looks like that might change," said Karl, placing his quivering hand on Spencer's shoulder and grinning.

Nobody else attempted to catch a ghoul, and Mr. Saunders made it clear he was very impressed with Spencer's efforts, much to the annoyance of Colin, who didn't speak to Spencer for the remainder of the session.

Saunders spent the time remaining discussing equipment, the various types of Plasmerisers, and a step by step guide on ghoul catching procedures, picking out good points from Spencer's effort and, embarrassing Karl, the bad points from his.

At the end of the session, Saunders came over and spoke to Spencer. "Great work, son," he said and winked.

"Thanks," Spencer replied.

As Saunders walked away, he shouted at the group. "Homework will be updated in your tablets. Now get out of here."

Spencer followed the group back through the chamber and into the locker room. He changed out of his suit, put his Plasmeriser back in its case, and placed it in his locker. He collected his holdall and left the session with Karl, who had now stopped shaking, apart from the odd twitch or two.

"I wonder what the homework is," Karl said as they headed for the dinner hall.

Spencer didn't answer. His thoughts had returned to catching the ghoul, the ectoplasm still in his canister, and Colin's reaction. "Does your brother always say stuff like that?" he asked Karl.

"Like what?"

"You know. What he said back there."

"Oh, yeah. He's a jerk and he'll do anything to win," replied Karl.

As they walked along the corridor, Spencer's tablet bleeped from within his holdall.

"Homework," assumed Karl.

It was a text message from Frankie, 'I have some news. Come to the library after lunch. Alone.'

Karl looked at him and smiled. "Homework, right?"

Spencer didn't answer. He didn't like lying so he tried to steer the conversation in a new direction. "We have a free period after lunch, what are you going to do?" Spencer was hoping he had something planned, leaving him free to see Frankie.

"Ah, nothing much. I'll hang out with you if you don't mind."

Spencer hesitated, unsure what to say. "Well, Okay. I'm going to the library, might be a bit boring."

"Na, that's cool."

All through lunch, Spencer wondered what Frankie wanted to tell him and hoped that Karl would eventually get bored and leave him to meet her alone, but he didn't. After a stodgy helping of toad-in-the-hole, they both set off to the library.

As they approached the door, he saw Frankie waiting outside. "Hi, Spence," she said, and beamed a broad smile. "I heard about your training. Congratulations."

"How do you know about that?" replied Spencer, surprised.

"Everybody's talking about it."

"It was only one ghoul," said Spencer, trying to shrug off his achievement like it was nothing.

"Yeah, but Albert said it's rare that anybody catches a ghoul first time using no ecto," she said and giggled. "Anyway, listen," But she stopped mid sentence and her face quickly changed when she noticed Karl standing behind Spencer.

"What were you going to say?" asked Spencer.

Frankie looked away quickly. "It doesn't matter. I'll tell you later," she said as she turned and walked into the library, quickly followed by Spencer and Karl. They climbed the steps to the first floor and Frankie sat on her own in one of the large soft chairs. She crossed her legs and grasped her holdall to her chest. Spencer and Karl sat opposite. The silence was awkward, but Karl hadn't noticed. He grabbed a book off a nearby shelf and started leafing through it.

Frankie started looking at her watch and making silent gestures at Spencer, instructing him to get rid of Karl. Spencer didn't know what to do. He simply shrugged.

It wasn't long before Karl got bored. "Right, I'm going to find Colin," he said and jumped up. "I'll catch ya later, man."

"Okay," said Spencer, lifting his right arm to wave.

They waited until Karl was out of sight before talking. "I didn't think he was ever going to leave," sighed Frankie.

"Me neither. What's up?"

"I asked Albert what's behind the locked door. There is definitely a realm cube in there. He's going to show me in about half an hour and I convinced him to let you come too."

Spencer looked at her in disbelief.

Frankie nodded silently.

He remembered Karl telling him that he thought there might be a cube behind the door. But the information came from his brother, so it wasn't the most reliable source.

"Albert also said if anybody finds out about this, his job will be on the line, so we have to keep it quiet," she whispered.

He could see now why she didn't want Karl around. He didn't want to pass up the opportunity. It was one of eight realm cubes used by the ancients. He had to see it. "Okay, let's go," he said.

Spencer and Frankie made their way down to the holding pens to meet Albert who was early and standing outside waiting for them.

"Remember what I said. Tell no one," reminded Albert.

They stepped into the entry chamber and pulled on the silver suits. The pens were eerily quiet. Just the deep, mechanical hum could be heard, with the occasional faint crackling from inside the pens. As Spencer past the Soul Stalker pen, he paused and glanced into it, remembering what it did to him the last time he saw it, but the chamber was still.

"Give me your tags," said Albert. Spencer looked at Frankie confused, but took it off nonetheless and handed it to Albert. "Listen you two. I'm showing you this cause I owe Frankie a favour. I don't want any trouble so you've got to keep it quiet. Don't tell a soul. Is that clear?" insisted Albert.

Spencer and Frankie nodded together.

"Now we need to fool the bods downstairs into thinking that it's only me going in there. I'll leave your tags here," said Albert and placed them on the floor by the door.

Spencer remained quiet, as did Frankie. As he stood in the dimly lit holding pens in the eerie silence, Albert tapped in the security code and the door hissed open. They all stepped into a small chamber. When the door closed, Albert opened another.

Spencer's jaw dropped and Frankie let out a soft gasp.

The room was cold enough that Spencer could see his breath. The walls, ceiling, and floor were glowing blue-white. In the centre of the room, beneath a glass dome, a stone pedestal poked up through a hole in the floor. A small, shimmering cube sat on top.

Spencer took a step forward. A hand grasped his shoulder. "Stop," said Albert firmly. "Don't get any closer."

"Where did it come from?" whispered Spencer. He wasn't sure why he was whispering, but it felt appropriate under the circumstances.

"It was found in a pile of rocks when the Tezlas discovered the ancient Portdoor," Albert explained.

Spencer looked at it carefully. He could see there were many smaller cubes, but it had more sides and it was bigger. He could also see there were symbols etched into each face. Spencer had seen Japanese symbols and he thought they looked very similar. "So why doesn't the academy use it?" he asked.

"We're not sure how to use it safely. The smaller cubes can twist and have an endless amount of combinations, possibly more than there are realms. And if we could use it, we're not sure where the Portdoors would lead us when activated. Some research has been done, but we have a long way to go before we understand its true power.

"I don't understand?" said Spencer. "We have Portdoors here that work perfectly. What's the difference?"

"Our Portdoors allow us to travel locally, inside our own realm," said Albert and smiled. "But the academy has had very little success when travelling to other realms. With the help of the basement, Drake has detected several realms but has only mastered getting to a few of them. Finding realms and pin-pointing safe Portdoor locations is a blind science at the moment."

"What if somebody steals it?" asked Frankie.

Albert laughed. "Nobody can get in here. Only select personnel have access to this chamber. You see that hazy shimmer around the cube, if you touch it, your hands will burn so it's impossible."

The moment he finished speaking, his smile disappeared and he spun around to face the door. "Shh, somebody's coming."

Spencer shot a look at Frankie. She was giving Albert a concerned lingering stare. Footsteps were clanking up the metal pathway. Angeline and Drake appeared in the doorway. Their tags dangled from Angeline's hands.

"What's going on here?" she said in a loud, demanding voice.

Spencer and Frankie exchanged glances.

Albert took a step forward. "I was showing them the cube, Angeline, that's all," he said, shakily.

"But you know this is a secure chamber and nobody is allowed in here. What were you thinking?"

"But I thought—" began Albert, but Angeline raised her hand and silenced him.

"You thought nothing of the consequences, Albert. Drake, guide these two out of Tezla. I will deal with them tomorrow. Albert, you stay here," instructed Angeline, glaring at him. Spencer snatched a look at Drake who had a wry smirk on his face and looked as though he was enjoying Albert's predicament.

Angeline handed Spencer and Frankie their tags. Drake turned and walked out of the chamber followed by Spencer and Frankie. Drake led them to the changing room, waited for them to climb out of their suits, and then guided them out into the corridor. Without uttering a single word, Drake pointed to the entrance hall and left them alone.

"Albert's going to be in big trouble and it's all my fault," said Frankie.

"It's not your fault, Fran."

"What if they dismiss him?"

Spencer shook his head. "I don't think they'll do that. They need him. Who else can look after the pens as well as he can?"

That didn't appear to appease Frankie. Spencer could tell by her distant quietness that she was worried.

As they made their way back through the house, Spencer thought about the cube and began to understand Drake's obsession. How did it work? Where could it lead them? What wonders might be waiting for them to discover?

It was late afternoon when they stepped outside into the warm summer air. It was scented with Honeysuckle and he heard the faint hum of bees lazily going about their business. Spencer liked stepping outside after being at the academy all day. It was energizing to breathe the fresh air.

Spencer left Frankie at his garden gate as he always did and went inside. His mother was doing her housework, as usual, and somehow Spencer knew that attending the academy was going to help her. He now knew what happened to Oliver and one way or another he was going to prove it to her once and for all.

CHAPTER TWELVE

Drake's Plan

Spencer woke early the following morning. A thumping headache had got the better of him during the night. He lost count how many times he woke with images of Angeline throwing him out of the academy and Albert being fired. He wasn't sure what to expect today, but he knew one thing: he was closer to finding Oliver than ever before and he couldn't stop his search now.

He got dressed and had breakfast. When he arrived at the Willow tree at nine o'clock, Frankie was waiting. She was leaning against the wall, toying with a stone beneath her foot, "Hi, Fran," he said.

She didn't look up. "Morning."

"What's up? Are you worried about Albert too?"

"Well, yeah, but it's not just that. I'm going on holiday next week."

Spencer frowned. "What's wrong with that?"

"We're going to Spain. I was looking forward to it, but now I don't want to go. I want to stay here with you, and go to Tezla."

"Oh."

"There's more," said Frankie quietly. "Do you remember I

told you my Dad may have a new job?"

"Yeah."

"Well, it's in Manchester and Dad said we might have to move up there," she kicked the stone away and started up the path. "Everything seems to be going wrong all at once."

Spencer ran to catch up with her. A chasm had opened in the pit of his stomach. If she moved away, he would lose his best friend. "Have you told them how you feel about it?"

"Of course. Dad says it'll be fine and I'll make new friends, but he doesn't understand. Grown-ups think they know best, but they don't. Anyway, we'd better hurry or we'll be late." She scrambled through the hole in the wall.

Spencer followed.

~ ~ ~

The Tezla Portdoor chambers and the gigantic entrance hall were quiet and there were only a few cadets passing through. Spencer spotted Hazel, dressed in her white coat walking toward them.

"Hello, Spencer," Hazel said with a broad welcoming smile as she approached.

"Hi, Hazel. Is everything alright?"

"Everything is fine," she replied. "Angeline has asked me to walk with you to your first Seeper session, that's all. She spoke to Albert about the incident yesterday, and he explained that it wasn't your fault, so she won't be taking the matter any further."

Spencer and Frankie swapped glances. "Doesn't she want to see us at all?" asked Spencer.

Hazel shook her head.

"What about Albert? What's going to happen to him?" said Frankie.

Hazel simply shrugged.

Spencer was confused. Angeline was very angry when they found them in the chamber yesterday. It was a realm cube after all and Albert broke the rules. Something didn't feel right.

Frankie, filling an awkward pause said, "Do you need to escort me too?"

"Nobody said I should escort you, Frankie, only Spencer."

Frankie turned to Spencer and shrugged. "Okay. Well, I'll meet you in the dining hall for lunch. Then we'll go to the library."

Spencer nodded. "Okay," he said, still trying to figure out why Angeline was being so lenient.

Frankie turned and strolled across the hall toward the holding pens.

"What are you researching?" asked Hazel.

Spencer's mind was still full of Angeline and he was curious to know why she didn't want to see him. "Researching?" he said.

"The library?" Hazel reminded him.

"Oh! We're looking for records on Oliver's kidnapping. We thought there must be some sort of record of it in the library, but it looks like they've all been removed."

Hazel lowered her head and looked at the floor. "Oh, really?"

"Do you know anything about that?" asked Spencer.

Hazel shook her head, looked ahead and rushed across the hall, "we must hurry or we'll be late," she said.

As they entered the corridor and passed through the glass walkway, Spencer became aware of the whispers.

"It's him, there he is," said a girl standing with a small group waiting for an elevator. They gawked and pointed at him like he was some oddity.

It was as if Hazel had heard his thoughts. "They know about your training session yesterday. Everybody's talking about it," she said. "Nobody catches a ghoul on their first try without using a single drop of ectoplasm. Nobody."

"So I'm told," said Spencer. "But it just felt natural."

"That's a good sign. The mark of a true Seeper," replied Hazel, smiling. But it was a forced smile. Spencer sensed she was trying hard to be friendly.

They reached the door to the Seepers lab. Hazel stopped, hesitated, and turned to face Spencer. "I'm sorry, Spencer. Listen, Drake has been acting odd lately. He's putting so much time into his latest project that it's beginning to take its toll. He may seem moody today, just don't take it personal."

"Um, okay," replied Spencer, a little dumbfounded.

Hazel opened her mouth to speak again, but whatever she was going to say, Spencer would never know. She closed her mouth, turned, and opened the door. She entered the chamber and Spencer followed. When he stepped through into the Seeper lab, Drake was sitting at his console studying a small flat screen in front of him. The three larger screens on the wall were blank and the group of cadets Spencer had met in the first session were already seated at the back of the room.

Drake spun around in his chair to face them. "About time," he said sharply. "Take a seat."

Spencer noticed Drake glare at Hazel. He didn't say a single word, but Hazel seemed to know what he wanted her to do. She turned and hurried out of the room.

Drake waited for her to close the chamber door before speaking, while Spencer found a seat in the front row.

"Okay. Let's begin," announced Drake. "Today, I'm going to explain what I hope to achieve over the coming weeks." He turned to face the three large screens looming down at them and pressed a button on the console. His next words made Spencer's spine shudder with excitement. "We are going to destroy Arrawn," he said, and then paused while staring up at the screens.

Spencer shifted uneasily in his seat and glanced around at the other cadets who were looking troubled.

Drake continued. "Our sole mission is to rid Asgard of this tyrant. He is evil in purest form."

The centre screen burst to life, displaying thousands of tiny glowing particles amassed in a hazy blue loop, like a galaxy.

Drake reached out his arm and pointed at the screen. "These are realms," he said with a hint of pride in his voice. As Drake stared at them spiralling gently around the enormous screen, he began to relax his callous exterior. "Asgard is here," he said. A white ring appeared on the screen, circling one of the glowing realms.

Spencer stopped breathing for a second. Oliver was his first thought. If he was alive, that's where he would be.

"We have numbered the realms in order of discovery, our realm being zero. We reference them using our own numerical positional guidance system," said Drake highlighting another realm near the centre of the swirling mass.

Spencer remembered what Albert said about the realms, 'finding them was a blind science.' With Drake relaxed, Spencer thought he would brave a question. "How did you find them all?" he asked, noticing his voice was slightly higher than usual.

Drake reeled around, face stern. For a moment, Spencer thought he was going to be scolded for speaking freely.

"Using our highly specialised equipment, we can detect their noise," replied Drake, and without further explanation, turned his back to them again.

"Dr. Tezla discovered that the realms were once permanently connected by Portdoors which remained open, allowing free passage from one realm to another. The ancients built this elaborate transport system and, as far as we know, extended it to all realms."

Spencer stared up at the screen wondering what marvels might exist within these places. It was phenomenal to think about and he could easily understand how Drake had become so consumed with discovering new worlds and new civilisations.

Drake continued, "It's believed the veils between realms, the walls that separate one from another, are forming splits and more of the realm's inhabitants are seeping through to places they don't belong. Once they slip through there's no way back. If they slip through to our realm, it's our job to capture them and bring them here, as you have seen in the holding pens."

Drake pressed more buttons on his console and the left screen stuttered into life. The view had zoomed into the cluster, displaying a handful of realms. Spencer noticed the name 'Asgard' on the left of the screen and above the name were three, five digit numbers. Branching from the name was a straight line attached to a small circle, illustrating the exact location of the realm.

Spencer was spellbound, but then he was struck by a sudden curiosity. If a Portdoor was needed to get around realms, how did Arrawn travel with such pinpoint accuracy without using one? He wondered if Drake would know the answer.

"How does Arrawn get from one realm to another and into places without using Portdoors?" he blurted out.

"That's a very good question, Spencer," said Drake as he glanced over his shoulder and smirked. "We're certain Arrawn has a realm cube and he's learned how to master it. He activates an ancient Portdoor at the centre of Asgard, and by tapping into the cube somehow, he seeps through into another realm of his choosing. We believe with sufficient knowledge, the user can manipulate the cube to determine a specific time and location rather than a Portdoor. The cube then creates a temporary wormhole, in which he can travel with precision. However, we believe the wormhole doesn't remain open for any great length of time and it causes a lot of damage to the veils, causing them to rupture and split."

The room was silent. Nobody moved. The others were enthralled and Spencer could hardly believe his own ears. Then it suddenly dawned on him. What he had witnessed in his bedroom when Oliver was taken—the bright light and the hole Oliver disappeared through. It must have been a wormhole created by Arrawn using a cube and he had seen it with his own eyes.

Drake continued. "It was believed for a long time that only the ancient Seepers could manipulate the cubes, but we were wrong."

"Has anybody ever found any of the other cubes?" said a boy behind Spencer.

Drake turned and paused briefly before answering. "Many of the eight are yet to be discovered. We know the realm pirates of Puya have one, maybe two. A Seeper once encountered the pirates on a scouting mission and overheard them bragging about a cube like it was a pot of gold. As far as we know, they do not have the knowledge or power to use it, but it's only a matter of time before they do."

Drake turned to gaze questionably at the screens. "Of course, Arrawn also has one, but he wants them all. With all eight cubes, he could travel to the edge of realms, vanquishing each realm as he goes. More importantly, he could access the sacred Seeper chamber where the ancients once observed and controlled the realms using the eight cubes. If he reaches it, he could destroy everything and everyone and attain his goal of complete control. It is our job to prevent this from happening."

Spencer noticed how passionate Drake sounded. He spoke with conviction and determination, but it was hatred for Arrawn that engrained his voice.

"Can we stop him?" asked Spencer.

"That is our intention," Drake replied. "But it's not that simple. We have detected two Portdoors in Asgard that we suspect can be activated. We have since sent probes deep into Arrawn's lair where one of these Portdoors exist, but the probes have disappeared without a trace. It appears that the second Portdoor is our way in and our initial investigations have proven successful," Drake said, but was interrupted by an alarm indicating the end of the session. "That's all for now. Homework will be sent to your tablets. Make sure you complete it before we see each other again next week."

Spencer left the session agitated. He had been fed so much information and so many wonders had arisen that had no answers. As he strolled toward the canteen, he could still hear his name being uttered around the academy, but he didn't let it bother him, he had too much to think about to let it get to him.

While riding the elevator, he couldn't stop thinking about Oliver. Was he still in Asgard? Was he dead? What had Arrawn done to him?

Frankie was in the canteen eating her lunch when Spencer arrived. She was sitting alone and gestured toward an empty seat next to her. Spencer nodded. The queue to the serving hatch was short and it took little time for him to collect his tuna salad sandwich and settle in the seat next to Frankie.

"Hi, Spence. How was your session with Drake?"

"It was okay," he prodded his lunch with his finger.

"Are you alright?" asked Frankie.

"Yeah, I'm fine," he replied, but he was distracted by Karl's unmistakable voice.

"Hi, guys, how has your day been?" Karl slid into a chair next to Spencer. Before giving anybody a chance to answer, he spoke again. "Hey, did you hear about Albert?"

Spencer's eyes met with Frankie's. "No. What happened?"

"He's been summoned to the council. The rumour is he's going to get fired."

Both Frankie and Spencer sat in complete silence not really knowing what to say.

"I wondered why I didn't see him this morning," said Frankie eventually. "What did he do?" she added trying not to sound guilty.

"I don't know, but it's just a matter of time before I find out," Karl said as he tucked into his sandwich. He fed his face but it didn't take him long before he piped up again. "What do you think about our little trip on Monday?" he said.

All thoughts of Albert were suspended while Spencer looked at him and frowned. "Trip? What trip?"

"We're going on a retrieval mission. A real life in-the-field kick ass ghoul retrieval, it's going to be awesome," said Karl.

Spencer and Frankie exchanged glances and then looked back at Karl.

"How do you know?" asked Spencer.

Karl frowned. "Didn't you receive your schedule for next week?"

Spencer reached into his bag and pulled out his tablet. The little green message light was blinking. He placed his thumb on the pad and flipped it open. On the screen was the text;

2 New Messages

With his finger, he touched the envelope icon and the first message opened. Karl was right. They were going on a real life mission, but it didn't reveal any details. It simply read:

Meet in the training ground at 9.00 am Monday morning for a mission debriefing. Collect equipment from locker and be prompt - DS.

Spencer closed the first message and opened the next. Nothing could have prepared him for what appeared on the screen. It read:

Do not attend the training mission on Monday, or you will DIE!

Spencer gasped and sat taut in his chair. He looked at the 'from' box. It was empty.

How can that be?

Without thinking, he blurted out the one name that popped into his head, "Colin."

"Colin what?" asked Karl.

Spencer quickly deleted the message, closed the tablet, and swiftly slipped it back into his holdall. "Oh…nothing," he said. "Are you ready to go?" He rose out of his seat quickly to avoid any further questioning and headed toward the door without waiting for Frankie or Karl.

"Spencer, wait up," Frankie called as she ran up beside him. "Are you okay? You're acting really strange today."

"Yeah, I'm fine." he glanced over his shoulder to see where Karl was. "I'll tell you about it later."

Frankie looked at him and frowned, but didn't push any further. They made their way up to the library. Spencer peered around every corner and the cadets still gawped at him as they passed. It seemed that everyone was still talking about him.

Frankie had already decided what they were going to do with their free time. She instructed Spencer to search the 'Buildings and Land' section for any records of an intrusion at his old house in Hertfordshire, while she searched the 'Unexplained Intrusions' section. But it was a fruitless afternoon. There was no trace of Arrawn in either.

As they journeyed home, a sense of foreboding crept into Spencer's mind. He had never received a death threat before, except from Billy and his cronies, but that was a normal everyday threat. He could handle them. This was different. It was real. He kept it from Frankie. She was going on holiday for a week and he didn't want her to worry about him the whole time she was gone. Instead, he told her he was upset by Drake's session and the fact that it brought back memories of Oliver's disappearance, which was mostly true anyway.

CHAPTER THIRTEEN

The Retrieval

The weekend went by slowly and was terribly boring. Spencer spent most of the time in his bedroom reading. He skimmed through the Paranormal Observer three times, flicked through his induction manual twice, picked up several books and scanned the first page of each, but found it difficult to concentrate on any of them. The only thing that kept his attention for any length of time was an article in the Paranormal Observer titled 'The Twin Strikes Back'. The reporter, Blanch Rokbottom, whom Spencer had never met, had written an article about Oliver's abduction and how Spencer would be joining Tezla Academy to avenge his brother's death. Where she got her information was anybody's guess, but he was used to seeing articles like this in real newspapers after Oliver disappeared, and it didn't leave an impression on him.

On Sunday, Frankie went on vacation to Spain. Knowing that she wasn't there made him feel uneasy. He was lonely without her. Frankie was the only person who knew how he felt and what he was truly going through.

That evening, he finished an assignment he had been sent via his tablet, an article on 'Ectoplasm Sources and Uses' from

Miss Nerts, which had been surprisingly more fascinating than he had expected.

He woke on Monday morning excited by the sudden realisation that he was going on his first real retrieval mission. He glanced at his clock. It read five past eight. He slid out of bed, got dressed, and rammed his books and tablet into his holdall. Halfway down the stairs, he paused on the landing outside his mother's bedroom. The door was slightly ajar. He stood for a moment and peered through the gap into the room. His mother was fast asleep, but even as she slept she didn't look peaceful. She turned and twitched beneath the blue duvet. She had been like that ever since Oliver left and it wasn't getting any better. He wished he could make her well, give her life again, see her laugh and smile like she used to.

He skipped breakfast, scribbled a quick note to his mother saying he was going out with some friends from school and left the house by way of the back door. The weather was a stark grey contrast to recent days. The air was cool and a spattering of raindrops hit his face.

It was the first time Spencer ventured through the old house alone. Without Frankie, it was darker and more sinister. Lonely.

Upon arriving in the bustle of the entrance hall he headed for the elevator and rode it up to the residence floor. He knew Karl would be in the relaxation room and would go with him to the briefing.

As he entered, a group of young cadets were standing near the doorway and Karl was among them. He spotted Spencer and immediately peeled away from the group and hurried toward him.

"Hey, Spence. I can't believe it, man. We're really going out this morning. You only just made it—we have to be in the training ground for a briefing in five minutes," said Karl, clearly excited at the prospect of a capture.

Before Spencer could open his mouth, Karl's tablet bleeped repeatedly. Karl flipped it open, tapped the screen and smiled. "Time to go," he said and marched toward the door.

Spencer followed.

The warning Spencer received on Friday continued to trouble him as they made their way to the training ground. As far as he knew, he hadn't done anything to receive that sort of threat.

"You Okay? You're very quiet," Karl asked as they walked up to the training ground door.

"Yeah, I'm fine," Spencer said. He was pretty sure Karl would blab it to the entire academy.

They entered the training ground lobby just as Saunders appeared at the doorway wearing a silver body suit.

"Quiet please," Saunders yelled. "Can everybody please go through into the training ground for a briefing?"

The cadets shuffled through the chamber and into to the training ground. Spencer noticed many of the cadets had a distant nervousness about them, while others were laughing and joking about what they might be catching today.

"Where do you think we're going?" Karl whispered.

Spencer shrugged. "Don't know, but I think we're about to find out." He nodded at Saunders who came and stood in front of them.

Before Saunders spoke, Spencer had the strangest sensation,

like fingers lightly stroking his hair. He turned, but nobody was there. Then, out of the corner of his eye, he glimpsed a silhouetted figure standing in the shadows, motionless, high up in the viewing chamber. Spencer didn't know how he knew, but he was certain he was being observed.

"I know this is only your second week of training," Saunders began with a clear booming voice. "But our belief is that some of you are naturally gifted and there is no better way to hone your abilities than to do it in the field. So, today will be your first true test.

"As most of you are Retrievers, we'll be remaining in our own realm and will be travelling to the Tower of London."

A scattering of whispers and gasps echoed around the group.

"Cool!" said Karl. "I've always wanted to see that place."

"This will be no holiday I can assure you," Saunders said sternly.

Spencer looked up at the viewing box again. The figure was still there, unmoving. Was it his assassin, he wondered? He leaned closer to Karl. "There's somebody watching us in the viewing box."

"So?" shrugged Karl. "There's always somebody watching, that's what it's there for."

"Quiet down please," insisted Saunders. "I need your full concentration today." He waited until everyone had settled and continued. "The towers are a regular hot spot for ghouls leaking into our realm. Throughout time, the veil in and around the castle has worn extremely thin and ghouls often seep through. However, they quickly discover there is no way of returning and create complete havoc. We have reports of two Haunters and a Soul Stalker causing the visitors some considerable distress, and it's our job to capture all three and bring them back here."

Another wave of gasps and whispers rippled through the group.

Saunders held up his hand for silence. "It is the responsibility of the D.D.G. to deal with the public that have seen ghouls. Their memories will be wiped, so you needn't worry about being seen by the public. The D.D.G. have cordoned off sections of the castle to allow us to enter without further disturbance." He paused and fixed the group with his penetrating stare. "Any questions?"

Predictably, Karl's arm shot up in the air. "Is there a Portdoor nearby?"

"Yes, of course." Saunders rolled his eyes. "How do you think we're going to get there, by train?" Everybody laughed. Karl's face went scarlet. "The castle has one of the original Portdoor sites built by Dr Tezla. He discovered the weakness in the veils in that location and decided to use it for his studies and subsequently part of the training programme. The castle is a perfect environment for our needs. Are there any more questions?"

The cadets seemed spellbound by the task ahead. Some of them were frantically tapping notes into their tablets as Saunders spoke and Spencer wondered for a moment whether he ought to be doing the same.

"We'll be taking some additional equipment with us that I hope will prove indispensable," Saunders said, striding toward two silver boxes next to the door and carrying them over to the group.

Once again, Spencer glanced up at the viewing box. The figure hadn't moved. Nobody else seemed bothered by the onlooker and Spencer wondered if paranoia was getting the better of him.

Saunders placed the boxes on the floor and flipped open the lids. "We'll all be wearing one of these," he held up an earpiece. He pushed it in his ear. "They have a broad range and will allow us to keep in contact with each other while we're out in the field. And remember, to switch it on and off, gently tap the side with your finger."

He pulled out what looked like a pair of binoculars from the second box. A rubber strap hung from the long viewing tubes. Saunders stretched them over his head and rested the lenses on his eyes.

The group laughed.

"Okay, calm down. These are Plasoptics and they have several modes. Primarily, they will help you see in the dark. However, if you're not gifted with Seeing, these will also help you see ghouls before they materialise.

"What's Seeing?" whispered Spencer.

"Some ghouls can hide themselves, they become invisible. Seeing is the ability to see the ghouls while in that state," said Karl and he gave Spencer a questioning look. "You really should do your homework," he added.

"I want you all to take a pair of these and then wait over by the door," Saunders instructed as he pushed the Plasoptics to his forehead.

Everybody surged forward, but Karl was the first at the box.

"One at a time, please," Saunders bellowed.

Spencer stood back and waited for the scramble to diminish. Then he proceeded to lift an earpiece from the white foam packing and grab a pair of Plasoptics off the tangled pile.

The cadets started pretending to communicate like astronauts, including imitating all the radio static.

Saunders stepped forward again. "Listen up. When you leave here, I want you all to collect a suit from Cheryl at the counter, take out your utility belts and your EP-V3s, strap them on, and make your way quietly to the entrance hall. Please ensure you are wearing your ID tags," he instructed. "The Portdoors are programmed to stop you if you're unfortunate enough to leave your tag behind. Is that clear?"

Everybody mumbled and nodded confirmation.

"Okay, move out," Saunders ordered.

Before leaving, Spencer glanced one last time up into the viewing box. It was empty.

As they pulled on their suits and strapped on their equipment, the mood had changed dramatically. They were no longer joking around. The realisation of an actual mission had finally settled in their minds.

Once equipped, they all ambled down to the entrance hall and gathered in the centre. Spencer noticed the broad physique of Colin striding toward the group. He was alone with his usual smirk smeared across his face. He walked directly up to Karl and slapped him on the back.

"Hi, Bro. Thought I would come and wish you good luck, man. You're gonna need it," he laughed.

Spencer watched him carefully. Perhaps it was Colin that

was standing in the viewing box?

"Read it and weep," said Colin, as he nodded toward the leader-board that was displaying his name at the top. Then he turned and glared at Spencer. "What are you gawping at, Quinn?"

Karl stepped between them. "Leave him alone."

Colin grimaced and then looked down at Karl. "I've got to get going. I'll see you later, bro, if you come back alive," he sniggered and strolled away.

"What's his problem?" whispered Spencer.

Karl swept his hand through the air. "Ignore him. He's messing with your mind, that's all."

"Okay everybody, listen up," Saunders shouted. His voice startled Spencer. "Portdoor twenty five has been programmed to take us to the tower. I will leave first. Then I want you all to follow one by one, but watch the lights. Only leave when the green light is lit. Matt Stamper, get up here." A tall boy with short brown hair scurried to the front. "You will be in charge of seeing them all through."

"Yes, sir," Matt replied, beaming.

"Is everything clear?" requested Saunders as he turned and glared at the group. He waited. Everybody confirmed with a nod. "Okay, let's move out," he marched over to the Portdoor chamber marked twenty five. Just inside the chamber, the Portdoor was active and ready to receive passengers. "Form an orderly queue, and remember, only one cadet at a time."

Spencer's stomach rolled as nerves got the better of him. The mood of the group had changed even more dramatically. Hardly a word was spoken. The girl in front of Karl was sliding the zip of her suit up and down and Spencer noticed that even

Karl had stopped talking, which was unusual for him. He then observed Smith and Pattel staggering across the hall toward them carrying two large silver boxes.

"What are in those?" Spencer asked.

"Don't know," Karl replied.

"Good luck everyone. See you on the other side," Saunders said.

Everybody leaned sideways and watched him step into the Portdoor and disappear into the liquid wall. The green light on the Portdoor frame flamed red but within five seconds, it reverted to green.

One by one, the cadets stepped into the Portdoor and the queue shortened. While Spencer waited, he looked at each cadet in turn, wondering if any of them were capable of killing him, but he knew most of them couldn't even catch a ghoul let alone kill a human being. The thought had occurred to him that it might be a practical joke, but he had to keep his wits about him.

Now it was Karl's turn to step into the Portdoor. He fidgeted nervously, waiting for the light to turn green. Spencer knew Karl hadn't travelled as often as he had, so he understood his apprehension.

"Are you alright?" Spencer asked.

"Yeah, why do you keep asking?" said Karl as the light turned green. "I have to go. I'll see you there." He half smiled and stepped into the Portdoor.

Spencer watched Karl swirl into the liquid wall. He stared at the light while waiting for it to change. When it flared green he hesitated, but then stepped into the cool liquid. He had gotten used to the nauseating whirl and the cool silk air that surrounded him. He had mastered control of the sick feeling and let the Portdoor do the work and not fight it.

CHAPTER FOURTEEN

Belly of the Tower

The air was cold. The room was small and dimly lit. The floor and walls were constructed from large sand stones many centuries old and the ceiling was low enough for Spencer to reach up and touch it.

He paused briefly as he mentally grasped his surroundings. Saunders stood in front of him, gesturing for him to step forward, away from the Portdoor. The group of cadets standing behind Saunders were laughing hysterically, presumably at him as he swirled into focus and stumbled out. Spencer joined them and spun around to watch.

The Portdoor was set back in the wall inside an open cupboard. It came as no surprise to Spencer to see a boy standing nearby holding a red bucket. As the cadets stepped out of the Portdoor, many of them looked pale and sickly. A short boy, who had stood behind Spencer, came through and vomited, but he completely missed the bucket and covered the boy holding the bucket with chewed chunks and yellow, stringy slime. The whole group roared with laughter.

When the last cadet staggered into the room, Saunders spoke. "We've arrived in the bowels of The Tower of London.

The basement is out of bounds to the public and is restricted to staff, security and the D.D.G. only."

As he spoke, a soldier wearing a camouflage uniform, whose head almost touched the ceiling, entered the room through a narrow arched passage. He wore a red beret. On the front was a gold badge with three inscribed wings. Spencer noticed he was a sergeant by the three white chevron stripes on his sleeve. He came and stood next to Saunders, saluted, and stood to attention. Saunders responded with a salute and also stood to attention. After a few seconds, they both seemed to relax.

"Good morning, sir," said the soldier. "Are the boys ready?" he asked.

"Almost, I was allowing them to recover from their journey," replied Saunders as he looked at the group and grinned. One boy was trying to wipe vomit off his sleeve.

The soldier smiled at the cadets and nodded. "Yes of course. Very well then, when you're ready, come up to the briefing room and we'll go through the details." The soldier turned, stooped to avoid hitting his head, and left the room through the arched doorway.

Saunders turned back to the group and said, "You'll be travelling in pairs so select a partner." He then bent down and opened one of the silver cases Smith and Patel had carried with them. It was full of ecto-phials. "Equip your Plasmerisers with one empty and one full. When you're done, check your partner has inserted theirs correctly. I don't want any screw-ups. Is that clear?" He paused and scanned them. The usual nods and mumbles ensued. "Smith, Pattel, follow me and bring that box," he ordered pointing at the remaining closed silver box.

Saunders strode out of the room with Smith and Pattel on his heels carrying the small box between them.

The group sorted themselves into pairs and Spencer had plenty of offers from potential partners, but Karl had already elected himself for that position.

As they were installing the ecto-phials into their Plasmerisers, Saunders marched back into the room. "We've identified the targets," he announced. Silence descended and everybody turned to face him. "Smith and Pattel are setting up the plasma shield in the surrounding area. When activated, the targets will not be able to penetrate it and will be confined to the tower. When the shields are up, you'll see them appear on your EP screen. Activate your earpiece and scanner now," he ordered.

Spencer tapped his earpiece, which proceeded to unfold. Then he pressed a small silver button next to the scanner on his Plasmeriser. The screen flickered and illuminated green and he could see three small glowing targets. Two of them were moving very slowly as a pair, while the other was stationary at the bottom of the screen.

"The three blips on your screen are the targets," said Saunders. "The two roaming together are the Haunters and the other is a Soul Stalker."

"That is so cool," whispered Karl, clearly impressed by the whole event.

Saunders tapped the side of his earpiece. "Smith, Pattel, can you read me?"

A crackle sounded in Spencer's ear followed by a boy's voice. "Yes, sir."

"How are the shields coming?"

"They're up and ready now, sir," replied the voice. As he said the words, Spencer saw a green ring appear on his EP scanner, encircling the Haunters, the Soul Stalker, and everybody in the vicinity.

"Okay. Stay where you are. I'm sending more cadets to join you."

"Yes, sir."

Saunders looked hard at the group. "Unit, listen up. Two pairs will circle the shield perimeter in opposite directions. Another pair will defend the middle sector and together, you will trap the Haunters. Remember what you've learned. Is that clear?"

"Yes, sir," the cadets said excitedly, although Spencer wasn't feeling overly enthusiastic or confident. Only a few of the cadets had experience catching ghouls.

Saunders spoke into his microphone again. "Smith, Pattel, move around the perimeter clockwise."

"We're on it, sir," a voice said in Spencer's ear.

"Enter the dining hall, turn left, and follow the wall. Do not stray. Do not speak unless there's an emergency or you're asked to speak. Understood?"

"Yes, sir."

Saunders then pointed to a girl and a boy standing to Spencer's right. "You two will move anticlockwise. Same rules apply. Go and join Smith and Patel, now." They quickly left through the arch. Spencer noticed Karl was standing on his toes and jiggling in desperation, hoping Saunders would pick him for something.

"And you two," he said, pointing to two boys at the back.

Karl slumped back onto his heels. Saunders continued. "You take the centre, and whatever happens, do not leave your position. Is that clear?"

The boys nodded silently.

"Go."

Saunders peered into his scanner inquisitively. "That leaves the Soul Stalker," he mumbled in a curious tone as he tapped his Plasmeriser screen. Then he looked up at the group.

Karl sprung up onto his toes.

"Spencer and Karl. I want you two to clear the Soul Stalker," he said. Spencer and Karl exchanged glances. Karl was beaming.

"Make your way to the basement of the West tower. To get there, leave this room through the arch. Go to the end of the passage and take the steps up on your right. When you reach the top, turn right again. Walk along the passage until you reach the tower arch. A spiral stone stairway will descend to your left. Go down the steps and turn right. Is that clear?"

"Yes, sir," Karl said enthusiastically.

Spencer nodded.

"Once you're in the hallway, make your way to the end. The Soul Stalker appears to be in the last room on the left. The area has been cleared and you're good to go. One more thing, keep the channel clear and only speak if you get into trouble," he said finally.

"Yes, sir."

Karl wasted no time. He darted out of the room and Spencer quickly followed along behind.

Karl turned right to ascend a spiral stone stairwell wide enough for only one person. At the top, a soldier greeted them and led them along a passage to a small wooden door. He yanked it open and gestured toward another set of steps descending into darkness. "Good luck lads," he said and smiled. Spencer smiled back and then followed Karl down the steps.

The stairwell was exactly like the other, but as Spencer descended, he could feel a cold breeze drift up from below. They reached the bottom and stepped into a long wide passageway. It was much colder than above and Spencer could see the breath plume from his mouth. The ceiling was high and arched and the floor was grey flagstone. Large arched wooden doors lined the walls on both sides and Spencer wondered for a moment if the rooms beyond were once ancient dungeons now converted into storage rooms. Spencer squinted along the dim passageway, lit by the faint glow of electric lights fixed to the walls, which looked out of place in such an old building.

"Where is it?" murmured Karl. His voice had changed from excitement to concern. Spencer gazed down into his Plasmeriser screen. A single green blip was stationary in a room at the end of the corridor.

"Down there," replied Spencer nodding forward.

They had only crept three steps when they stopped dead. The muted sound of crashing came from a room at the end of the hall.

"What was that?" blurted Karl who had dropped back and was now standing behind Spencer.

Spencer turned and looked at him with a raised eyebrow. "What do you think it was?" he said in a sarcastic tone. "Come on, let's go."

He led the way as they crept further along the corridor until they reached the door and stopped outside. More crashing and banging came from behind the door.

"It doesn't sound very happy," said Karl.

Mr Saunders voice sounded in Spencer's ear. "Spencer, Karl. Are you two in position yet?"

"We're at the door, Sir, and we're going in," whispered Spencer.

"Okay, keep me informed of progress, and keep that chit chat down, Karl."

"Yes Sir, sorry Sir."

Spencer looked at Karl. His cheeks were as red as a tomato.

"I'll go first," Spencer said, making it sound like he was in control of the situation despite his nervousness. He reached for the handle, turned it, and pushed the door. A bitterly cold blast of air rushed out as the door swung open. A still, dark void rested beyond, waiting to swallow them.

"Switching to night vision goggles, Sir," said Spencer. He pulled the Plasoptics down over his eyes.

"Understood," crackled Saunders's voice.

Everything turned mint green. The room was still a little murky, but he could see it was large and he could make out the remains of furniture. Desks, chairs, and bookcases were scattered all over the floor in pieces.

"Entering the room now, Sir," said Spencer. He could feel and hear the dull thud of his heart and his breathing deepened as he crept slowly into the room. It was like stepping into a giant refrigerator.

He stopped.

He scanned the room, probing every corner with his eyes,

but he couldn't see the Soul Stalker. He glanced down at his EP screen. The green blip was still there. He pressed the magnify button next to the screen and it zoomed in, displaying the outline of the room in more detail.

"There you are," whispered Spencer. The Soul Stalker was skulking in the far corner. Spencer recalled what Albert had said during the induction tour 'Soul Stalkers remain invisible unless they need to materialise'.

"Karl, are you ready?" asked Spencer.

Karl nodded but he didn't speak.

"Okay then. I'll move along the right wall and you go down the left," said Spencer, gesturing toward the other side of the room.

"Take it steady, boys," came Saunders's voice.

Karl hesitated and then nodded again. Spencer wasn't sure if Karl was actually listening. He certainly didn't look in Spencer's direction when he spoke.

Spencer gestured his hand forward. "Approaching target, Sir," he said.

"Understood," came the reply in his ear.

Spencer navigated his way through the debris. He had got halfway along the wall when he noticed Karl had stopped and was standing quite still. He was aware that Saunders was listening to them and began waving his arms trying to get Karl's attention, but it was no use.

"Karl," he whispered. But no reply came. "Move along the wall, Karl," he added more urgently. Still no reply came.

In the far corner of the room, splintered wood and pieces of furniture began launching into the air as if an invisible bull was charging through the room. The Soul Stalker was heading straight for Karl, who was anchored to the spot, his face rigid with terror.

"Karl!" Spencer bellowed, but it was too late. The Soul Stalker pummelled straight through him and sent him crashing to the floor.

Karl's head hit the wooden floor hard and Spencer flinched at the cracking sound. He ran toward Karl, but stopped abruptly as a chair came hurtling through the air. Spencer ducked. It careered over his head and smashed into the wall behind him, sending pieces clattering to the floor.

Kneeling ten paces away, Spencer could see that Karl was alive. He was trembling, though much more than he did in training.

"Karl is down, Sir," said Spencer while his eyes darted around the room in search of the Soul Stalker.

"Understood, we're on our way."

Spencer switched his Plasoptics to 'seeing' mode. The room turned inky blue and it was difficult to identify objects easily, except for one. In front of him was an enormous, heaving globule, like a glowing body of water that hung in the air. It had no fixed shape and moved slowly, like a jellyfish.

Spencer raised his arm. In his mind's eye, he focused the blazing ball to his shoulder, like he had done in training.

He waited.

In a split second, the Soul Stalker came charging, ploughing through the debris like it wasn't there. Spencer quickly released his power and pushed it down his arm, but when it reached the Plasmeriser nothing happened. It was like a candle being dabbed out by a damp finger. What was wrong? He had done the exact same thing he had in training.

Spencer looked up. The Soul Stalker was still charging toward him. He quickly dove and rolled across the floor, skin bristling as the Soul Stalker brushed past him. It didn't stop. It turned and came back at him again. Spencer got to his knees and gathered the energy from his stomach to his shoulder and drove it down his arm, but again, it fizzled and popped like a damp match. He dove to the floor again, this time face down, flat to the floor. The Soul Stalker swished over his head, sending a shiver down his spine. Spencer glanced over his shoulder. The Soul Stalker had stopped at the end of the room.

Spencer started banging his Plasmeriser with his fist. What was he going to do?

"What's going on, Spencer?" said Saunders in his ear.

"Karl is down, Sir, and my Plasmeriser isn't working."

"Hold on, son. We're almost there."

Spencer noticed Karl's wide, bloodshot eyes staring up at him like a crazed lunatic. He couldn't speak. The only thing he could do was tremble.

Spencer crawled toward him, watching and listening for any signs of movement from the Soul Stalker. He reached Karl, but he didn't know what to do. Karl kept flicking his eyeballs, as if he was drawing attention to something in his pocket. Then Spencer grasped what he was trying to tell him. Karl was signalling to his Plasmeriser. Spencer quickly released both guns. He dropped his to the floor and slipped Karl's onto his arm. It was like putting on someone else's shoe until it adjusted and settled on Spencer's arm.

A thunderous crash came from the far end of the room. Spencer spun his head around. The Soul Stalker had darted down the right wall and was turning at the bottom, gathering speed as it hurtled toward them.

It was now or never. Spencer stood up and took a deep breath. He held his position and raised his arm. "Come on you bag of air," he screamed at the top of his lungs. The anger swelled in his chest and the blaze of power was bigger and more powerful than he ever experienced before. His whole body trembled and his right arm began to shake. The Soul Stalker bolted straight at him. Floorboards were torn from the floor. Chairs and tables were cast aside like children's toys.

Spencer released the fiery ball and the ectoplasm burst from his Plasmeriser. The ferocity of the ectoplasm stream forced him to take a step backward. He scowled as the Soul Stalker began to reveal itself, changing and morphing. Screams of pain whirled out of the writhing, blinding, mass, like all hell had been released. Suddenly people burst into the room behind him. He heard something in his ear, but it didn't register. His concentration was intense. He simply raised his left hand, indicating that he had it under control.

Then the second moment came. The Soul Stalker stopped thrashing among the coiling ectoplasm. Spencer twitched his right hand. The mass rushed at him and vanished. Silence and darkness filled the room.

Spencer slumped to the floor, breathless. His chest heaved and his arms and legs were shaking.

The silence was replaced with gasps from the group behind him. Spencer pulled off his Plasoptics, dropped to the floor and glanced over at Karl who raised a trembling thumb into the air. Spencer smiled briefly.

"Great work, Spencer," Saunders said, now standing over him. Before Spencer could gather his breath, Saunders spoke again. "What happened, son?"

"My Plasmeriser, Sir, it wouldn't work."

Saunders picked it up off the floor and examined it closely, turning it one way then another. "It looks like it's been tampered with," he said. "The injector is blocked. Your power wouldn't have been able to get through. This is not the sort of thing that happens without a forced hand," he added curiously.

Spencer struggled to his feet. "Who would do such a thing?"

"I don't know, but this will be investigated by security," insisted Saunders.

As Spencer detached the full ecto-phial from his Plasmeriser and handed it to Saunders, he suddenly remembered the message he had received. Was the tampered with gun an attempt on his life? Should he mention it to Saunders? No, Spencer decided. Saunders probably wouldn't believe him and he didn't want to cause any more trouble.

While they had been talking, members of Saunders's group had helped Karl to his feet. Spencer scanned the room. It looked like a truck had driven through it. Deep grooves had been carved into the floor and the floorboards were twisted and splintered. He couldn't believe that a Soul Stalker could do so much damage.

"Gather around," Saunders shouted. "A breach of security has taken place here. Luckily, Spencer was able to handle the situation quite spectacularly."

Spencer blushed.

Saunders continued. "But I can assure you, there will be a full investigation and no one is to discuss this with anyone, is that clear?" He shot a stern glare at everybody, more intense than he had done before and stepped forward. "Okay. Let's move out."

CHAPTER FIFTEEN

Unwelcome Guests

The mood was low amongst the cadets when they arrived back at the academy. A photographer and reporter from the Paranormal Observer were loitering in the entrance hall foraging for any scraps of information they could lay their hands on. Spencer wondered if they had already heard about the incident before they had arrived back. Secrets didn't last long in this place.

The cadets were prodded with questions as they came through the Portdoor, but nobody said a word. They just walked by with their heads stooped. Spencer skirted around the edge of the hall to avoid them completely.

~ ~ ~

The next day, despite Saunders' warning, the news had quickly rippled through the academy. The cadets could talk of nothing more than Spencer's Plasmeriser failing and how he had probably saved Karl's life. There were also several attempted guesses at who had tampered with his Plasmeriser.

"I bet Colin Povey did it, he's scared Quinn will catch his score," he overheard one boy say on his way to Ectology.

"Na, that's not Colin's style," replied another.

The next couple of days were the same; whispers leaked out of every corner, speculation was rife, and he was sure bets were being taken on the identity of the saboteur. The digital notice boards around the academy warned everybody to be vigilant, to lock away belongings and not to leave anything unattended. Spencer also overheard somebody say there was another reporter from the Paranormal Observer lurking around the hallways, asking questions about him.

Spencer wished Frankie was here, at least then he'd have someone to talk to. He was surprised how much she filled his thoughts. It had been five days since she had gone and he was looking forward to seeing her again. If her father took her away to Manchester, he wasn't sure what he would do.

He was making his way to training when he passed Karl's brother, Colin, and two of his cronies in the hallway.

"Look who it is? Wonder Boy," Colin said sarcastically.

Spencer continued walking and found the courage to glare at him as he went by.

"Lucky escape, eh Quinn? Maybe next time you won't be so lucky," Colin laughed. "Watch your back, Wonder Boy." An elevator swallowed him and took him up to the second floor.

"Wonder Boy," muttered Spencer in disbelief. Is that the best he could come up with?

Spencer was the last one to arrive. As he walked into the training ground, everyone turned and looked at him. Spencer's face burned.

Saunders called him to the front. Spencer thought he was going to reprimand him for being late.

"Spencer," Sanders began. "I have something for you," he said. He walked over to the edge of the room, picked up a Plasmeriser case, and strode back.

"What is it?" Spencer asked, turning his gaze to the group with surprise. They were all smiling at him and Karl looked extremely excited, but then again, he always did.

"It's the new EP-V4. We want to give it to you. Your old Plasmeriser is in the lab being stripped and analysed," said Sanders. "You performed like a true pro at the tower. We're also going to double your ecto-points as a bravery award," he said.

Shocked by the announcement, he simply said, "I thought they were prototypes," and nodded at the Plasmeriser.

Saunders laughed. "Not anymore. They've been fully tested, but are only issued to those who can handle it." It was the first time Spencer had seen Saunders smile since he'd been there.

The group erupted in applause. It was the first time he had received an award or won anything in his whole life. He was speechless.

His handling of the Soul Stalker at the tower was the talking point and case study for the remainder of the session. After class, Spencer placed his new Plasmeriser in his locker and left for Phantology. After being caught red handed in the realm cube chamber, Spencer wondered if Albert was going to be teaching. He had heard that he still had his job, but the head council had given him an official warning.

It was a boring session. Albert didn't make eye contact with Spencer and managed to avoid speaking to him altogether. After giving them the simple task of considering the abilities of Soul Stalkers, he paced the front of the theatre in deep thought, his eyes to the floor. Then, while Albert explained why they were studying Soul Stalkers, he glared at Karl and said that some of them clearly weren't listening the first time.

Spencer found it difficult to concentrate throughout the session. He couldn't wait to leave, and for the first time since he came to Tezla, he was looking forward to going home.

He left the session with Karl and stepped into an elevator. Karl got out on the second floor after saying goodbye. Spencer continued to the ground floor and made his way through to the hall. The majority of Portdoors were out of use at this time of day and the vast space seemed eerie in the quiet dimness.

Spencer stopped and gazed up at the leader board as he crossed the vast empty space. The list of names scrolled slowly up the board and his name appeared at number twenty two. A little smile crept across his face. He had never achieved anything like that before in his life.

As he stood admiring his name on the board, he heard somebody whisper from a corner of the hall. "Psst, Spencer."

He turned to his left.

"Over here."

Spencer squinted toward the waiting room. Hazel was standing in the shadow of the doorway frantically gesturing for him to come closer. She was shooting looks around the hall and over her shoulder as if she was hiding and didn't want to be caught.

Spencer started toward her.

"Quickly," she said waving at him with both hands.

Spencer hurried. "What's wrong?" he asked. Hazel's brown eyes were wide, wild, and bloodshot like she had been crying.

Fear was etched on her face. She shot another glance over her shoulder and then across the hall. "I'm really sorry, Spencer," she whispered.

Spencer shrugged. "Sorry about what? What's wrong?"

"That message. I sent it."

"What message?"

"The day you went to the tower. It was me. I didn't mean to frighten you and I didn't tamper with the Plasmeriser. I swear," she pleaded.

Spencer gasped. "You mean the do or die message?"

Hazel nodded. "I'm so sorry."

"But, why? I don't understand, Hazel."

"I'll explain, but there's little time. There's more. I've been watching you. You know, while you've been training. I needed to know if it was true," Hazel stressed.

"If what was true? You're not making much sense, Hazel. Why would you do that?"

"Like I said, I needed to know if it was true."

"If what was true?" said Spencer, clearly too loud for Hazel's liking. She cowered slightly and glanced over her shoulder at the doorway.

"There's something you need to know. Drake is—"

But before she could finish, Drake burst through the doorway behind her and put his hand on her shoulder. "Hazel," he said bluntly, his face contorted with fury.

Spencer looked at Drake and then back at Hazel. Tears filled her eyes and trickled down her cheeks. She mouthed something, but no words came out. It looked like she was saying 'help me', but Spencer couldn't be certain.

"What's going on, Drake?"

"It's a family matter. Leave us, Spencer. We'll see you tomorrow." He pulled Hazel back through the door. Hazel was shaking her head and her eyes were wide and frightened.

Spencer took one step forward as the door shut in front of him. He stood in the shadow for a moment. What was she going to say? They were brother and sister, surely she couldn't be in any sort of danger, right? They always seemed to be arguing about something.

Spencer thought that he shouldn't get involved. He slowly turned and began to walk away, but stopped. He glanced back at the door. Why was she watching him? What did she need to know? Drake told him to leave and he would see him tomorrow. He continued toward the Portdoor, and all the way home he puzzled over what Hazel was going to say to him before Drake interrupted.

That night, Spencer found it difficult to sleep. Even though he had found out who had sent him the message, Hazel's fear-filled expression and what she had said plagued his mind. The events at the Tower also troubled him. What was going on?

He only realised he'd been asleep when he woke the following morning at ten minutes past eight. He pulled on his dressing gown, quickly went downstairs, and dropped into a chair in the dining room. His mother was in the kitchen and seemed to be busier than usual. There were no breakfast dishes at the sink and the kitchen surfaces were clean and clear.

"Have you heard from Frankie since she's been in Spain?" asked his mother.

Spencer shook his head. "No."

"So, who are these boys you're hanging around with, Spencer?"

Spencer hesitated. "Uh...just some friends from school," he lied.

"Where do you go?" she asked as she placed a plate of toast in front of him.

"To...Billy's house...in Baker Close. Number thirty-four. We play Xbox and stuff," he lied again. It was the first name and place that popped into his head. He didn't want to tell her the truth about Tezla, not now, but he hated lying, especially to his mother.

"Okay, as long as I know where you are, that's fine."

He knew she would never come looking for him unless there was some kind of emergency, which was unlikely.

It was eight-thirty and he was chewing on his last piece of toast when the phone rang. His mother dried her hands, rushed into the living room, and picked up the receiver.

"Hello," she said. There was a long silent pause. Spencer took a bite of his toast and watched the enthusiasm drain out of his mother's face. She looked up at the ceiling, sighed deeply, and then looked back down at the phone before she began rubbing her forehead with her free hand.

"What time are you coming over?" she asked. Spencer immediately knew she was talking to his father. She always spoke in a flat, riled tone when he called.

"Fifteen minutes? He's only just got out of bed," she said.

When she had finished speaking on the telephone, she turned and said, "Your father will be here in fifteen minutes. He has some news for you that I think you need to hear," she said. Her voice quivered slightly and Spencer wondered what the news could be. Then a thought suddenly struck him. It was Drake's session at the academy. He had to check in with Hazel too. He couldn't miss it. If his father was coming here to take him out, he couldn't go with him.

"You had better go and get changed," said his mother.

He slid out of his chair, rushed through the hallway and up the stairs. By the time he reached his room, pulled on his clothes, gathered up his tablet, and filled his holdall, sounds of the doorbell echoed up the stairs.

Spencer left his room, but stopped outside the door and leaned over the banister to listen. He heard adults talking in the hallway and he was sure there were more than two voices.

His mother bellowed up the stairs. "Spencer, can you come down here, please?"

"Coming," he replied.

He ambled down to give him time to practice different hellos with the voice in his head. When he reached the bottom, it wasn't only his father standing there. Beside him was a woman he had never seen before. Spencer glanced at her fleetingly and then looked at his father. He noticed they were holding hands and his mother was standing in the kitchen doorway, propped against the doorframe staring silently at the floor. His father was clean-shaven. He was wearing jeans, a loose short-sleeved blue and white shirt and his hair was cut short with the grey bits dyed back to brown.

"Hello, son," his father said.

Spencer paused before replying. "Hi." He pushed his hands into his jean pockets. He forced a one sided smile as he looked at his father. It was probably the most awkward moment of his life, as if he was talking to a total stranger.

"Hello Spencer," the woman in a soft voice said. Spencer looked at her again. She was blonde, and very pretty, he thought. "My name is Mary," she stepped forward and held out her hand. But then a look of confusion swept across her face. At the same time, he noticed the same frowned confusion on his father's face.

"What is that?" his father said, pointing at Spencer's chest.

Spencer looked down. He gasped. Through his shirt, he could see the rim of his identity badge pulsing red, which meant only one thing. There was an emergency at the academy.

He looked at his father who continued to stare feverishly at Spencer's chest. Mary was staring at him, waiting for an explanation. His mother had walked into the hallway, curious to see what they were looking at.

His grandmother appeared at the top of the stairs. "Why is everyone standing in the hallway," she asked, but no one answered.

The whole world was closing in around him.

"Are you alright, Spencer?" asked his mother. But Spencer remained silent. He looked at all three of them in turn and over his shoulder to his grandmother. Then he looked down at his flashing ID tag. The academy needed him. For the first time since Oliver's abduction, somebody truly needed him. He wasn't needed here. His father only came to see him when it suited him and he had never met Mary in his life. Why should he stay? He didn't give it another thought. Without a single word, he rushed past them, through the kitchen and bolted out the back door.

His mother called out after him. "Spencer."

He didn't stop or even look back. She was still calling him as he dashed down the path. Her voice grew more urgent with each call.

Spencer ran past the willow tree and arrived at the hole in the wall. He dropped to his knees, scrambled through as quickly as he could, darted through the garden, and burst into the old house. Without giving the groundskeeper a seconds thought, he ran up the stairs and, following the dog, bolted through the maze of corridors until he reached the Portdoor room. He closed his eyes and leapt straight through.

Spencer arrived in the Portdoor chamber at running speed, lost his footing, and tumbled onto the floor. Dizziness caught hold of him, his stomach heaved unpleasantly and he was sure his breakfast was about to make an appearance, but managed to keep it down.

The lights in the room were pulsing red and the woman's voice began to speak.

"Emergency, proceed with caution," she repeated in the same monotone voice as her other messages. Spencer didn't think it portrayed a sense of urgency at all.

Spencer got to his feet and swayed. The wall rotated in its usual way and as the entrance hall came into view, his ears were flooded with shouts and screams. He stepped out and looked around, frantically trying to identify the source of the panic. His first thought was an escaped ghoul, but he couldn't see one. People were fleeing in all directions.

A thunderous crash, like somebody had fired a cannon ball, shook the entire lobby to its foundations. Bits of glass fell from the ceiling and hand scanners bounced off the reception desks and crashed to the floor.

Saunders was hurrying toward him from the direction of the ancient Portdoor with a look of alarm on his face.

"Spencer, follow me," he ordered. His voice was loud and abrupt. This was no training session, thought Spencer. He ran closely behind Saunders to the far corner of the hall where a row of Retrievers, armed with Plasmerisers, stood in formation in front of the ancient Portdoor. Twisted, broken metal stuck out of the wall where the door had been and debris lay twisted and splintered across the floor.

Spencer stood behind the Retrievers, his eyes fixating on the hole in the wall.

When he saw it, his mouth fell open in shock.

The monster was a gigantic translucent worm the size of a tree trunk with thrashing tentacle arms. Its body split at the neck and formed two heads, both with enormous mouths and razor sharp teeth. Its liquid-like body was covered in stripes like a zebra, and Spencer could see its innards. The creature was sticking out of the ancient Portdoor as it lashed out its tentacles and snapped its glistening jaws.

"What is that?" said Spencer.

"It's a giant rat worm, a fine example of realm gutter scum," bellowed Saunders, bending over and picking up a Plasmeriser. "Catch, and take the right flank," he added as he threw Spencer his EP-V4.

Spencer caught it and slipped it on as quickly as he could. Boxes of full and empty ecto tubes were scattered around the floor. He pulled out an empty and full one from a box nearby just in case he needed them, and loaded the Plasmeriser.

Suddenly, there was an almighty crack and the air filled with static as the Retrievers released their ecto at the creature. The beast thrashed and writhed in pain. The lobby shook with every blow the beast threw with its tentacles, its screech deafening.

Spencer noticed Colin instructing the attacking squad of Retrievers and Saunders organising the outer flanks. Spencer went and stood next to another boy he had never met. The boy shook like a frightened rabbit. "You okay?" Spencer shouted. The boy nodded quickly without looking at him, his wild staring eyes fixed on the rat worm.

Then the Retrievers stopped.

"Front line, fall back. Right flank move in," commanded Colin.

The line of Retrievers stepped back while Spencer's group shuffled sideways in full view of the beast. Spencer took a sharp intake of breath. The creature glared at them, each head drooling like a hungry rabid dog. Spencer had never seen anything like it. Fear flowed through his veins, but he stood his ground, ready and armed. The beast reared up and hesitated for a moment, like it was surveying them, deciding what to do next, but then quickly thrashed its tentacles against the wall and heaved its giant jelly body further out of the Portdoor.

Spencer heard Colin holler behind him, "Take two steps back and stand by." Spencer did what he was instructed and stood feet apart with his right arm outstretched. He conjured his power and held it ready for release, all the time not taking his eyes off the beast. "Not until I give the order," Colin added, sensing that they were eager to release.

The beast gripped the walls and lunged forward again. Its two heads were now in the entrance hall as they let out synchronous high-pitched screeches. Spencer flinched. He could see its two forked tongues licking the air, and green saliva dangled from its razor sharp teeth.

"Release!" screamed Colin.

Spencer released his power. All the Plasmerisers discharged jets of ectoplasm, which gripped the beast, trapping it like a fish in a net. It writhed and squirmed, each tentacle lashing out like a worm that had been pulled from the ground.

"Hold it steady," hollered Saunders from behind.

Spencer gripped his right arm with his left hand for support. The tug of the beast pulled him closer as it slowly, but reluctantly, began to retreat.

Saunders shouted again. "Stay with it."

They were inching closer and soon the beast would be within tentacle reach. Spencer watched his arms start to shake. He wasn't sure how much longer he could hold it. A boy on the other end of the line collapsed. Saunders dragged him away by his arm, as if he was a rag doll, and another boy quickly took his place.

Suddenly, the beast found new strength. It seized a piece of wall debris the size of a television, and hurled it toward the cadets. They all ducked as it flew over their heads and crashed into the counter behind them.

Spencer could feel sweat trickling down his spine. His clenched fingers ached with stiffness. His nails dug into his palms and his legs began to shake.

Colin and Saunders joined the battle. They were a step ahead of the group shouting obscenities at the creature. This spurred the cadets on and they shuffled forward quicker and more aggressively. They were winning. Spencer watched the beast squirm back into the Portdoor. Now, only its two heads and one tentacle were protruding.

With one last yell from Saunders, the beast slipped back into the Portdoor and vanished. The cadets ceased fire, and for a moment, all Spencer could hear was the residue of ectoplasm cracking in the air. He slumped to his knees from exhaustion, as did all the others.

The cadets around him began asking questions.

"How did it get through?" asked one boy.

"I don't know, but there will be hell to pay," said another, breathlessly.

"Are you okay?" asked a familiar voice. Spencer looked up and saw Saunders standing over him.

"Yes," Spencer replied as he stood up. "How did it get in?"

"I don't know. It didn't crawl in without help, that's for sure," Saunders retorted, looking disagreeably at the Portdoor. "Anyway, you did good, son. Well done." He smiled, turned, and walked away to assist the others, some of which were lying flat on the floor among the debris.

Spencer took a long lingering look around the lobby. It looked like a war zone. He had only seen this sort of thing on television. One boy was on his back on the floor while several medical staff nursed a bloody gash across the boy's belly. People were rushing in all directions, some carrying medical kits, others carrying stretchers.

Spencer looked into the Portdoor chamber. The elliptical Portdoor was still intact, but everything around it had been smashed and twisted. Then he recalled what Albert said. 'This Portdoor is out of action'. If that was the case, somebody must have activated it for the beast to come through.

He spun around quickly as a boy burst into the lobby calling for Saunders.

"Yes son, calm down. What is it?"

The boy was panting heavily and his eyes were wild and wide. "I've come from the pens, Sir. It's the cube, Sir."

"Spit it out boy. What about it?"

"It's gone, Sir. Somebody has stolen it."

CHAPTER SIXTEEN

The High Council

Saunders stood for a moment glaring fiercely at the boy. It was as if he was absorbing the consequences of what the boy had just said. The cadets around him crept closer. "We had a cube here?" gasped one boy.

"Stay here and help," instructed Saunders, and he bolted across the hall and out of the door.

Spencer walked up to the boy. "Did you just say the cube has been stolen?"

The boy nodded, but kept looking over his shoulder toward the door Saunders had just left through, as if he was expecting something to burst through it at any moment.

"Who took it?"

The boy shrugged. "I don't know, I was just sent to deliver the message," his voice trembled and he sounded frightened.

Spencer turned slowly and surveyed the devastation as he pulled off his Plasmeriser and placed it carefully in a large silver box on the floor. Luckily, no one had died, he thought, but there were several wounded. It felt as though a hole had opened in his chest as he thought of Karl. He couldn't see him. Then Frankie flashed into his mind and he was glad that she was away from all of this.

The large woman he met when he first arrived at Tezla was ushering dazed cadets into the waiting area, including Spencer. He walked to the darkened room wondering how all this could happen.

From the waiting room, he watched while men in silver suits unfolded a silver barrier to cover the ancient Portdoor. They carried metal cases and scientific instruments into the chamber and came out empty handed. Two burly men marched into the hall and went and stood guard either side of the Portdoor.

All around, cadets had formed little groups and were discussing what had happened. A group standing behind him was in awe of the monster's huge powerful tentacles and its two snapping heads, but another group seemed more concerned that the cube had vanished.

"The monster was a decoy," suggested one boy.

"I'd like to know who switched on the Portdoor and let him in. There aren't many people here who could do that," said another.

"And why would somebody take the cube? They'd never figure out how to use it."

"I bet it was Albert. I heard he was caught sneaking around in there last week."

Spencer wanted to spin around and defend Albert, but he didn't. They had a valid point. There were only a handful of people at the academy that could get into the cube chamber and only a few people who could open the ancient Portdoor, but who would have done this?

The women at the desks began diverting cadets around

the debris as they came and went through the Portdoors. The Paranormal Observer had turned up and started taking pictures of the damage, but there wasn't much to see except a silver barrier that hid the Portdoor well. Even though people were going about their business, a sense of foreboding hung in the air and as cadets wandered past the ancient Portdoor, they stopped and looked, before moving on again.

The large woman who guided them into the waiting area came striding toward them. "You can all go to your sessions now, don't hang about, move along quickly."

Spencer suddenly realised that in his haste to get out of the house, he left his holdall at home in his bedroom. As he stood wondering if he should go back and confront his mother and father and suffer the consequences, he felt a tap on his shoulder.

"Hey!"

Spencer spun around. "Hello, Karl." he said, relieved.

"Looks like I missed all the action again. I had to go home last night, my Grandma was ill and Mom was worried. I've only just got back. It must have been awesome," he said in his usual awe-filled manner while looking across the hall at the ancient Portdoor.

"It was really scary actually," replied Spencer. He didn't think Karl had quite grasped the severity of what had happened. "Colin was here. Why did he stay?"

"He's a senior so Mom and Dad let him stay, but she wouldn't let me." Karl's tablet started bleeping. He pulled it out of his bag, opened it, and read the message silently. Then he frowned.

"What is it?" asked Spencer.

Karl looked up at Spencer. "We have to go to the lecture theatre, right now. The principal has called an emergency meeting. We better go."

They left the hall quickly and walked through the corridors toward the theatre. When they arrived, the room was packed with people and there wasn't an empty seat in sight. Cadets were standing and sitting all over the floor and up the stairs. Spencer and Karl zigzagged between the excited bodies, made their way up the stairs, and stood on an empty step near the back.

Silence quickly filled the room. Spencer looked down to the front of the theatre. The principal had entered the room, stepped up to the podium, and was looking back at them with her hand in the air.

"Today has been a day that will be recorded in Tezla history," she began. "Today we were violated, but more significantly, we were betrayed by one of our own." She paused and briefly lowered her gaze to the pedestal. The room filled with gasps and frantic whispers.

The principal raised her hand again. "We have detained the perpetrator. She is being held by security and is currently being questioned."

More excited mumbles rolled around the room.

"She?" whispered Spencer.

Karl shrugged, his gaze fixed on the principal.

"The principal just said 'she is being held captive'," repeated Spencer. Karl didn't respond.

Spencer noticed Drake was sitting alone, cross-legged, in his usual place. He was smirking while thoughtfully twisting his foot in the air like he was thinking about something else, unaware of his surroundings. Spencer looked for Hazel, but she wasn't there.

The Principal waited for the room to settle before she began. "You're all aware of the troubles in Asgard. This is no secret. I have been informed the creature that breached the Portdoor came from Asgard aided by our suspect. We can only assume it was sent by Arrawn." More gasps filled the room.

"The high council have held an emergency meeting and concluded that the time has come for us to advance into Asgard and put an end to this tyranny. For too long we have waited and navigated around this beast, but we can wait no longer. Asgard is bathed in darkness, stained with blood from the atrocities inflicted upon it. And now, it spills into this realm. We must put an end to it and we must do it now."

The room erupted with applause. Cadets jumped up, whooped, and punched the air.

"This is a job for our Seepers," shouted the principal into the microphone to be heard over the noise.

Karl looked at Spencer wide-eyed with eyebrows raised. "That's you, Spence," he said, nudging Spencer in the ribs. Spencer was dumfounded. Surely they didn't mean him? He had only been here a few weeks. Then a thought struck him so hard he stumbled on the spot. Oliver was in Asgard. Was this his chance? Maybe he could find his brother and bring him home.

The room settled and the principal continued, "Mr Saunders and Mr Jones inform me that the Seepers are ready, and that we have gathered enough intelligence to guide them to their goal. It is a time for unity, a time for the spirit of Tezla to unite and work together to destroy the evil that has plagued us for so long."

The cadets applauded again.

The principal raised her voice. "All Retrievers must remain on full alert. Guard posts have been identified around the academy and resident Retrievers will receive a patrol schedule shortly. All Seepers must make their way to Drake's laboratory immediately upon leaving the theatre for a briefing." She paused and looked around the room with a look of pride on her face. "Together, we will defeat this tyrant. We have overcome bigger obstacles in the past and we will do it again. Thank you."

The Principal gave a small nod, turned, and walked out of the theatre. The lecturers, including Drake, followed her.

The cadets' voices increased in volume. There was an air of concern coupled with excitement. Spencer's stomach stirred.

Karl looked at him differently now, with wide eyes and unease. "You had better go," he nodded.

Karl led the way as they weaved through the excited crowd and down the steps toward the door. "Who do you think they've got in custody?" Spencer asked.

"The Principal did say 'she.'" Karl replied, glancing over his shoulder.

"Yeah, and I noticed Hazel wasn't with Drake either." He had a horrible feeling it was Hazel they were detaining, but somehow it didn't feel right. He wondered if that's what she was trying to tell him yesterday before Drake pulled her away. She did say sorry, but for what he had no idea. Why would Hazel do such a thing?

They reached the door and stepped out into the corridor.

Karl grabbed Spencer's hand and shook it. "Good luck, dude. Make sure you come back." He didn't laugh or smile, his eyes were fixed on Spencer's.

"Of course I'll come back," Spencer laughed for him, trying to disguise his own fear. Truth was, he hadn't even considered not coming back, but now that Karl had mentioned it, he realised there was a real possibility that he might not.

Spencer watched Karl walk away. Then he turned and made his way toward Drake's lab.

CHAPTER SEVENTEEN

Asgard

Spencer nervously approached the lab door while a hollow feeling settled in the pit of his stomach. There were several twins standing in the corridor waiting for Drake to open the chamber door, including Smith and Pattel who nodded and smiled at him. Even though he had trained with them and he was a twin himself, Spencer felt awkward, like he shouldn't be there. Nobody spoke. They simply waited silently, deep in their own thoughts.

Spencer knew if he did go, it wasn't going to be a training session, nor was it like the Soul Stalker mission at the Tower, this was for real, in another world. There would be no Mr. Saunders to help him if he got into trouble. No Miss Nerts to suck up escaped ectoplasm, and no friends patting him on the back when he did something right. He would be alone. He thought about his mother, his father, and how he ran from them, but more than anyone, he thought about Frankie. He really wanted to see her now; she would know what to say to make him feel better. Would he ever see any of them again? He couldn't be sure. His thoughts settled on Oliver.

The chamber finally opened. Everybody stepped inside and

walked uneasily through to the lab. Drake was standing next to his swivel chair waiting for them, looking more serious than Spencer had ever seen him.

He glanced around the dim room in search for Hazel, but she wasn't there. It was unusual for her not to be helping Drake, particularly on such an important day as this.

Drake glared at Spencer with one eyebrow raised, "Take a seat as quickly as possible," he demanded in a flat tone. The severity of his voice seemed to hurry everyone along. When they were all seated and quiet, Drake began.

"As you are all aware, today we were attacked. Arrawn violated our academy and threatened all of our lives. In the words of the principal, 'we can never let that happen again'. It's our duty as Seepers to go into Asgard and destroy this monster once and for all. We need all hands in the field for this mission. Everybody in this room will be going." He looked directly into Spencer's eyes as he said the last sentence. Spencer's face burned and he shifted uneasily in his seat.

Drake went on and reiterated everything Angeline had said in the lecture theatre. Just as he was coming to a close, Spencer's eyes darted across the room and settled on the chamber door as it whirred to life and began to open. Was it Hazel? Perhaps she was okay after all. His hopes were soon dashed as Mr Saunders strolled in. He was carrying various bits of equipment and placed them on the table behind Drake. They acknowledged each other with a small nod.

"Are there any questions?" Drake asked.

Spencer wanted to know where Hazel was and what she had tried to tell him. If anybody knew her secret, surely it would be Drake. Spencer raised his hand. "Where's Hazel?" he asked.

For the first time, Spencer noticed Drake shift awkwardly. He narrowed his eyes, "She's been called away for other duties."

What did he mean? Something was wrong. Spencer knew she wanted to tell him something important "When is she coming back?"

Drake's anger flared like a struck match, "Why do you insist? Hazel is of no importance right now. We have far more pressing issues to deal with."

Spencer recoiled. All the cadets shifted and looked at one another. Now he was certain something was very wrong. Mr Saunders stepped forward and placed his hand on Drake's shoulder. Drake glowered at Spencer and then turned away.

Mr Saunders took over the briefing. "We've been working on this plan for some time based on the information Drake has retrieved from Asgard over the last few months. We didn't expect to execute it this early, but the mission will involve you all and will require you to be at your very best. No mistakes. You will be leaving immediately. We have no time to waste."

Saunders was direct and always to the point. Spencer felt a little more comfortable knowing that he was going to be overseeing the mission.

"You will not be using the main Portdoors in the entrance hall. Drake has chambers specially designed and built for Seepers who are travelling to other realms," he indicated to his left, toward the two Portdoors at the edge of the room. "Before we proceed, I want you all to change out of your civilian clothes and get into your Tezla uniform. You will find everything you need in the changing room." He pointed to a door at the back of the room. "Go now. When you're ready, come out and I will run through the mission with you."

Spencer swallowed hard. The same sickly feeling he had when he first started school stirred in his stomach. This was really going to happen.

He tentatively followed the other cadets into the small, white changing room. Small booths lined the walls, reminding Spencer of the changing cubicles in a clothes store. Each booth door was open and he glanced in as he walked past. A pile of clothes lay neatly folded on each bench beneath a mirror. The only difference between the booths was an illuminated panel above each door displaying the intended occupant's name.

When told, they all filtered into their respective booths. Spencer's was directly ahead at the end of the room. He stepped inside and the door automatically slid closed behind him. Once inside the sterile cubicle, there was no handle or lock, only a small green button set at waist height.

He turned and looked down at the items on the bench where a silver suit with the academy's 'T' emblazoned on the pocket was neatly folded. Next to that was a rolled up utility belt and placed beneath the bench was a pair of black, laceless, ankle high boots.

He pulled the silver suit up onto his shoulders and slipped his arms through the sleeves. It felt heavier than normal and Spencer could feel a slight stiffness in the arms and legs as if wire strands were embedded in the fabric. Once he slipped on his boots, he left his regular clothes in a neat pile on the bench and walked back into the lab. Drake and Mr. Saunders were watching and smiling proudly as each Seeper came out and returned to the seats facing them.

As soon as the last Seeper was seated, Saunders stepped off the console platform and began pacing in front of them. “In approximately thirty minutes, you will be transported to Asgard, via these Portdoors,” he began. “Your target is Arrawn and he resides in the heart of his lair. His lair is a maze of tunnels hollowed out of a cliff face and the whole place is centred on a Portdoor that you will arrive through. Once there, we will close the Portdoor to prevent the creatures in Asgard from seeping back through.”

Saunders paused.

“Uh, excuse me, Sir,” said a girl sitting behind Spencer. “Why are you sending us directly to him? Wouldn’t that be bad?” she asked in a concerned tone.

Saunders stopped pacing and looked directly at her. “We have to strike hard and fast. If he knows we’re coming, he will send an army of Gobblers and amass the vilest of creatures to hunt you down and kill you. Make no mistake. Going directly to him will give us a better chance of success. He will be caught off guard, giving us the advantage. Asgard is swarming with evil. Arrawn’s lair is surrounded by a black forest that is teeming with creatures that resemble the walking dead. It would be almost impossible to penetrate the fortress from the outside. We have to go to the heart,” he said as his gaze drifted past Spencer to the boy next to him who had his arm in the air.

“How much do we really know about Arrawn?” the boy asked nervously.

“We know enough,” replied Saunders nodding. “Arrawn is essentially a Soul Stalker. He has the strengths and weaknesses of a Soul Stalker, but he's also developed the abilities of a shape shifter. He can form into many beings, but only beings he has seen with his own eyes. But every villain has a weakness. Just like you have learned in training, he will have two moments of vulnerability. It will be the sharp eyed among you that spot them. But do not be fooled by what you see. It isn't real. He will play tricks with your mind and have you begging for your life in no time.

"In a moment, I will be issuing each of you with a new V4 Plasmeriser. One or two of you have already used this model. The power it generates is significantly greater than the standard EP-V3. It uses ectoplasm much more efficiently while providing greater power during engagement." He turned and plucked some objects from the table behind him. A pair of Plasoptics hung from his fingers and in the other hand Spencer recognised a communication device they had used in training.

Saunders held it aloft. "The communicator is similar to those used in training, except this one will allow you to transmit and receive through realms. It is plugged into your suit and powered by ectoplasm which drip feeds from your Plasmeriser," he demonstrated as he waved a fine wire strand branching from the device. "Don't worry; you won't get tangled in wires, the Plasmeriser and the communicator plug into your suit's internal veins. Once the Plasmeriser detects a connection, it will take care of the feed, so you can forget about it. But make sure the phials never empty or you'll lose contact."

Saunders turned again, placed the objects back on the table, and picked up a utility belt. "This has the capacity for four Ectophials. One will be full and will power your equipment, but three slots will be empty and require filling with Arrawn's ectoplasm. Two should be sufficient, but a backup is there if you need it." He dropped the belt back on the table and paused in front of the group for a moment.

"Which brings me neatly to the task at hand: Arrawn's capture. Upon successfully defeating him, Drake will re-open the Portdoor, which can then be used for your return. It will only be activated the moment Arrawn is dead. We cannot risk opening it before that time. In our estimations, the entire operation should take no longer than thirty minutes."

Spencer was feeling apprehensive. He sat among Seepers, but he didn't know them any more than he knew Drake. Frankie was on holiday in Spain and Hazel was attending to 'other duties.' To top it off, he was about to put his life on the line. To dispel any doubt, he quickly reminded himself why he was doing this. He recalled the look of horror on Oliver's face the night he was dragged through the hole. He was doing this for him. If there was a chance he could bring him home, it was worth the risk.

Drake stepped forward and instructed the cadets. "Could you all stand up one at a time and retrieve the items from the storage room, starting with you Spencer, as you are the closest." Drake walked over to a door in the corner of the room and placed his finger in a hole.

Spencer followed.

The door slid open revealing a small, dimly lit, shelf-lined room packed full of gadgets and equipment. Spencer walked in and examined the objects neatly placed on the silver shelves as if someone had taken great care laying them out. He eyed several items Drake hadn't mentioned, like numerous small, pen-sized objects that were laid out in trays. And what looked like eggs in cartons, but they were metallic and had no marks on the surface. He could only wonder what they might be used for. Spencer plucked the earpiece, Plasoptics, and the empty phials from the shelves. He clipped the Plasoptics to his utility belt, placed the phials into the empty belt slots, and fixed the earpiece over his right ear. Then he picked up a Plasmeriser. It felt familiar and powerful. The metallic silver coating was gleaming like it had been polished. He suspected it had never been used. He turned and left the room. As he walked to his seat, he was conscious of the eyes upon him and tried to remain composed, but inside his stomach was churning.

The other cadets followed Spencer's lead until the entire group was standing in front of Drake and Saunders, fully equipped, like a military squadron ready for combat.

"There are full Ectophials in the boxes by the Portdoor. Shortly, as you approach, take one and lock it into your Plasmeriser. Is that understood?"

Everybody nodded.

"Are there any last minute questions before I activate the Portdoors?" asked Drake. There was silence. Nobody spoke a word, but Spencer could feel the tension in the room.

Saunders visually checked each cadet one at a time. He looked into their eyes and scanned their equipment, checking their belts were tight and their Plasmerisers were securely fastened to their arms.

"You will go in pairs, except for you Spencer, you will be the last person to leave. Upon arriving in Asgard, listen to my instructions very carefully. If by some chance we lose contact,

Smith and Pattel will take command. Is that clear?"

Everybody nodded again.

"One more thing that is vitally important. When you arrive in Asgard, you must eat or drink something from that realm. This will bind you to Asgard. If you fail to do this, it could be fatal. You will have about ten minutes before you start to feel the effects, so make sure you consume something fast. There is plenty of water in the caves so move quickly and source it."

"Finally," Drake announced in a duller, flatter tone. "None of you have to do this. You can walk away now if you have any doubts."

There was a moment of breathless silence. Spencer had no doubts whatsoever. He wanted to go for Oliver if nothing else. He had been waiting for this moment for over a year.

Drake continued. "Form two queues, one twin at each Portdoor and Spencer you take the right hand Portdoor and stand at the back of the queue." He walked over to his console, sat in his swivel chair and began tapping at his keyboards.

Saunders stepped forward. "Good luck everyone. See you in thirty minutes." He put both thumbs up and then went and stood between the Portdoors.

Everybody shuffled into position and watched the Portdoors slide open. The liquid panels were already active. Spencer stared at them. Right in front of him was a doorway to his brother who was being held captive. All he had to do was step through.

Drake gave the order for them to begin. Saunders handed out a full Ectophial to each cadet as they came forward. Smith and Pattel were first to leave. They casually stepped into the liquid panels as if passing through a real door.

There was a delay.

"Smith, Pattel, can you read me?" requested Drake.

A crackly voice replied through a speaker high up in the ceiling. "Yes, we arrived safely, Sir. It's very dark here."

Drake gave the order for the remaining Seepers to step through. Spencer observed the cadets melt away into the Portdoors two at a time until finally he was standing alone with Saunders, waiting for Drake's order.

It seemed to take longer than the others.

"Spencer, give me a minute. The last two are taking their time reaching their destination," Drake said.

Saunders frowned and glanced toward Drake. He looked back at Spencer. "Relax son, it'll be fine," he smiled.

Spencer waited, looking over at Drake and then back at the Portdoor. He could hear Drake clicking away at his keyboard. Then he gave the order, "Okay, go."

Spencer took the filled Ectophial from Saunders, placed it into his Plasmeriser, stepped into the Portdoor and didn't look back.

CHAPTER EIGHTEEN

Jack in the Realm

The journey through the Portdoor was similar to the ride home, shunting, falling, and the rush of wind. It may have taken slightly longer and the nausea still swirled in his stomach, but before he knew it, everything stopped and fell silent.

The ground was solid beneath his feet. He staggered. A cool gentle breeze brushed his face and he could hear his heart pulsing in his ears.

It was dark. His eyes gradually adjusted to the light and he peered through the gloom. Slowly, he turned and saw the Portdoor practically floating in the air. There were few remains of an ancient Portdoor structure. A small piece of rock at the base and the start of a frame that began to curve up on one side, but there was nothing more than that. A small crumbling ruin and Spencer wondered how it ever worked in this condition. The actual Portdoor window was like a sheet of suspended water and was very difficult to see unless you knew it was there. It quickly evaporated like somebody had simply switched it off.

Spencer suddenly became aware that he was alone. There was no sign of the others. He found himself standing in a decrepit stone building with four crumbling stone walls surrounding him.

It looked like a war torn church that had taken a serious battering. The roof of the building had completely eroded, exposing the cloud filled sky. But it was not a sky Spencer was familiar with. The clouds were thick and heavy and tinged with red. At the far end of the building, the top half of the wall had crumbled, leaving a section of a large round window. It certainly didn't look like the maze of tunnels Drake had described, Spencer was sure of that.

"Smith, Pattel, where are you?" he whispered urgently. He wasn't sure why he was whispering because by the look of the place, it was deserted.

"Hello," he called out, thinking they might be hiding close by, but there was no reply.

As he turned to survey his surroundings in more detail, he squinted through the murk and saw a shimmering ghostly image at the far end of the building. He moved slowly towards it, cautiously treading around the rubble on the ground. The image was distorting and twisting like a badly received TV signal. Then he realised it was Drake. He rushed forward and swept his hand through the image, but felt nothing.

"Drake, is that you?" said Spencer hopefully. "I can see you."

Spencer couldn't identify any objects or furniture, only a ghostly image of Drake who appeared to be sitting, just as he was when he left him.

"Can you hear me?" said a crackly voice, which sounded like it was desperately clinging to existence.

Spencer tapped the earpiece. "Yes, but only just," he replied. "What happened, Drake, where is everyone?"

He waited for a response, but it never came. Instead, in the distance, he heard a haunting howl that sounded like something that had crept out of a crypt.

His earpiece suddenly crackled to life again. "Did you say you could see me?" Drake asked. His voice was much clearer this time.

"Yeah, well sort of, but you look like a ghost," replied Spencer, comforted by the fact he could hear at least one other person, even if it was Drake. "Where is everybody?" he asked. "I don't think I've come to the right place and the Portdoor has vanished."

Silence settled in his ear once again. His Plasmeriser started bleeping. He looked down and saw that it was the radar. A single red spot was pulsing and moving slowly across the screen.

"Oh no!" muttered Spencer. He quickly pressed one of the many buttons at the edge of the screen to deactivate the alarm sound.

Drake started talking again. "What's wrong Spencer?"

"There's something here. It's getting closer," Spencer replied, looking around frantically. There was only one way out and that was through an arched doorway, but if he went in that direction he would walk straight into whatever was approaching.

"What is it, Spencer? Tell me what it is," Drake demanded.

Spencer looked down at the tiny radar screen and noticed another red blip on the scanner, but this one was much further away.

"I don't know. I'm picking up two entities now," Spencer replied, but it was too late to say anymore. He heard a squelching sound outside the door like something was wading through thick, wet mud. He shot quick glances all around him, searching for somewhere to hide and spotted a large pile of rocks below the dilapidated window. Without much thought, Spencer ran toward it, jumped over the pile, ducked out of sight, and waited silently.

As Spencer hunkered down, trembling with fear, something beyond the doorway snorted and grunted, like a pig foraging for food. He restricted his breathing, desperately trying to remain as quiet as he could.

Shifting his weight, he peered over the rocks at the doorway. He recognised the creature instantly. It lingered for a moment, searching, waiting to attack at the first sign of movement. It was much larger than the Gobbler Spencer had seen at the academy.

Its wet, sweaty skin was a dark, mottled green. At the back of its large, blubbery potato-like head were the two pathetic leathery wings that didn't look as though they could lift a sparrow, let alone the hideous heavy beast they were attached to. Below the wings were long, bony arms and huge club hands, but its most overwhelming feature was its mouth, splitting its head from side to side with a fat bottom lip that protruded like a shelf and was dribbling stringy slobber from the corners. Its nose was wide and flat and framed by two large pointy fangs protruding upwards from its bottom jaw almost poking out its bloodshot, bulbous eyes.

Spencer stared as the Gobbler searched the shadows, its wings twitching one way then another seeking the slightest of movements, but it hadn't yet seen Spencer. It sniffed the air and grunted disapprovingly.

The two red blips on the radar quickly reminded Spencer that the Gobbler was not the only creature lurking nearby. Maybe there were two Gobblers, he thought, but the second blip was coming from a different direction and moving much slower than the Gobbler in the doorway.

His earpiece crackled again and Drake began muttering something that he couldn't make out. Spencer ducked out of sight. "Shhh! I can't talk now," he whispered, hoping that Drake had heard him and the Gobbler hadn't.

As he stared at the approaching red blip, he noticed that the Ectophial in his gun bathed the rocks in a soft green glow. He quickly slipped his arm inside his suit to block the light.

When he bobbed his head up again, he accidentally put his hand on a loose rock and it clattered down a pile of rubble, landing with a thud on the ground next to him. He gasped. The Gobbler clumsily flapped its wings and lumbered through the doorway toward the centre of the building using its long gangly arms like legs. It stopped in the middle of the building and faced the pile of rocks where Spencer was hiding. It knew he was there. Slowly, the Gobbler opened its cavernous mouth and displayed its two razor sharp fangs. Its tongue lolled out like a giant slab of raw beef. It began to wail a hollow, haunting sound that increased in volume and seemed to penetrate his skin and tug at his organs. Spencer slapped his hands to his ears and dropped to his haunches in pain.

Spencer knew he had to confront it before the scream turned his bones to dust or ripped him apart, but he had only one chance to get it right.

He swallowed hard and was spurred on by the ceaseless Gobbler shrieking. He jumped out from behind the rock and ran toward the Gobbler. It seemed startled to see him and the wailing stuttered for a moment as it stumbled backwards on its fists. Spencer pointed the Plasmeriser directly at it and it didn't seem to flinch at all as it regained its stance and heightened the screech to a more intense, flesh shredding sound. Spencer was sure he could feel his skin begin to ripple.

It was difficult to concentrate, but he managed to summon the blazing fiery ball. It writhed in the pit of his stomach. With intense concentration, he guided it up to his right shoulder and held it there as he began side stepping, keeping the Gobbler in focus. His arm was shaking. His chest heaved with every breath.

Without warning, the Gobbler stopped screaming, which was a relief if nothing else. It gargled and stared at him with its huge bulbous eyes and suddenly rushed forward.

Spencer released the fiery ball with such ferocity, the burst of green ectoplasm exploded out of the Plasmeriser. A green stream of light attached itself to the Gobbler and coiled around its quivering, blubbery body, forcing it to shake and convulse as if it was being electrocuted. The force of the Plasmeriser shunted Spencer backward, but he was ready for it and remained on his feet.

The Gobbler let out another ear piercing shrill. Its arms flailed. Its body shook more violently. Its eyes became even more bulbous and Spencer was sure they were going to pop.

Spencer's entire body trembled. As he held the squirming mass in front of him, he waited for the second reveal. He knew it would come, if only he could hold on. Like a desperate, trapped animal, the creature would use its last moments of existence and pounce again. He was hoping it would be soon, before his energy drained completely. Luckily, it didn't take long. The

Gobbler stopped writhing. Spencer instantly twitched his wrist and dug his heels into the dirt. The Gobbler bolted toward him and the tug of the Plasmeriser was near violent. In the blink of an eye the creature was extracted from the air and a spattering of moisture hit his face as it was consumed by the Plasmeriser.

Spencer dropped to his hands and knees and breathed deeply. What was this place, he wondered, shaking his head? Where had Drake sent him?

He looked up. A pungent stench was left hanging in the air and Spencer quickly covered his nose and mouth with his left hand. He lifted his right arm and looked at the glowing, swirling ectoplasm in the half filled phial.

He got to his feet and after a moment of calm, Spencer tapped his earpiece. "Drake, can you hear me?" he whispered, but there was no reply. "Drake, if you can hear me, you've got to open the Portdoor and get me out of here. Drake. Drake."

He sighed heavily and remembered what Drake had said about consuming something from the realm. If he didn't he would die. He looked from one end of the crumbling building to the other, but there was nothing but rock and dirt. Not a single drop of water.

The silence was broken by Spencer's Plasmeriser bleeping rhythmically. Before he could look at it, he noticed out of the corner of his eye a red light glint on the doorframe.

"Oh no, not again," he muttered. He looked down at his scanner. The second blip was here and he could now hear footsteps just beyond the door. It couldn't be a Gobbler, he thought, they didn't make footstep noises. They didn't have a red light either.

It was too late to hide behind the pile of rocks, he was too far away from them. The stone ground outside the door was slowly bathed in red light and it began creeping across the floor and through the doorway.

Spencer shot a look to his right, leapt into a dark shadowy corner, and pinned himself against the cold, stone wall. He stuffed the Plasmeriser inside his suit to hide the green glow, held his breath, and waited.

What entered the room surprised Spencer. It wasn't a foul smelling creature at all, but a man. He must have been six feet tall with long dark straggly hair streaked with grey and he was wearing a long, heavy overcoat that draped to his knees. He was carrying a long, smooth staff. It looked like a branch from a tree with its bark stripped. It was thinner at the bottom and twisted to a loop at the top. Hanging from the loop, was a small cage, a little larger than a teacup. Inside the cage, flitting about like an angry moth, was a red ball of light, glowing intensely.

The man spoke in a deep voice. "Where are you, son?"

Spencer gasped, causing the man to look in his direction. "Are you hiding from me, boy?" asked the man.

How does he know I'm here, thought Spencer?

Leaning on his staff, the man limped toward Spencer and held his lantern high above his head allowing him to peer past the light and illuminate the corner where Spencer was hiding.

"There you are," said the man stopping five paces away. Spencer slowly pulled the Plasmeriser from beneath his coat.

"You'll not need that," the old man smiled. "Why don't you put it away, son," he added calmly.

"Who are you? How did you know I was here?" Spencer

asked. He didn't lower his Plasmeriser. For all he knew, the old man could be Arrawn, a shape shifter or some other creature in disguise.

"I make it my business to know who is coming and going from Asgard," he replied. "But before we get into any verbal exchange, we must leave this pitiful place before they get here."

"Before who gets here?" asked Spencer.

"You have just killed an Iroquois, a demon head. I heard it half a mile away."

"You mean the Gobbler," said Spencer.

"Yes, whatever you want to call it. Anyway, its cry would have been heard for miles around. This place will be swarming with them any moment now. You must follow me," the man insisted. He turned to leave.

Spencer took a step forward. "But how can I trust you? I don't even know your name."

The man stopped and looked over his shoulder. "My name is Jack. Now that we have exchanged formalities, let's get out of here before we're lunch to that lot," he said nodding over his shoulder. He then turned and left through the doorway.

Spencer could hear the Gobblers' haunting screams. The sound radiated all around and they were getting closer. There must be hundreds of them, he thought.

Jack poked his head back around the corner and shouted. "Move it!"

Spencer had three options. He could stand and fight hundreds of Gobblers, which he didn't think was really an option. He could run for it, but he had no idea which way to go and would probably get lost or caught. Or he could follow Jack.

He didn't think about it for too long.

He ran toward the doorway and stepped out of the building. A cool breeze brushed his face and the foul stench of Gobbler rot filled his nostrils.

The dilapidated building was standing on a solitary hill. To his left a sea of shadows moved quickly across the open plain. In the distance, he could see mountains silhouetted against a deep red sky. Spencer turned and looked down to his right. Jack had already negotiated half the crooked stone steps. At the bottom, they met a vast towering cliff-face that stretched into the distance and disappeared into the gloom.

"Quickly! Now!" shouted Jack, gesturing him down the stone steps. Spencer looked back at the mass of shadows gliding toward them at an alarming rate. Fear drove Spencer down the steps.

"This way," Jack shouted, hobbling into a small opening in the cliff face. Spencer reached the bottom step with the sound of the Gobblers close behind him, scratching at his heels, snorting and slobbering like hungry dogs. He darted through the opening into a small dark hollow.

"Stand back," Jack demanded. He kicked a log wedged between the ground and a large wooden wheel protruding from the wall. As soon as he did, the wheel spun and a gigantic stone fell from above the opening. The boulder slammed into the ground with a dull thump, kicking up a cloud of dust, covering the hole entirely. Spencer heard faint thuds as the Gobblers slammed against the stone, unable to stop. He could only imagine the mangled pile of Gobblers against the rock.

The hollow was small with only the glow of red from Jack's lantern revealing the walls.

Spencer coughed and glared at Jack through a cloud of dust.

Jack stared back, unable to speak through his heavy breathing.

CHAPTER NINETEEN

The Ancient Tunnel

Spencer stood on the soft ground as the pale menacing cries of the Gobblers wailed beyond the impenetrable rock. He paused to gather his breath, eyes searching the cool hollow.

The chamber walls and ceiling had been chiselled smooth and straight. Jack's lantern now bathed them in a soft golden yellow. In one corner of the hollow, a perfect rectangular passageway branched off into darkness.

Spencer could see Jack more clearly now. His face was rugged and gaunt, framed by long straggly hair. Deep lines webbed out from the corners of his sunken eyes. Two of his top teeth were missing and the remainder were black and pointy.

"Who are you and what is this place?" Spencer demanded.

Jack raised his left hand with his palm facing Spencer. "Slow down, kid. I need to get my breath back." He leaned on his staff and took more deep breaths.

"Don't call me that. My name is Spencer. Not boy or kid."

"Okay. okay. Calm down, Spencer. I got it."

"Well?"

"I was sent here to meet you."

"Where's Arrawn…and the others?"

Jack laughed and then sighed heavily from exhaustion. "Arrawn is on the other side of the rip, a long way from here my friend. As for the others, I have no idea what you're talking about."

"The other Seepers. They came through here before me."

Jack shook his head. "Nobody has come through here in years," he replied, but Spencer noticed Jack shift uneasily. He began to wonder if Drake had made a terrible mistake and sent him to the wrong place.

"So who sent you to meet me?" Spencer asked abruptly, trying to make sense of it all.

"Rina," Jack replied.

"Who's Rina?"

"She's the Mudhead Shaman. She told me you would be on the mound. I know, I know, I was a little late and I'm sorry about that. The legs aren't what they used to be. It's good you had that thing with you," Jack said, nodding at Spencer's Plasmeriser.

Spencer ignored his comment. "What's the mound?" he said.

Jack waived his thumb over his shoulder. "The old Portdoor you came through sits on the mound. It's been out of use for years. Until you showed up."

"You know about the Portdoor?" exclaimed Spencer.

"Of course. The Mudheads discovered it long ago. It flickers to life from time to time, but they've never been able to control it. They built these tunnels so they could move freely between their village and the mound." Jack said, nodding toward the passageway. "The tunnels run parallel with the cliff face and will keep us safe from those slobbering monstrosities."

Spencer shook his head. "I think there's been a mistake. I'm not supposed to be here. I need to go back," he said.

Jack laughed again and shook his head. "No. You can't. There's no way back. Like I said, we can't control the Portdoor from here, all that was destroyed long ago."

Spencer suddenly had an overwhelming sense of isolation. He was standing in a dark, dingy passage with a strange old man he had never seen before in his life, in a dark world full of Gobblers with no communication with Drake, and no way home. How did this happen? More importantly, how was he going to get back?

As he tried to make sense of it, the chamber began to spin. His knees and hips began to stiffen and he struggled to move his arms. He stumbled like an old man and painfully placed a hand on the wall for support.

Jack rushed forward and grabbed Spencer's left arm to support him. "Oh darn it. I forgot." From inside his robe, he pulled out a small glass bottle full of clear liquid and pulled the stopper from the top using his teeth. "Here, drink this quickly," he said, and held it up to Spencer's lips.

Spencer jerked his head away. "What is it?" he breathed.

"It's only water. Quickly, drink it. If you don't, you'll die."

"I'm not thirsty, I'm a little dizzy that's all."

"No, no. You don't understand. This water originated here in Asgard. You need to absorb something from this world or you'll die."

He opened his mouth and allowed Jack to pour in the liquid.

Jack smirked. "You don't trust me?" he said.

Spencer never replied. He held the water and swirled it

around in his mouth. It was mildly warm, but it did taste like water. He swallowed. As it trickled down his throat, a gentle bristle rippled over his skin. It was a sensation Spencer had never felt before. What had Jack just given him?

"What's happening to me? I thought you said it was water?"

"Relax. It is water. Your body is acclimatising to this realm, that's all. It'll pass in a few moments."

He was right. The stiffness in his joints, the dizziness, and the prickling sensation gradually eased and vanished.

Spencer took a deep breath and sighed with relief. "Thanks."

Jack stared back at him with his piercing dark eyes. "No problem."

Spencer stood up straight. "So what now?"

"We must go to Rina. She wants to see you."

"I don't understand. How did she know I was here?"

"She knows everything," Jack smiled. "Come, let's go."

Spencer had no choice but to go along with Jack. What else could he do? Jack turned toward the tunnel. His feet scuffed the ground as he entered the dark passage. Spencer followed.

The tunnel was narrow. Spencer could reach out his arms and touch the smooth, flat walls on both sides. The ceiling was high, well out of arms reach. As they walked, Spencer became more curious about Jack. "Why did the Mudheads send you, Jack?"

Jack didn't answer immediately. "Well, I guess you could say I'm their runner. Although I couldn't run anywhere these days," he laughed. "Since Arrawn came here and destroyed everything there are few places left for sanctuary. The Mudheads provide me with shelter, and I run errands for them in return."

As Spencer followed, he noticed Jack was sluggish and his limp was more evident now.

Jack continued. "We're reasonably safe here. Arrawn's lair is on the other side of the rip and the Mudheads pose little threat to him so he leaves us alone."

"What's the rip?" asked Spencer.

"Long ago, before Arrawn showed up, Asgard's land was torn apart. The ground shook violently and opened up a bottomless gash across the land, thirty paces wide and stretching hundreds of miles in both directions. Overtime, bridges were built, but Arrawn destroyed them all and the only way across is by air."

Spencer was beginning to wonder if there was any hope of finding Oliver alive. Not only was there no passage home, there was no way to Arrawn either, the place where he should have arrived after stepping through the Portdoor.

They walked deeper into the tunnel, through the darkness. The air was cool and damp and it reminded Spencer of the old house when Frankie and he first entered the maze of corridors. The memory seemed distant now, but he would give anything to have Frankie by his side right now.

"So, how did you get here, Jack? I mean, have you always lived here?" asked Spencer.

"Yes, of course. But it's not like it used to be. When Arrawn arrived, everything changed."

"What was it like before Arrawn came here?"

"It was a pleasant, peaceful place. Tribes worked and lived off the land and the sun actually shone here once. But that's all gone now. Asgard is riddled with darkness and shadows. But enough talk. We must move quickly."

As Spencer shuffled along behind Jack, he gazed at Jack's lantern, which had now turned aquamarine. "Why does your lantern keep changing colour?" he asked.

Jack chortled. "It's not exactly a lantern, Spencer. This is a woodland sprite that once populated the forests of Asgard. I found it hiding amongst some rocks, frightened. Probably the last of its kind. We've become great friends. Even though it cannot speak or hear. It can feel. It'll glow red when it senses danger or golden yellow when it's safe. It can also be happy and sad and the colour will change depending on what it's feeling. Some days it can be stubborn and remain white, not changing at all."

The light pulsed orange for a moment and darted around the cage, before settling into a golden yellow.

They ambled deeper into the tunnel, turning one way then another, up a slope and down the other side, but the walls remained smooth and constant.

"Who are the Mudheads?" asked Spencer.

There was a pause before Jack answered. "You'll see."

Spencer didn't ask any more questions and followed Jack closely, occasionally glancing over his shoulder searching the creeping blackness behind him. Jack's woodland sprite became their guiding light, remaining calm and sun yellow, casting enough light to illuminate the way ahead.

Spencer didn't have a watch, but he was sure an hour had passed since they started through the tunnel. He wondered how much longer it would be before they reached the Mudheads. They passed several branching tunnels on their right, but Jack ignored them. He seemed to know the way, like he had travelled the tunnels many times before. The only sound was the soft crunch beneath their feet as they sunk into the sandy ground.

"What does he want?" Spencer asked, as they turned a sharp corner.

"Who? Arrawn? Nobody knows for sure. We do know he's taking children from your realm in search of something, but exactly what that is we don't know."

"And we're meant to stop him?"

"We?" said Jack, glancing over his shoulder.

"Yes, we, the Seepers at Tezla."

"Oh I see. Is that what they call you these days? Seepers?" His voice sounded troubled. "Listen, I don't have all the answers to your questions, Spencer. The Mudheads will tell you everything you need to know, I'm sure. What I can say is this: if Arrawn isn't stopped, great evils will pour into your realm and the darkness will shift there too, just like it has here."

That remark halted further questioning from Spencer. The thought of his world ending up like Asgard was too much to bear.

They walked for another half an hour in silence when the tunnel dipped, ascended, and turned several sharp corners before it came to an abrupt end.

They entered another small hollow like the one at the beginning and stood before another large rock door. Jack walked over to a wooden wheel next to the rock and started to turn it. As he did, the rock slowly began to rise. A gap at the bottom appeared and a gentle, cool breeze swept in, bringing with it a foul stench like rotting meat.

“What about the Gobblers?”

“They can’t get this far up the valley. The mountains block them and there is no way over them. Anyway, they’re too fat to get off the ground and those wings are pretty pathetic,” Jack replied while struggling with the wheel.

Spencer rushed over to help him and it didn’t take them long before the rock was high enough to walk under.

“Are you sure it’s safe to go out there?” asked Spencer apprehensively.

“I wouldn’t be opening it if they were out there, would I?” Jack threw Spencer a sideways glance.

With one hand holding the wheel, Jack picked up a log that lay on the ground and guided it through the rungs of the wheel and into a smooth round hole in the rock. Gently, he let the weight of the rock hold the wheel in position.

Jack stood back, sighing deeply, and reached for his staff. “Okay, let’s go,” he said, turning to face the door.

Spencer followed him out of the chamber into a clearing surrounded by enormous grey rocks. On the opposite side of the clearing two gigantic wooden gates stood as tall as a house. They were hinged on two wooden poles as thick as tree trunks and covered in intricate carvings of human faces and ugly creatures that Spencer had never seen before. A nerve-shredding squawk echoed up the valley.

“What is that?” asked Spencer.

“Oh, it’s probably a hungry Boargle,” Jack replied, as if it meant nothing.

CHAPTER TWENTY

The Mudheads

Spencer gazed up in awe at the colossal wooden gates "What's behind there?"

"Mudheads," Jack replied in a tone that stated the obvious.

Judging by the size of the gates, Mudheads were either very large or they wanted to keep something very large out. Spencer stood and examined each carving like it was a work of art. "Why are the gates covered in these?" he pointed to a detailed snake that coiled around the post several times

"In the days when Asgard was thriving, before Arrawn came, every clan was symbolized to represent their beliefs. The coiling snake you see here is the Mudhead symbol. They believe the snake has many lives. It sheds its skin and then moves on symbolising a new beginning."

As Spencer absorbed the information and tried to understand what it all meant, Jack turned to the right and walked toward several large boulders.

"Where are you going?" asked Spencer.

Jack looked over his shoulder at him, "Follow me."

Spencer followed. Behind the boulders, next to the colossal gateposts, was an opening in the rock the size of a narrow doorway. They entered a short tunnel, turned left, and emerged in a small, dark room constructed from log posts. It had no visible openings, apart from the one they came through. It was a small rectangular space and the only way out was back the way they came.

Suddenly, a man's voice started shouting from the other side of the wall. "Who's there?"

Spencer was startled and looked around nervously. "Did you hear that?" he whispered.

"Yes, it's only the gate keeper," replied Jack. Then he shouted back. "It is I, the Crow."

Spencer looked at him perplexed. "The Crow?"

Jack looked down. "That's what they call me, for reasons I would rather not divulge."

The man's voice spoke again. "Did you bring the boy?"

"Of course," Jack replied, still gazing down at Spencer.

They stood in silence for a few seconds before the entire wall in front of them began rumbling and groaning as it slowly moved upwards. Trails of dust spiralled from the ceiling and the ground gently vibrated.

Spencer placed his hand on his Plasmeriser. He had been saved from the Gobblers and he assumed Jack and the Mudheads didn't want to hurt him, but could he trust them?

"Quickly, come out where I can see you," ordered the voice.

They stepped out of the enclosure. Spencer stopped at the entrance and his heart sank at the scene before him.

Located behind the large gates and at the base of a deep crevasse was a bedraggled village that looked as though it was clinging to the edge of existence. The sheer, grey cliff face towered above like a city skyscraper, almost touching the heavy swirling clouds above, but it was a useless shield from the hands of time.

The voice Spencer heard came from a man who now stood in front of them. His hair was black with grey streaks, long and matted into thick tubular clumps, like he hadn't washed it for a very long time. His skin sagged and was pale and weathered. But the most striking thing about the man, thought Spencer, was the tattoo on his torso, resembling the carving on the gate. The snakehead began at the base of the man's neck and wrapped around his body with its tail finishing below the belly button. Other markings of creatures and symbols covered his arms, from his shoulders to his fingertips. Curious tiny bags the size of thimbles hung from a necklace around his neck. His feet were bare and his trousers were made from some sort of animal hide, bound together with heavy stitching.

The man spoke, but there was no welcome in his voice and no introduction. Only one simple word, "follow."

Jack and Spencer did as they were instructed. They walked along a dusty path that weaved through the crude village, deeper into the crevasse.

Spencer slowly surveyed the frail community. This was no ordinary village. Decrepit lean-to shacks constructed from stone, logs, and mud sat in the shadow of the cliff. They were small, the size of a single room, lopsided and crooked. Painted masks and trinkets hung in the doorways of the shacks and were attached to poles sticking out of the ground nearby, as if they were carefully placed to ward off evil.

Dotted around the village, plumes of smoke poured

from holes in the ground where blackened steaming pots sat suspended on wooden frames.

Spencer noticed the children weren't playing, but sat helplessly and silently on their haunches in the doorways of the shacks. Some wore paint on their gaunt faces, decorated in the same way as the masks, making them look scary. They were meagrely clothed in threadbare cloth hanging from their frail bodies. Occasionally they waved their hands feebly to brush away the insects that swarmed around them, but mostly they sat unmoving, as if disconnected somehow from their surroundings.

"What happened to them?" whispered Spencer.

Jack didn't answer. He simply looked back at Spencer and gently shook his head, signalling for silence.

As they continued, more villagers came out of their shacks and stared, cautious and wary of the stranger among them. Seeing a boy dressed in bright clothes with shiny gadgets, Spencer wondered what they were thinking. He must have looked alien to them.

They approached a set of narrow steps carved out of the rock that ascended up the cliff face. As Spencer turned and began to climb, he looked over the rooftops, across the crevasse, and noticed more cave entrances opposite. There were too many to count, but Spencer was certain they must be a natural formation as many were out of reach and too small to walk into. More villagers began to emerge from the caves; small groups of children, mother's carrying babies, all glaring at him.

They reached the top of the steps and stopped. Before entering a cave to their right, the tattooed man turned to Jack and muttered something in a foreign tongue. Jack simply nodded.

"What did he say?" asked Spencer.

"He wants me to translate what is spoken," replied Jack in a low voice.

They followed the man into the cave. It was a large, bulbous space, but not so that Spencer couldn't make out the smooth walls and ceiling. Fire torches clung to the walls causing long shadows to dance across the floor. In the middle of the cave, small boulders had been placed in a circle in which an old woman sat cross-legged on a rug with her eyes closed. She looked much like the others, but wore a headdress full of red, yellow, black, and white feathers, with several bone trinkets around her neck and many piercings in her ears.

The guide spoke and Jack translated.

"Please sit," he said, gesturing at a rock. Spencer walked over and sat down. Jack sat next to him.

"Who is she?" whispered Spencer.

"Rina, the Shaman I told you about. She's a very, very wise lady. She can talk to ancient spirits and she knows and sees things that seem impossible to us."

The old lady opened her eyes.

Spencer sat up straight and shifted uncomfortably. There were no pupils in her eyes, only pure white orbs.

"Welcome," said Rina in a soft tone as she bowed her head slightly. She spoke slowly and although Spencer couldn't understand her, her voice was gentle.

Spencer looked at Jack, unsure if he was supposed to reply. Jack pouted his lips again and continued interpreting.

"We have been expecting you." There was a long, deliberate pause.

"You have seen the despair that clouds our people and you know of the evil that brought this despair to our land," she said.

Spencer nodded slowly, but he wasn't sure if Rina could see him or not. Jack took a moment to translate what she was saying.

"We once lived on the plains, feeding off the land, but now we exist as prisoners in our home, like many in this realm.

Rina spoke effortlessly as if she had rehearsed the words a thousand times. She reached out her twisted hand toward Spencer.

"Take her hand."

Spencer extended his hand, palm up, and let the old lady rest her hand on his. There was a delay, a quiet moment as if she was absorbing Spencer's thoughts and feelings.

"I know what your heart seeks. You have come to this world to seek your brother. His spirit is here, but is being restrained."

The old lady stopped talking. Spencer shot a glance at Jack and back at Rina. His breathing deepened as he fought back tears.

"I can feel you are troubled."

Jack looked at Spencer and tilted his head toward the Shaman.

"Is he alive?" Spencer stuttered slowly, unsure if he wanted to hear the response.

"I cannot see. Something is shielding him, restraining him. His spirit is trapped, but senses you are close."

Finally, some hope. "I must go to him. Where is he?" he blurted as quickly as the words would allow.

"You must confront Arrawn, but the journey to Hollow Cove, over the rip, is a perilous one. The plains are full of death.

Deep within the black forest roam the walking dead, guarding Arrawn's fortress like it is their own. You must begin at the gates to the black forest. You will travel to the frozen city by air."

"The black forest? The frozen city? I don't understand."

"I will be your guide Spencer. You needn't concern yourself with that," Jack replied.

"The black forest is shrouded in darkness. I cannot see inside. You must go with caution."

"What about the rip? If we go outside the village, the Gobblers will kill us. Surely, we can't walk there!" said Spencer.

"No, no. We will fly on Boargles."

"Boargles?" exclaimed Spencer curiously.

"You'll see."

The Shaman continued. "You must go now. Waste no time. He will take your world soon, like he has taken ours," she said. "There is one more thing." Jack went silent while the old lady spoke. When she had finished, Jack looked down at Spencer, but he didn't speak for a few seconds as if he was trying to think of how to translate what the old lady had said.

"What did she say, Jack?" asked Spencer.

"She said that all is not what it seems. You must be wary of all that is around you."

"What does that mean?"

Jack shook his head and shrugged. "I'm not sure."

The old lady closed her eyes, placed her hands back onto her knees and her head slumped as if she had fallen asleep.

"Is that it? I have so many questions. What about the others? I need to know where they are."

Jack put a hand on Spencer's shoulder. "It doesn't work like that, Spencer. That's all she has. At least you know what you have to do."

The guide that had led them there spoke and Jack stood up.

"He's going to lead us to the Boargles. They're feeding now but will be ready to fly soon. We can eat while we wait and discuss the journey," said Jack. He turned to follow the guide out of the cave. "If you're friends are there, it might be a good idea to get there as quickly as possible."

They turned right and walked along a narrow ledge. Jack and the guide ambled along casually, inches from the ledge and taking no notice of the height. Spencer was fully aware that there was a sheer drop to the crevasse floor only inches away to his left. One slip and he would plummet to his death. He simply didn't look, fixed his eyes to the back of Jack's grey straggly hair, and felt along the cold rock face with his right hand as if somehow it made it safer.

They reached another cave entrance and went inside. A cool breeze swept past him. The cave was much deeper than the Shaman's cave and he noticed two tunnels branching from it. One led away to his left and the other to his right.

The guide grabbed a flaming torch from a wooden rack and strode toward the left tunnel.

It was only a short walk, but dark nonetheless. The tunnel did a noticeable zigzag before emerging into a gigantic cavern, thirty or forty footsteps across.

He noticed several smaller caves around the edges, lit by flaming torch light. To his left, a circular opening like a giant mouth overlooked the vast plain below.

Then he saw them, three enormous creatures standing side

by side, tearing at raw, bloody flesh with razor sharp teeth. They were holding the meat under their giant trotters as they ripped it apart and then swallowed it without chewing. A chain stretched from the cave wall to a brace around their necks. Spencer couldn't decide if he was looking at a bird or a giant warthog. Huge tusks curled from its snout and wrapped around the back of its head. Attached to its bulky, black body were enormous, grey leathery wings. The creatures weren't shorthaired like normal hogs. They had a bushy mane and were covered in long matted hair that draped to the floor. Much bigger than a normal wart hog, their bodies were more like a pony. Strapped to their backs were saddles.

The guide led them to one of the smaller caves where several Mudheads were sitting at rickety tables, eating from wooden bowls with their hands.

"Sit there," Jack said, gesturing toward several large rocks that had been placed around the tables. The guide wandered off through a small opening, but soon came back with two large bowls of steaming meat.

Spencer looked at it curiously. "What is it?"

"It tastes like chicken," Jack replied with a smile. It didn't quash Spencer's curiosity, but he didn't probe any further because he was hungry and if he knew what it truly was, he may not want to eat it.

He picked out a piece of the warm meat and put it in his mouth. Jack was right. It really did taste like chicken. As he ate, Spencer thought it might be a good time to probe deeper into Jack's life.

"There's still something I don't understand Jack," Spencer

began.

"And what's that?"

"How they knew I would be there. I was supposed to go to a different place, a different Portdoor."

"I don't have the answers, Spencer, but I do know one thing. The Shaman is in touch with spirits across many realms and some say they can see into the future. I do as I'm told and I get fed." Jack stuffed more meat into his mouth.

"If they can see into the future, why didn't they stop Arrawn from doing this to them?"

"Shaman can see things, but it doesn't mean they can prevent things from happening. Things happen for a reason. If you start meddling with what is meant to be, things will get terribly messy."

The Mudhead guide returned with two jugs of water. Spencer wasn't sure where he got it from, but it was cold and fresh and it was just what he needed.

"Why do you hang around here?"

"It's safe. Until Arrawn is out of the way, I don't really have a choice," Jack said, sounding annoyed, as if Arrawn had ruined his plans.

Spencer glanced over at the Boargles. "I need to find the rest of the Seepers before we can go to Arrawn's fortress," he said. "I can't do this alone."

"I will guide you and I'm sure you will find your friends on the other side."

Suddenly, a deep, loud horn echoed through the caves.

"Ah, the Boargles have finished eating. Finish up. We should go and talk to the keeper." He stood up, took a gulp of water, and walked back into the large cavern where the Boargles had been feeding. Spencer stuffed as much food into his mouth as he could and washed it down with the remaining water. Hunger had crept up on him and he wasn't sure when he would see food again.

He jumped up from the table and followed Jack into the cave. He froze when he came face to face with the Boargles. The thought of climbing onto them and soaring through the skies made him feel sick.

A man stood nearby sweeping away scraps of meat the creatures had left scattered around the floor. Jack approached him and started talking while Spencer stood back and watched. He could tell something was wrong. The Mudhead started arguing with Jack, but Spencer couldn't understand what they were saying.

Jack turned and walked back toward Spencer, his face rigid with fury. "We can take two Boargles to the edge of the black forest. They will not fly over the forest, they're too frightened," he said.

"What are they frightened of?"

"A Windigo."

"A what?"

"There's a myth that a giant un-dead creature lurks in the forest, waiting for anything to cross its path. The story goes that once they're in the forest, it hunts them down and eats them alive, leaving their bones scattered on the forest floor," said Jack rolling his eyes. "It's all nonsense. Nobody has actually seen it."

"Okay, but if we can't fly over, what are we going to do?" said Spencer.

Jack stared at him for a moment. "Not we, you," he said.

"You mean you're not coming?"

"The Boargles will only fly to the frozen city. I am too old to hike through the forest. My legs won't make it. Besides, I have to guide the Boargles back here," Jack said, looking at the Mudhead who had started sweeping again. "It's the only way we can get there."

"So, you want me to go through the forest alone?"

Jack began talking quietly as if he didn't want anybody else to hear what he was saying. "Listen, if you want to see your friends and family again, you had better do as you're told."

Spencer stepped back. Was that a threat? "I want to go back to the mound and back through the Portdoor right now," he demanded loudly. The Mudhead looked up at them.

Jack glanced around and composed himself. "Look, it's impossible, I've already told you, you can't do that."

"Why not?"

"Like I explained before, we have no way of controlling it."

The thought of wandering through a black forest alone repulsed Spencer. But if he wanted to see Oliver and get back home, he would have to go through it and find the Portdoor on the other side.

"Spencer, stop fretting. There is no Windigo in the forest," assured Jack. "There are Soul Suckers that will attack the Boargles if we fly over, but they won't touch humans," he added, but he didn't look at Spencer when he said it. Spencer was sure Jack wasn't being entirely truthful.

Jack turned and strolled toward the Boargles. Spencer also approached. His eyes were fixed on the creatures, the sheer size and aggressive nature of the beasts made him nervous. Their trotters cracked against the rock floor as they shifted on their four powerful legs.

The Mudhead stopped sweeping and stroked the Boargles with his dirty, bony fingers, speaking to them in a calm voice.

"Come on, I'll help you up," Jack said.

Spencer hesitated. He had an overwhelming rush of fear. He suddenly became aware of himself standing in an alien world, being led by a strange man that he had only known for a couple of hours. He thought of his mother home alone and a hollow feeling settled in his chest with the thought that he may never see her again. He thought of Frankie lying on a beach somewhere in Spain. He would give anything to have her here with him right now.

Jack must have noticed something on his expression. "Are you alright, Spencer?" he asked.

Spencer nodded. "Yes," he replied, pulling his thoughts back to the present.

Jack patted him on the back and said, "Okay, let's do it. Here," he locked his fingers together to form a step. "Up you get."

Spencer gripped the edge of the saddle, put a foot on Jack's hands, and heaved himself up. He dropped onto the saddle and the creature swayed and staggered as if surprised somebody had mounted it, which would have sent Spencer to the floor if he hadn't been gripping the lip of the saddle.

Sitting on the beast put him much higher than it had looked from the ground and he swayed as the powerful body of the creature moved beneath him.

"Put your feet in here," Jack said, lifting Spencer's foot and tucking it behind the wing into a leather loop. "Grip the tusks," he added. Spencer leaned forward, reached out, and gripped the two tusks in front of him like they were handlebars on a bicycle. The tusks had ridges down its shaft, which gave him a firm grip. The Boargle seemed to settle the moment he touched them.

Jack climbed onto the Boargle next to Spencer. "When we take flight," he said, "keep a firm grip and don't let go. You'll not need to steer, I'll take the lead and your Boargle will follow. Despite the look of them, they are gentle creatures. Just relax and enjoy the ride."

Spencer nodded, but he didn't feel comfortable and he certainly didn't feel relaxed.

The keeper walked away.

Jack's Boargle started toward the large opening and without so much as a nudge, Spencer's followed. The swaying motion surprised Spencer and he almost slid off the saddle. He gripped the tusks with both hands and began moving his body in rhythm with the Boargle.

He watched Jack as his Boargle stood at the edge of the cave mouth overlooking the vast, ghostly plain below. The wind was brisk and whistled through the opening.

Jack glanced over his shoulder and gave Spencer a nod and a smile. Spencer nodded back, but he didn't smile and he certainly didn't feel as confident as Jack appeared.

Then, without warning, Jack's Boargle leapt from the overhang and vanished out of sight. It reappeared, gliding majestically and getting smaller as it flew into the distance.

Without any instruction, Spencer's Boargle stepped forward

and stood at the edge. It's squeal and screech echoed across the plain. Spencer looked over the side and saw the spread of insipid landscape below as a vast hoard of creatures moved slowly across the ground. Above, red clouds hung menacingly in the sky.

Spencer took a deep breath.

The Boargle leapt.

Spencer momentarily left the saddle as the Boargle plummeted and then swooped after its mate. He gripped the tusks until his knuckles were white and pushed his knees to the sides of the creature. He crouched low as if somehow it would make him more aerodynamic. The cold wind rushed against his face and the breath was snatched from his lungs. The Boargle's body heaved with every thrust of its powerful wings.

As he began to level out, Spencer heard a scratchy noise in his earpiece. Was it Drake trying to contact him? "Drake, is that you?" he said, finding it hard to speak as the air rushed around him. No reply came. Spencer didn't attempt to speak again. He needed all his concentration to stay on the Boargle as it banked one way, then another.

Below, Spencer saw a deep, dark chasm that split the land in two. Then, up ahead, he saw it, the blackness of the vast forest spread out like a growing cancer on the land, waiting to consume anything that ventured into it.

CHAPTER TWENTY ONE

The Frozen City

Spencer's stomach lurched as the Boargle dropped out of the air, preparing to land. Below, angular rocks were strewn across the landscape, but as he got closer, he saw they weren't just rocks. They were ruins and dilapidated buildings. Long stone pillars lay on the ground, some broken in two as if they had been snapped and tossed aside. Then he noticed statues of small people. They were everywhere. Groups of them, some in a running pose brandishing large axes and other weapons.

The ground rushed toward Spencer at an alarming rate. The Boargle did a final thrust of its wings to slow their descent, kicking up a cloud of dust. It touched down, surprisingly gently, on a dusty, sunken path and went into a trot before coming to a standstill.

Up ahead, Spencer could see the entrance to the black forest. Two crumbling pillars intersected an enormous stone wall that stretched to the left and right. The forest appeared lifeless. The trees cracked in the wind and were charred black like they had been in a fire.

Suddenly, a haunting shriek echoed from the forest. The Boargle jolted like a startled horse. Spencer was caught off guard and slid off the saddle. He landed painfully on his backside, which was already sore from the ride.

As he got to his feet, he turned and noticed Jack had landed on the other side of the path to his left and was walking toward him smiling.

"What is this place?" asked Spencer. "Why are all these statues placed like that," he said.

Jack came and stood next to him. "They're not real statues. They were a tribe of Tantillians that lived in the city," he said. "There was an immense battle when Arrawn came. The Tantillians fought for their land and for peace. Arrawn wanted power so he sucked the life out of them and turned them to stone. They've been like this for years. Unfortunately, there is no way back for them."

There was a silent pause as Spencer looked out over the vast loss of life and the crumbling city. He imagined what it might have looked like at one time with huge columns propping up vast ornate buildings once thriving with Tantillians.

"Well, we should get a move on. You have to go that way," said Jack turning and pointing at the forest.

Spencer turned toward the black creaking trees.

"One rule will see you safely through," began Jack. "Stay on the track. Do not stray," he added, but Spencer interrupted him.

"You said there was nothing in there."

"Well, they're only small. A few Tree Ghasts and Soul Suckers, but if you stay on the track they will not come out into the open."

"Tree Ghasts!" said Spencer in alarm.

"Yes. Some Spectres too, maybe," Jack added quickly.

"What! So let me get this right. There's nothing in there apart from a few Soul Suckers, Tree Ghasts, and the odd Spectre here and there," shouted Spencer angrily. "Are you sure you don't want to throw in the odd Windigo to even up the numbers," he added furiously. It was like he was about to walk through a long dark alley in the most dangerous part of a large city. Then he noticed Jack's lantern, the light inside was glowing red and darted in random directions like a moth on the other side of glass trying to reach a light.

"Look," he said, nodding at the lantern. "I thought you said when its red there's danger nearby."

"Take no notice. It doesn't like to fly, that's all," Jack replied, but his voice was pitched higher than normal and Spencer knew he was lying.

Spencer shook his head. "I can't do this, Jack."

Jack turned and stood in front of him. "If you don't go through there, Spencer, you will live with the Mudheads and you will end up like me," he said sternly. "Is that what you want?"

Spencer shook his head slowly. "Why can't you come with me?"

"I'm too old. My leg won't make it. Besides, I need to guide the Boargles back to the Mudheads." The sincerity in his voice had completely vanished and Spencer began to doubt anything he said.

He stepped around Jack and looked toward the forest. Fear breathed down his neck, raising the hairs on his skin. It felt as though it had hold of his heart and was about to rip it from his chest, but he knew Oliver was on the other side.

"What are Spectres?" asked Spencer, stroking his

Plasmeriser.

"They are apparitions. They're a white shimmer, tall and thin, but you will not see them if you look at them directly. They should cause you no trouble. They have a taste for our furry friends here, not the human kind. Arrawn keeps them fed and thus they shield him from any creatures that may wander over or through the forest. "

Spencer swallowed hard. "And the Tree Ghasts?"

"Well, they were once peaceful dwellers of the forest when it was green. Now they've turned black and evil and feast on any living soul that passes through. A few Mudheads recently vanished and we suspect they were victims. If you confront them, I'm sure that contraption of yours will be a worthy protector," Jack said, nodding at his Plasmeriser.

As he stood peering into the dense, black forest, he longed to be at home with his Mum and Dad and Oliver back in Hertfordshire where things were normal and safe. But he knew Oliver would be on the other side of the forest, in what form he was unsure, but he was there. Encountering a Tree Ghast or two seemed a small risk if that was all that lay between him and Oliver.

Jack continued. "When you get to the other side, you'll see Hollow Cove and Arrawn's fortress ahead of you, sitting at the foot of the black cliff. It was once an old trading post used by merchants that travelled this land. It goes deep into the cliff and it may be guarded. Be cautious, Arrawn will be waiting at the heart."

"If I make it that far," he said, looking sideways at Jack.

He took a few more steps toward the forest. The trees were

enormous, giving the appearance of a huge black void. The dusty path stretched up to the two pillars and then vanished beyond the wall into the gloom.

"We should be moving on, Spencer. Good luck," Jack said.

Spencer turned to face Jack. He was more frightened than he had ever been in his entire life. "What if I fail?"

Jack stared back at him, "Arrawn will become more powerful and more realms will fall into darkness until he eventually conquers them all. You are here for a reason Spencer, of that I am certain. You will not fail."

"How can you be so sure?"

"I see it in you, Spencer. Rina would not have asked me to guide you to her if she didn't believe you were somehow part of the solution. It's up to you now. You can do this," Jack replied more sincerely than he had ever spoken. Spencer believed him this time. It was going to be the biggest challenge of his life, but Spencer remembered one thing that gave him hope and drove him forward: Oliver.

Jack snapped back from his moment of compassion. "I must return the Boargles, they're getting irritable," he clambered onto the beast and looked down at Spencer one last time. "Good luck my friend."

With a giant swoop of its wings, the Boargle leapt into the air leaving Spencer standing in a cloud of dust at the gates of the black forest, alone once more.

CHAPTER TWENTY TWO

The Black Forest

Spencer watched the Boargles, his only lifeline to any kind of existence, shrink to a spot in the sky. With a pounding heart, he turned to face the creaking forest and crept warily along the dusty path. He hesitated between the two stone pillars and peered into the shadows of the trees. The forest cracked and groaned like an old man, but there was no sign of any life, only the wind, barley brisk enough to rustle his hair and stir the dust on the path. The tangled canopy of gnarled branches blocked any light from getting through. The only light he had was the glow from his Plasmeriser, but then he remembered his Plasoptics. He reached around his belt, unclipped them and placed them over his head. The forest lit up in a luminous yellow. He could see clearer and much further now.

Ten paces into the forest five statues peered up into the dark canopy, as if something tall had attacked them. They were adorned in heavy garments, protective chest plates, and shoulder pads, and looked as though they had been placed there deliberately, like a child's toy soldiers. They carried bows and arrows over their shoulder and a moment of sheer terror was cemented on their faces. Spencer could only wonder at what had frightened them.

He kept Oliver in the forefront of his mind. He was close to seeing him, close to setting him free. All he had to do was walk through the forest, find his friends, and defeat Arrawn, but Spencer stood and reasoned with himself. If an army of Tantillians couldn't defeat him and the Mudheads couldn't defeat him, what chance would Seepers have? He comforted himself with the fact that he had a technical advantage, but would that be enough?

Again, a sound crackled in his earpiece. Spencer gasped with hope. He poked at it wondering if it might be faulty, and prodding it like that would somehow fix it. "Drake, can you hear me?" he said, but again, no reply came. He really was alone. Perhaps the others were waiting for him on the other side.

He stepped into the forest, peered into every shadow and behind every tree expecting fear to be hiding there, stalking him and waiting for its moment.

He checked his Plasmeriser and ecto phials, adjusted his Plasoptics and crept further along the path. His eyes darted among the black trees that had begun to swallow him as he wandered deeper into obscurity. It looked like the tree canopy had never been pierced by sunlight, leaving the forest floor in a dark, death-like trap of gloom. The crooked trees creaked and moaned as if they were complaining that somebody was stepping on their roots and their giant gnarled hands seemingly ready to snatch him if he got too close.

He looked fleetingly one way, then the other, expecting a Tree Ghast to leap out at him. A few uneventful minutes passed, and then there was a loud snap, like something had ripped a branch from a tree. Spencer was certain it wasn't the wind. The sound was too loud and purposeful. A chill curled around him, his skin began to crawl. He heard another snap, much closer this time. He took a deep, shuddering breath and started to move faster, almost jogging, careful not to trip over the thick roots twisting out of the ground. He gripped his Plasmeriser and repeatedly glanced over his shoulder, but he couldn't see anything.

Something crunched under his foot as he ran. He recalled the rotting stink from the old house, and now, the same stench filled his nostrils. He looked down and gasped in horror. Bones were strewn across the forest floor as if the trees were shedding them like rotten fruit. Matted hair clung to crushed skulls and limbs. There were so many bones covering the path that the ground was barely visible. Where did they come from? Some were clearly fresh. Instantly a horrible thought filled him; what if they were the other Seepers? He swallowed back the nausea and moved on.

The snapping of branches became more frequent and louder. Spencer glanced over his shoulder and saw something moving among the trees. He noticed a large blip flashing on his Plasmeriser radar. Whatever it was, it was moving toward him, approaching from behind, and fast.

Spencer sped up, running as fast as his legs would carry him. With every stride, the bones on the ground became denser, cracking and snapping beneath his feet, making it difficult to run. His foot slid off the slippery bones and he stumbled on several occasions.

He leapt over a tree root, dodged a large rock jutting into

the path, swerved left and then right, while keeping his hunter behind him. Spencer didn't look. He could see on his radar it was gaining on him. Then several smaller blips appeared behind the larger one, like an army falling into flank, following in the wake of their leader.

Spencer tried to run faster, but it was hopeless. What was the thing closing in on him? He caught a glimpse of an enormous figure over his left shoulder as he bolted between two trees. He remembered what Jack had said and this was too large to be a Tree Ghast. It was human formed and big, probably three times his size. It bounded toward him purposefully.

"Help me!" Spencer muttered breathlessly. "Somebody, please help me."

His voice was lost without reply.

As the creature pounded closer, the stench became stifling and the air grew cold. Beads of sweat trickled down Spencer's face and his chest heaved as he gasped for air.

He spotted a small hole in the rocks up ahead to the right of the path. A cave perhaps? It looked big enough for him to crawl into and possibly small enough to keep that thing out. He didn't care what lived in there. It couldn't possibly be worse than the thing chasing him.

He veered to the right and ran toward it. When he reached the entrance, he dived toward the opening and with one swift scoop of his arms, brushed a pile of bones to one side and scrambled frantically in to the hole, half expecting the creature to grab his heels as he went.

He spent no time examining the cave and stood up quickly, cracking his head on the ceiling as he did so. He dropped to his knees and rubbed his head trying to rid himself of the pain.

Trapped like a rabbit in a warren, he sat on the hard ground and pushed his back against the cold rock, pausing to catch his breath. His teeth ached from the cold sharp air that scraped his lungs. Exhaustion overwhelmed him and his eyelids descended over his eyes. Darkness filled his mind.

~ ~ ~

Spencer woke with a start. How long had he been asleep? The cold air gripped him and the shock of his situation made him instantly alert. His feet were numb. He banged them on the ground to get some feeling back and looked down at the radar. He could hear bones crunching outside the cave entrance. The creature was close. Before another thought passed through his mind, a thunderous crash came from above and the entire cave shook. Small pieces of rock clattered all around him. Spencer reached out his hands as if to steady the cave walls. His left hand touched something wet and slimy. He looked down. It was a skeleton slumped against the rock. Maggots filled the skull and wiggled all over the decaying flesh that clung hopelessly to the bones. A Mudhead, he thought. Spencer shuddered and shuffled as far away from the body as he could get.

Fear had found him in the cave, laughing at him, taunting him. It swirled around him, fencing him in like a caged animal. He had to get out or he would end up like the corpse next to him.

Spencer peered out of the opening, but he couldn't see the creature. He glanced down at his scanner. The creature was very close, but he couldn't pin point it exactly.

He edged forward and poked his head out of the opening. He looked to his left, then to his right, but he still couldn't see it. Pulling his head back inside quickly, he knew for a heart stopping moment that he had to run for it. He had no choice. He knew the creature was waiting for him, waiting to pounce. It wasn't going anywhere. If he didn't try, he would die here for sure.

He took a deep juddering breath and scrambled forward on his hands and knees. He positioned himself like a sprinter ready to dash, took another deep breath, and darted out of the hole like a frightened rabbit from its burrow.

The blip was right on top of him. He didn't look back. He knew it was there. He could hear the smash of bones with every footstep and feel the ground vibrate as it bounded after him. Spencer ran, but it was in vain. Something clipped his right heel and knocked his foot sideways. He tripped and fell flat on his face. The jagged bones that covered the ground jabbed into his ribs and he grimaced in pain.

A heavy crunch landed behind him. He flipped over and sat up among the shattered bones. Spencer recoiled in horror. Looming over him was the vilest creature he had ever seen; a skeletal giant that looked as though it had just climbed out of a grave. It bellowed a throaty gargle. Loose flesh hung from its bones and Spencer could see its black withered heart inside its ribcage.

"I'll get you for this, Jack," he muttered under his breath.

This must be a Windigo, Spencer thought, and he was sure the Boargle Mudhead back in the cavern knew it was here and tried to warn Jack. But for some reason, Jack ignored him.

The Windigo took a giant step forward and placed its decaying foot next to Spencer. It stooped down and tilted its head like it was examining and playing with its prey before taking a bite, but it had no eyes that Spencer could see, only holes full of rotten mucus.

Spencer held his breath, the stench was overwhelming and it made him wretch. Then he realised what the creature was interested in. It was the glow from the Plasmeriser. It had probably never seen colour before. Spencer nervously lifted it to his chest and pointed it at the Windigo. The urge to scramble backwards was intense, like something was tugging him from behind, but Spencer forced himself to take slow, gradual movements.

The Windigo was mesmerised, tilting his skull from side to side like a curious kitten. Spencer climbed into a squat position while maintaining eye contact with the large skull that curiously followed the Plasmeriser as he slowly waved it from side to side.

A voice inside Spencer's head was telling him to stand and fight. Don't run. Fight, it repeated. In a sudden swift movement Spencer stood up and took a few clumsy steps back. A sharp pain shot up his leg, like something had stabbed at his ankle, but he simply gritted his teeth and absorbed the pain.

The Windigo was startled and smashed his fist against a nearby tree, followed by a bellowing, throaty, disapproval. The air turned bitter cold, and Spencer noticed frost forming on the trees and bones around him. Breath plumed from his mouth. He sensed the Windigo was winding up for an attack. He took another step back out of arms reach.

The creature crouched low and hunched its back.

Spencer hung on to his nerve for the moment the creature would reveal itself; the moment Spencer could pummel him with ectoplasm. He summoned the fiery ball in his mind's eye and held it at his shoulder.

The creature raised its arms with an almighty screech and lunged forward. Simultaneously, Spencer released the ball with an intense ferocity. The fiery bolt shot down his arm and a green explosion burst from the Plasmeriser with the force of a lightning bolt. The Windigo became enveloped in a ball of ectoplasm and the black forest was suddenly awash in a green glow.

Spencer took several, carefully placed, steps back. The creature squealed like a pig and thrashed its arms and legs in every direction. Pieces of flesh flew off the Windigo as the ectoplasm engulfed it.

Spencer held the Windigo with every ounce of strength he could summon. The creature desperately reached out for something to grasp. Spencer struggled to keep his footing on the loose, slippery ground. His right arm shook vigorously, his left foot slipped off a large bone and he stumbled backward, but somehow he managed to find a foothold again. He remained focused, carefully stepping this way and that, feeling his feet between the bones until finally, it happened. The Windigo halted momentarily like somebody had paused them in a silent pocket of time before it thrust itself at him. Spencer was ready. He twitched his arm. The Plasmeriser seemed to grip and engulf the Windigo like it had a mind of its own and it collapsed into a frenzied ball of fleshy bones. The force of the grip jerked Spencer forward. The thriving mass rushed toward him with such force it pushed him over onto his backside with a painful crunch. The last thing Spencer saw was the skull as it finally evaporated and disappeared into the Plasmeriser.

Spencer slumped where he sat. His arms and legs were drained of strength. He gasped for air as he watched the frost slowly melt around him. The forest fell into darkness and the wind was gentle as if the trees were heaving a sigh of relief.

Before he could gather his strength, he noticed more flashing dots on his Plasmeriser screen. Something else was approaching.

"No more, please," he sighed.

He struggled to stand and look down at his radar. It wasn't one thing. There were hundreds of them, honing in on him like a swarm of hungry bees.

Spencer scanned the forest, but he couldn't see anything through the Plasoptics. He glanced down at his radar and turned so the swarm was behind him. Then he started to run, but they were moving much faster than he could.

He shot a look over his shoulder, but he couldn't see anything behind him except the thick black forest. Again, he glanced down at his Plasmeriser. They were close, really close. He should be able to see them, but there was nothing there.

The bones on the ground thinned until they completely vanished and running became much easier. All of a sudden he burst out of the forest, as if emerging from a long dark tunnel. The swarm of dots on his Plasmeriser had stopped chasing him, but he kept running.

When he looked up, he slowed his running and gradually came to a halt on the open plain. The swarm quickly left his thoughts as he pushed his Plasoptics up on to his forehead and gawped at the sight before him. A sheer cliff face stretched into the clouds above him, higher than any building Spencer had ever seen.

At the bottom, hiding in the shadows, was a stone fortress. It was still some distance away, but Spencer could see a slope reaching down to the plain from an opening in a perimeter wall. Two towers stood on each corner and Spencer wondered if there was anybody occupying them, watching him. There was no shelter.

He heard a screech some distance behind him that sounded like an injured hawk. Spencer spun around. Then he saw them mingling amongst the trees at the edge of the forest as if there was some sort of invisible barrier they couldn't cross over. Dark shapes that were not quite distinguishable. When Spencer looked directly at them, they vanished. To see them he had to look to the side. They faded in and out of existence and changed shape like a sheet blowing in the wind. They must be the Spectres Jack mentioned.

Spencer turned back toward the fortress. It looked deserted, a dishevelled, white stone building, uninviting and ominous.

CHAPTER TWENTY THREE

Into the Lion's Den

The wind whistled among the black rocks at the base of the cliff. Drained and weary, Spencer ambled toward Hollow Cove across the loose, stony ground beneath a heavily laden sky. He hoped that the other Seepers would already be there waiting for him.

Arrawn's white stone fortress was elevated on a bed of rock huddled at the base of the vast, black cliff. He stepped on to the wide slope that led up to greet an arch at the top and paused. The slope wasn't steep, it was long and wide and it had four shallow ruts carved out of the rock, presumably by the wheels of carts rolling up and down the slope over many years.

He looked down at his radar, but that, too, was lifeless. Only when he was sure there was nothing lurking nearby did he start up the slope, listening and watching. He reached the top and stood at the entrance to an open-air courtyard. The entire complex was built from stone and Spencer staggered at the scale and complexity of the crumbling outbuildings that surrounded the yard, backing onto the perimeter walls. Wooden doors dangled at awkward angles. Decaying wooden carts, some of which had wheels missing, lay rotting in the corners.

Smashed wooden crates and piles of stones lay at the base of the crumbling walls. Ahead of him, hollowed into the cliff face was a gaping arched entrance like a giant mouth waiting to swallow him. This was not how he imagined Arrawn's fortress. He was expecting something much grander, more imposing and heavily guarded. At least some sign of life, some kind of resistance.

Spencer turned and gazed back across the landscape blotted by the black forest spreading far and wide. He shook his head and thought about Tezla. Would they be trying to contact him? He thought again about his Mum and Dad, and Frankie. Would she be back from Spain yet? And Oliver, the reason he came here in the first place. An aching pain stirred in his chest and tears began to fill his eyes. He turned back to face the courtyard. A feeling of helplessness overwhelmed him. How could he simply walk in there alone and face Arrawn? With a deep breath, he shook the thoughts from his mind and started toward the entrance.

He tapped his earpiece, hoping it would come alive and he would hear a human voice, one of his fellow Seepers perhaps, but it was as dead as the land he stood in.

With each tentative step, a stinging pain shot up his right leg. He looked down and noticed a rip in his suit and a bloody gash above his ankle. His once white sock was now stained red with blood.

As he paced slowly across the courtyard, he tried to imagine how it would have been before Arrawn destroyed everything. He pictured the festive atmosphere, bustling with traders haggling for a good price; children playing on the slope and buskers playing music as the folk of Asgard came and went. But all that had gone. It was now inhospitable and deserted.

As he approached the entrance, he raised his Plasmeriser close to his chest, half expecting hell to pour from the gaping hole, but again, there was nothing. He recalled what Jack had said. Arrawn would be hiding deep within the caves, but why leave them so exposed? He crept further forward, glancing left then right, scrutinising the empty doorways and the exposed rafters of the outbuildings, but nothing moved, not a mouse, not a bird, nothing.

He peered inside, but it was black. He pulled the Plasoptics back over his eyes and crept inside. The cave was larger than any of the Mudhead caves, although the roof was much lower. The walls were punctured with more tunnels snaking into the rock.

He still couldn't believe there was nobody here. He didn't expect to be greeted, but he didn't expect complete and utter silence either.

Suddenly, he froze. A gentle voice began singing from the gloom, like the sound of a choirboy humming softly to himself in the corner of a giant cathedral, but he couldn't make out the words and there was no sign of a boy. The voice appeared to be coming from the far end of the cavern, but it was difficult to tell for sure. He crept across the vast chamber, weaving between enormous stone pillars, occasionally stopping to listen and get a bearing on the direction.

After stopping several times, turning one way then another, Spencer concluded the singing was definitely drifting from a tunnel at the far end of the cavern. Surveying his surroundings as he went, he stepped up to the entrance and stopped. The soft heavenly voice was much louder here. He shot a look over his shoulder and stepped into the tunnel. He turned with his back against the wall, alternating glances ahead and behind him as he crept along. The floor of the tunnel was smooth from years of tread, but the walls were uneven like the rock had been chipped away with a sharp implement.

As he edged onwards, the tunnel curled left then right. A few minutes into the tunnel, and for no apparent reason, the singing stopped, like somebody had switched off a radio. He waited and listened. Another sound replaced it. He held his breath when he heard the echo of faint footsteps behind him. After five or six steps they stopped. He glanced down at his radar and sure enough, a single blip pulsed on the screen and appeared to be located near the start of the tunnel.

He shuffled forward as quickly and as quietly as he could and then stopped again. The footsteps mimicked his movements and the blip on his radar also moved and stopped. Whoever it was waited a few corners back. He was being followed, but by whom? They must be able to see him somehow. Maybe it was another Seeper. Maybe it was one of the others. Should he go back, call out? If it were a Seeper, surely they would come forward and show themselves. Why would they keep stopping?

He couldn't take the risk. He had to keep moving. Taking a deep breath, he crept further along the tunnel and turned several corners, but stopped again when up ahead, a light bloomed in his Plasoptics. He pushed them up to his forehead and gasped when he saw the luminous green light seeping around the corner. He glanced down at his scanner and he couldn't believe his eyes. The screen was glowing with life. So many blips it was impossible to count. They were all around him, yet there wasn't a soul in sight.

Spencer moved to the other side of the tunnel and crept into the shadow of the green light. He peeked around the corner. It was the end of the tunnel. Steps, carved out of the stone, ascended to what appeared to be a much larger cave. He gazed in awe at the green aura flooding the walls and floor.

Again, Spencer glanced back over his right shoulder expecting someone to appear at any moment, but there was no one.

He wondered where the other Seepers could be and why his scanner was glowing. Something prodded at his mind. It was the same feeling he had when he was with Angeline in the small room back in the academy, but this was more intense, almost painful. He pulled off his Plasoptics, dropped them to the floor and slapped his hands to his head in pain.

He stepped out and stood at the bottom of the steps. The pain dwindled. He looked up and his heart almost stopped beating at the sight before him. Oliver was staring down at him from the top step. His face pale and expressionless. His eyes unblinking.

Spencer became rigid. Was it really him? He was lost for words and didn't know whether to climb the steps and hug him or run away. Before Spencer made a move, Oliver slowly turned and walked away, out of sight. Spencer rushed up to the top the steps and stopped abruptly. He recognised the blue shirt and jeans. It wasn't Oliver, it was his mother.

"Mum?" said Spencer softly. "Is that you?"

She didn't answer. Instead, a slow, deep, contemptuous laugh echoed around the cave.

"Oliver," shouted Spencer desperately, but the laughing continued.

His mother began to turn.

Spencer gasped and took a step back. From the head downwards, her body began transforming. First the hair sprouted, long and black. Her clothes changed into a long black coat and her skin darkened and wrinkled until finally his mother became an old man with gaunt features and dark, sunken eyes.

"Who are you?" gasped Spencer. "What have you done with Oliver?"

His voice echoed around the chamber and the figure before him simply laughed louder and then said in a deep voice, "you finally came. What took you so long?"

Spencer stared at him with disdain and said, "Arrawn."

CHAPTER TWENTY FOUR

Secrets and Lies

The air was much colder here. It seeped through his clothes and pricked his skin.

"What have you done with Oliver?" he demanded.

Arrawn glowered back, his pearl black eyes pierced Spencer's mind like needles through cloth. "That's no way to greet your executioner," he smiled, approaching Spencer slowly. He didn't appear to walk, his black coat simply rippled around his feet as he moved, making no more noise than a breeze through leaves on a tree.

"I've been expecting one of you to show up for what feels like an eternity. Who would have thought it would be a weak little specimen like you?" he said, gesturing toward Spencer with his bony left hand as if Spencer was a subject and Arrawn was talking to somebody else.

Spencer glimpsed Arrawn's hand and saw it was more than simply bony. The skin was scarred and the fingers were twisted and bent out of shape. "Why wait? If you wanted me so badly, why didn't you take me like you did Oliver?"

That comment seemed to amuse Arrawn even more. "No, no, no," he sighed, "you simply don't understand. I wish it were that effortless. I don't know you and I don't know—what is it you keep calling him? Oliver? You're simply one of them. A touch special, I might add, but one of them nonetheless."

Spencer shook his head. He didn't understand what Arrawn was saying. He raised his Plasmeriser and rested it in his left hand, feeling its presence as if it were a protective shield. "What have you done with Oliver?" he asked again.

Arrawn drifted effortlessly to his left and smiled. "Let's just say, he has moved on."

"Moved on? Why are you talking in riddles? Tell me where he is!" Spencer screamed, his rage now at boiling point.

"Okay, okay, you seem adamant to find him. What does it matter, you'll be joining him soon anyway. Oliver is dead," Arrawn replied nonchalantly.

Spencer shook his head. "I don't believe you."

Arrawn laughed heartily. "You don't believe me? Oh, I see. Is that what you came here for, to find your brother? You misguided fool. What have they done to you?" he gestured. "Step over to the edge. See for yourself."

Spencer hadn't taken too much notice of the cave. He had become so enraged and transfixed on Arrawn. He looked around the edge of the cavern, glancing back at Arrawn every few seconds. A green aura radiated from a deep, wide channel that encircled the cave. The light was intensely bright at the base and faded into darkness the further it crept up the ragged walls. At the far right of the cave, over a stone bridge and nestled in a small inlet, was a Portdoor. It looked exactly like the ancient Portdoor in Tezla. He was certain of it.

Slowly side-stepping toward the edge of the cave, Spencer's

gaze never strayed from Arrawn for more than a second. When he reached the channel, he looked down into a deep, vast pit. A lingering layer of green mist capped it like a protective covering.

"Go, jump in, help yourself, it would save me the effort," Arrawn chortled.

Spencer stood rigid on the edge, shocked by what he saw. Thousands of glowing white orbs trailing wispy tendrils drifted aimlessly around the deep channel. Could Oliver really be one of them? He found it hard to believe; yet in his heart knew it to be true.

Spencer collapsed to his knees and any glimmer of hope he had was sucked out of him. The desire to grieve was immense, but he desperately fought it back. "What have you done?" he said, shaking his head. "All those people. What have you done to them?"

"Oh dear boy, you're unbelievably naïve! You have so much power, yet you are blind to it. Such a waste."

Spencer stood up and whirled around to face him. His grief suddenly cloaked with rage. Blood raced through his veins. "Why are you doing this?" he screamed.

Arrawn hesitated. He put his hands behind his back and drifted toward Spencer, stopping two steps in front of him. He fixed his pearl black eyes on him. Spencer's mind became heavy and disorganised. Arrawn rummaged through it like an old sock drawer.

"Of course, you don't know. They have told you only part of the truth," he said with a broad smile spreading across his pitted face as if the prospect of telling Spencer the rest of the story would give him great pleasure.

"The truth? The truth about what?"

Arrawn's smile broadened further as he watched Spencer squirm. "Where to begin," he gloated as he turned and drifted back across the cave.

"Drudging through what lingering brain cells you have, I can see they have explained the Seeper ancestry to you. They have also explained Reapers, haven't they?"

Spencer gasped. A sudden realisation hit him and if there was any glimmer of hope, it was now extinguished. "Of course, you're one of them. A Reaper. You steal souls and you…" he turned and looked down into the pit.

"Bravo," beamed Arrawn. "Maybe there are a few commendable brain cells up there after all. But there is more. They're not just ordinary souls. They are Seeper souls, each and every one of them, but not all are like you. You see, Spencer, you are special. I mean we're all special in our own little way, but you my little friend, are exceptional. You're not just any Seeper like these pathetic off shoots," he gestured. "You are a true descendant of the ancient Seepers, like I'm a true descendant of the ancient Reapers. You have pure Seeper blood running through your veins. You and I, we're the same, chips off the old blocks."

Like a bull from a stall, Spencer's rage burst out of him. "How dare you. I'm nothing like you. You're scum!"

He breathed hard and fast now. His fists were clenched. "I can't be a true descendant. My father is not a twin. It's impossible."

Arrawn continued to smile. "Oh but he was. Your father's twin was removed from your world, just like your brother. Before that and before your Grandfather's time, much of my work was done for me. However, birthing facilities are not as primitive as they once were and thus my workload has increased somewhat. Your father was like you, a twin, but once I had harvested his brother at a very young age, he became a Dud, of his own choosing I might add."

Spencer didn't want to believe him, but some things started to make sense. The night Oliver disappeared his father kept repeating 'not again, please' over and over again. It took weeks for him to accept what had happened. Spencer never understood this. Oliver always suspected his father knew they were different, but their father never let on. He also recalled the night his father came to the house with his new fiancée and the sheer look of horror on his face when he saw Spencer's tag flashing.

"Ah, I see it's all falling into place now," said Arrawn gleefully. "Of course, the fact that your father lost his brother almost destroyed him. He had to make a choice. Become a Dud or die. Fortunately for you, he chose to become a Dud."

"What's a Dud?"

"A dead Seeper of sorts. Something I strongly advocate," Arrawn laughed. "The academy can perform a small procedure that will remove your abilities and, in many cases, remove the memory of having it in the first place. Most weak Seepers can't live without their twin, but with this procedure, it gives them a chance at what they call normal life."

Spencer recalled the suggestion Angeline had made to him, that they could help him if he chose not to join Tezla. Now he understood what she meant. He felt sick. Why keep it all from him? Why didn't they tell him about his father? So many secrets.

He had been betrayed.

Arrawn continued. "So now you see. You have learned to control your power even though your brother is dead. This makes you very exceptional, Spencer. There are most likely others like you, but you are the first to come forward and make it this far. I congratulate you for that."

Spencer clenched his fists tighter. "I don't want your congratulations. I want you dead!" He screamed and then lunged forward fists first. Arrawn simply vanished and reappeared ten strides away. Spencer stumbled onto his knees.

"A fighting spirit, I admire that. We would make a great team."

Spencer shook his head. "Why. Why do you do this?"

"You still don't get it do you. Eradicating identical twins while they're young makes my work easy. Of course, I can't find them all, but I try to take them before their powers mature. I only need one of you. If they're a Seeper, the other will most likely die or become a Dud. But I knew eventually I would discover a descendant, and here you are," he smiled. "Not a particularly fine specimen, but you're here nevertheless. I have come this far, and now, I can't let Seepers regain control. You will not and cannot find the cubes. They will all be mine. And once I find them, I will have ultimate power over all realms and everything within them. Don't you see?" Arrawn sounded like a crazy, demented mad man. He reached into his black coat and pulled out a realm cube, which he held in the palm of his disfigured hand as it began to glow and radiate green shards of light. He closed his eyes and breathed deeply as if inhaling fresh air for the first time.

"The power I harvest is so delectable, so palatable, and

once I yield it all, nothing will stop me."

Spencer got to his feet. "That will never happen. Not as long as I'm alive."

Arrawn drifted closer to Spencer laughing uncontrollably and placed the cube back inside his coat. "Once I've destroyed you all and retrieved the cube from that pathetic institute you call Tezla, I will bleed into your realm like a deep wound, turning it black, sucking the life-force from its soul."

All of Spencer's thoughts came to a crashing halt. "You mean you don't have the Tezla cube?" he said.

A look of bewilderment fell upon Arrawn's face, which indicated to Spencer that he hadn't taken it when the rat snake came through the portal. But if Arrawn hadn't taken the cube, who had?

Spencer quickly changed the subject. "But why wait? Why haven't you taken my realm already?"

"Patience is a virtue, my friend. Time is but a passing of moments, of which mine are somewhat unlimited. My task will be easier without filthy, meddling Seepers scattered all over the place. I will destroy you all first. I knew the moment I sent my little pet through, they would send the troops, and here you are. One Seeper. How pathetic and predictable," he laughed.

Spencer began to side step back toward the centre of the cavern, his gaze never leaving Arrawn. A pain shot up his leg from the open wound on his ankle. Fear had long since left him, replaced instead with a deep loathing ache in his chest.

"You may have taken my brother, but you will never take me," Spencer yelled as his fingers ran over his Plasmeriser.

Arrawn glanced down at it. "You think that pathetic trinket

can harm me?" he roared. He began to shake violently and his body began changing shape again. This time it was no human. His black coat fell to the floor as his scaly body stretched tall, four times bigger than Spencer, transforming into a long red snake. Arrawn's arms and legs thinned and became tendrils that lashed out on either side of his serpent head.

Spencer stumbled backward, horrified, as he gazed up at the enormous creature.

Somehow, Arrawn still managed to laugh as he slithered closer. "Do you still believe you can defeat me," he hissed, looming over Spencer.

Spencer remembered what Mr Saunders had taught him, 'lock away your fears,' he would say and that's exactly what he did. He was tired of being bullied, tired of being shoved around, and tired of the betrayal. It was time to make a stance for him and for Oliver.

Arrawn slinked along the floor and began encircling Spencer, his tail whipping around behind him.

Spencer lifted his Plasmeriser. He pictured the ball of energy in his mind's eye like he had done with the Windigo.

Then, without warning, Arrawn lunged at him. Spencer leapt to one side, avoiding a pummelling from the enormous head, and released the ball of energy from his Plasmeriser. A stream of liquid green ectoplasm spewed into the air and wrapped around Arrawn. The serpent squirmed and screeched momentarily, but it quickly gathered composure and turned to face Spencer with fury and immense speed. The serpent's head swept down to meet Spencer, stopping inches from his face. The fork tongue slithered out of his mouth and his black liquid eyes swirled. The green ectoplasm seemed to be having little effect now.

"Is that all you have little boy?" hissed Arrawn.

Spencer had no time to move before Arrawn's tail coiled around Spencer's body. He lost his concentration and the stream of ectoplasm ceased. He glared up into Arrawn's black eyes. The last moments of his life were upon him. He thought of his mother alone in the world; he thought of Oliver trapped in the pit; he thought of Frankie; his school; his grandmother; his father and his old friends. His whole life reeled through his mind

His entire body went numb. Any fear he had had scampered away, and was replaced with flat, silent, rage.

The breath of Arrawn warmed the side of his face. "Are you ready to meet your sibling?" he said triumphantly.

Arrawn's grasp tightened around Spencer's body, squeezing the remaining breath from his lungs. Arrawn waved him in the air like a toy about to be hurled across the cave. As Spencer tried in vain to draw breath, the cave began to spin and his thoughts and vision became hazy. His muscles and limbs collapsed into the grasp of Arrawn. There was nothing more he could do. He was going to die.

His head flopped from side to side as he tried to focus on something—anything. Darkness crept from the corners of his vision when, at the distant edges of his mind, he heard a commotion. It was familiar, but his brain refused to connect the sounds to images. He couldn't see what was happening, but Arrawn suddenly released his grip and he slipped to the floor, landing with a thud on his stomach. A white hot flash shot through his mind as his head cracked hard against the stone, cold floor. The pain pierced his skull leaving a hazy numbness that immobilised him as he lay waiting to be devoured, waiting to be with Oliver.

With what strength he could muster, he desperately rolled over on to his back. His head lolled to one side. The vast shape that was Arrawn loomed over him, but there was another shape too.

A blurry human outline.

Somebody else was there.

CHAPTER TWENTY FIVE

Unexpected Company

Spencer breathed deeply and between the gasping breaths, his mind and vision slowly began to clear.

"What is this?" Arrawn bellowed from high above.

Spencer found some hidden strength and began to crawl to the edge of the cave. Arrawn was snapping at the figure like a vicious dog.

Spencer's vision became clearer and standing in front of him in full Tezla uniform was Drake. He looked down at Spencer with a smile and nodded once. But then a thought occurred to him. He's not a Seeper, why isn't he dying? More questions rushed through his mind, but he had no time to digest them.

Arrawn's head hovered above Drake.

"Look out!" Spencer screamed.

Drake turned and dived to one side as Arrawn's jaws snapped close to Drake's head and slammed into the floor with a mighty crunch.

Drake quickly got to his feet and rushed over to Spencer. "Can you get up?"

"I think so," Spencer replied. Drake flung Spencer's arm over his shoulder and hauled him up. "But how—" began

Spencer.

"Later. First let's deal with that," Drake interrupted, nodding at Arrawn. He reached over his shoulder and pulled something from a backpack. "Here take this," he said and handed Spencer a Plasmeriser, but it didn't look like his own.

"I have one," replied Spencer, holding up his arm.

"No, this one is new," explained Drake lifting his own arm. "It's still in development, but I had no choice. I stole them from the basement."

Arrawn had recovered from his nose bashing and had turned to inspect them.

Spencer couldn't believe Drake was here with him. A mixture of relief and curiosity overwhelmed him and his spirits began to rise with hope.

"It works in the same way as your Plasmeriser, but this one utilises your power more efficiently," said Drake. "Can you stand on your own?"

"Yes, I think so."

Drake released him and Spencer's legs wobbled, but he remained standing. He released his own Plasmeriser, tossed it to the ground and pulled on the new one. It was heavier, but it moulded perfectly.

Drake must have noticed Spencer's frown. "You'll get used to it. I did say it's a work in progress. Anyway, you stay here and I'll circle him. When I give you the nod, let's take him out."

Spencer nodded.

Drake sidled around the edge of the cave, his eyes fixed upon Arrawn.

"At last we meet," Arrawn hissed.

Drake remained silent. He stealthily moved away from Spencer, taking the focus onto himself.

Again, Arrawn lunged and snapped at Drake, but Drake was too quick and leapt out of his path.

"So you have a cube?" hissed Arrawn.

"What of it? We're here to destroy you, Arrawn, and that's what we intend to do."

Arrawn laughed. "I know what you really want and destroying me will only be the start of something much bigger. You're sightless, just like this fool," his head tilted toward Spencer.

Spencer glanced over at Drake who met his eyes. Drake subtly nodded and glared back at Arrawn. Spencer took that as 'get ready' and guided the fiery ball, along with a torrent of hate and fury, to his shoulder and held it steady.

Arrawn continued. "Greater things are at work here, you know that, Drake Jones. You cannot win."

Arrawn seemed distracted and exposed for a moment. Drake didn't waste a second. "Now!" he screamed at the top of his lungs.

Spencer's anger and hatred boiled to the surface all at once. A year of pain and torture burst out of him. Drake released simultaneously and the ectoplasm burst from both Plasmerisers like hungry radioactive snakes. Arrawn became smothered in frenzied streams of ectoplasm. The screams of a thousand souls echoed around the cavern and Arrawn writhed and flipped like an eel out of water.

"Hold it, Spence, hold it," Drake yelled.

Spencer gripped the bulky Plasmeriser with all the energy

he could muster. He stepped one way, then another as he was tugged and shunted with the force of the Plasmeriser.

Arrawn stopped writhing and released a spine shredding, defiant scream. Within seconds he exploded and ejected his green ethereal intestines all over the cavern floor.

Spencer's energy was spent. He dropped to his knees and turned to look at Drake, who was extracting Arrawn's vapour from the air. As it cleared, Spencer gazed across the cave. He glimpsed a small shimmering object on the floor, glinting like a star in the night sky.

It was a realm cube.

The cave fell silent.

Arrawn was defeated.

Drake strode over to Spencer, stood in front of him and held out his hand. Spencer grabbed it and pulled himself up. But before Drake uttered a single word the ground began to shake violently, like an earthquake had just triggered.

"What's happening?" Spencer said.

"I don't know," Drake replied and by the troubled look on his face, Spencer knew he wasn't lying. He surveyed the cavern further as small rocks clattered all around them.

With an explosive shudder the green pit around the edge of the room erupted and sent a shockwave around the cave knocking Drake and Spencer on to their backs.

Spencer sat up quickly.

Pouring from the pit all around them were thousands of stolen souls rising and swooping silently around the cave. They were intense balls of light the size of Spencer's fist with a hazy perimeter and trailing wispy tendrils. They illuminated the cave as if a thousand light bulbs had been switched on. Slowly, they formed a stream and began to drift out of the cave like a torrent of dancing vapour being sucked away.

Spencer's heart was heavy and an overwhelming sense of loss and sadness rushed through him. The ground ceased to shake and Spencer staggered to his feet.

He looked up at the lustrous stream and as he did so, a bright, sparkling white light broke away and circled the cave. It swooped and dived, eventually settling on the cave floor in front of him. It spread out into a hazy, transparent blur that slowly came into focus.

Oliver.

Spencer gasped and rushed forward. "Oliver, is that really you?" he said quietly.

Oliver smiled and nodded slowly.

Spencer didn't dare blink or avert his eyes for fear of losing the vision. He reached out. "I'm so sorry, Oliver," he choked, tears stinging his eyes. "I really did try to save you."

Then Oliver's spoke, but Spencer didn't hear the voice in his ears, it danced through his mind like a vivid dream.

"There was nothing you could do Spencer, it wasn't your fault."

"It was my fault. If only I had looked earlier when you were calling out, I could have pulled you back, I could have saved you."

Oliver slowly shook his head causing his image to blur into a ball of light. "I am saved. It happened the way it was meant to happen. There was nothing you could have done differently."

"But you would be alive," said Spencer.

"I am alive, Spencer, more than you know." Oliver's innocence and glowing smile hadn't left him. "I knew you would come, I knew you would set us free," he said brightly.

Tears seeped from Spencer's eyes and ran down his cheeks. He couldn't hold them back any longer. A year of emotion and guilt spilled out of him. He longed to see and speak with his brother again and now here he was. Question after question had plagued him since he was taken. He wanted to hug him and take him home.

"Mother will be fine, Spence, she'll be released from her sorrow and accept my fate, just as I have accepted it."

"How do you know that?" said Spencer. But as he spoke, he noticed Oliver's glow shimmer and weaken for a brief moment. "Oliver, don't go! You can't go!"

"It's going to be okay, Spence. It's not the end. It's only just begun. I have to go, the draw is so strong. It pulls you from inside, brother. Remember the feeling when we stood on the football ground? It's like that Spence, but a hundred times more."

Spencer simply shook his head.

"But there is something that must be done. The connections between realms must be closed and you must seal them. Arrawn has done so much damage, it must be repaired."

"I don't understand, Oli," said Spencer. "Close what connections? Seal them with what?"

"I don't have enough time to explain. You must destroy the cubes, Spence. You will find the answers at the place where it all began. You will know what to do. You have come this far, you can do it."

"Where what began? What are you saying?"

Oliver's image stuttered and shimmered again. "It's time, Spence. I have to go, but I will be seeing you again, brother."

Tears streaming from his eyes, Spencer stepped forward and reached out his hand, but Oliver suddenly vanished and all that remained was a glowing white orb surrounded by wispy tendrils that moved so quietly and gracefully, it was mesmerising. A final whisper echoed from the unkept corners of Spencer's mind.

"I love you, Spence. We will always be one."

The orb moved slowly away then swooped around him twice. It rejoined the celestial stream creating a dazzling burst of light.

Oliver was gone.

"OLIVER!" Spencer screamed, but there was no answer, only the echo of his cry dancing off the cave walls. Spencer gazed up at the spot where Oliver had vanished. His heart ached, like it had been squeezed dry by a firm hand.

The cave slowly faded into black as the final souls drifted silently away.

"He's gone," Drake muttered.

Spencer reeled around, wiped the tears from his face, and glared at Drake. He was barely visible in the darkness, lit only by the glow of Arrawn's ectoplasm and a small pool of light on the cave floor.

Drake turned and walked over to where Arrawn was defeated. He crouched down and picked up the glowing cube. He stood and held it up at eye level, turning it one way then another, examining it like it was a valuable diamond. The light highlighted the smile that stretched across Drake's face like a child who had been given a brand new toy. "There you are," he said softly.

"What are you doing here, Drake? You should be dead. Nobody can survive a realm unless they're a Seeper," said Spencer, his voice heated and abrupt.

"That's no way to speak to somebody who just saved your life," Drake reminded him with an air of arrogance.

Spencer ignored the comment. "Why aren't you dead?"

"Oh, didn't I mention it? I'm like you, Spencer, although, my brother died much younger than Oliver. Of course, it was an accident. There was nothing I could do." Drake didn't sound at all sorrowful or sincere.

"You mean—"Spencer began, but Drake interrupted him.

"Yes, I'm a Seeper. I can travel the Realm Portdoors just like you."

"So why didn't you do this yourself? Why send us? Me?"

A smile crept across Drake's face. "I know what you are. I knew it from the first day we met outside your school. A direct descendent of the ancients. I also knew you would make it through the forest. The other Seepers don't have the same strength as you, Spencer. They are weak in comparison. I needed to clear a path. And why risk my own life when somebody else is more than willing to risk theirs?"

Spencer couldn't believe what he was hearing. His own mentor had betrayed him. A torrent of rage gushed through his veins and he charged at Drake. "You!" he screamed.

Drake raised his arm and held the palm of his hand toward Spencer. "I wouldn't do that if I were you," he sneered. A sudden, invisible shunt in his chest forced Spencer backward.

"But why, I don't understand why you did this?" Spencer

pleaded.

Drake turned and took several steps before spinning back to face Spencer. "As I grew up, I learnt about the ancient Seepers. My father told me bedtime stories about them. After my mother died and my father vanished, I was adopted. From that moment on I became obsessed with the legends. I consumed every last drop of information in search of a single thread of evidence that the legends were true. I needed to know. I wanted to be one of them. Although I could never trace my own ancestry, I did discover one. I discovered you, Spencer."

Spencer stood and listened intently. This was not the Drake he had come to know. The person standing in front him was somebody completely different, draped in selfish desperation. A blood vessel protruded and throbbed in his temple as he spoke.

He continued. "I couldn't tell you Spencer. If you had known, things would have been different. I had to control you. Tezla would have had you under guard and we wouldn't be standing here right now. After searching for so long, I couldn't let that happen. Just to be sure, I removed all evidence about you from the ethereal library."

"That was you?" gasped Spencer.

Drake nodded. "Most Seepers develop one core power and your powers may seem limited right now, but you'll flourish, Spencer. An ancient is said to host many great powers," he said, looking at Spencer with a curious admiration.

Spencer shook his head. Arrawn had said the same thing, but surely he would know something this huge, this important.

"But why did you do it?"

Drake plunged his hand into his pocket and pulled out a

second cube. "For these," he said. He held them out, one in each palm. "Two of the lost realm cubes are now mine. For years I have been searching for them, and now I have two. They will take me closer to Kedjom, the sacred chamber at the centre of realms where the ancients once controlled everything."

Spencer realised Drake was no better than Arrawn; evil, corrupt, and deceitful. "You stole the cube from the academy and you let them believe it was Hazel?"

Drake thrust forward in rage and said, "It has taken me a very long time to get here, and I am not about to throw it all away for a snivelling girl. She knew too much, I had to get her out of the way before she blabbed. She almost blew it when she came running to you. I couldn't let that happen."

"But she's your sister, Drake."

"It's pathetic. She tried everything to stop me. She was loyal up to a point, I'll give her that. But then she threatened to tell. She wouldn't shut up. So I started to lay the trap. I tampered with your Plasmeriser before you went to the Tower and all I had to do is give the nod and Hazel would take the fall for it. She found out what I had done and tried to stop you from going by frightening you with that stupid message. It simply made my job much easier. Then, once I stole the cube and activated the ancient Portdoor, it was the final act for Hazel. She was going to the High Council to tell them everything. But whom do you think they believed? Coupled with a simple evidence placement that made it look like she had stolen the cube, it was a done deal. She was taken in and it bought me enough time to do what I needed to do.

Spencer was dumbfounded. "It was all your doing? The

realm worm too? Somebody could have been killed."

Drake shook his head. "No, no, no. I didn't send that through. How was I supposed to know Arrawn would be monitoring the Portdoor. As soon as he saw it was open, he sent it through. I just wanted to create a diversion, nobody was meant to get hurt. A slight oversight on my part, I know."

Spencer had never felt so outraged. "You scumbag! What about the other Seepers? What have you done with them?"

"Oh I sent them on a little round trip. They're fine. I couldn't have them come here, they would have been slaughtered."

"You can't go back to Tezla. Where will you go? What will you do?"

"I have no intentions of going back. I want the realm cubes, Spencer. I want all of them. The pirates of Puya hold some of them. I don't know how many, but one day, I will find them all and once I do, I will reactivate Kedjom and explore all realms."

"You can't do that, Drake. You must destroy the cubes. You heard Oliver, they must be destroyed and all open connections must be closed. Think about it, Drake, the ancients must have shut the Portdoors for a reason. If you open them up again, who knows what will pour through?"

Drake laughed and shook his head. "Destroy the cubes? You must be joking. They can't be destroyed. That is why they were hidden, scattered. Now it's time to take them back to where they belong. Come with me, Spencer. Join me. We'll make a great team."

Spencer sensed a hint of Arrawn in his voice and he looked at him sadly. He suddenly grasped that this is what Drake had hoped for all along, but it was never going to happen. He recalled the Shape Shifter taking on the form of Drake during Albert's tour, the mad staring eyes and the open mouth. He glanced down at his Plasmeriser and then back at Drake.

"Don't even try it, Spencer. This is your way home." Drake held one of the cubes aloft. "If you try anything you'll never go home and I will disappear."

Before Spencer's brain calculated its next move, something snatched his attention. He heard footsteps behind him. He spun around and saw Jack climbing the last step.

"Jack!" Spencer gasped and he ran toward him.

"Hello, Spencer," Jack replied. The light in his cage glowed orange and flitted irritably.

"What are you doing here? How did you get through the forest?"

"You killed the Windigo, remember? Now the Boargles are happy to fly over it." He looked over Spencer's shoulder. "Hello, Drake," he added and he threw Drake a small phial full of clear liquid. Drake caught it, pulled out a stopper and drank the liquid inside.

He looked at Jack and stepped away from him. He glanced at Drake, then back at Jack. "You two know each other?" he said.

There was silence. As sudden as a flash of lightning, he understood what he had done.

"I suspected you wouldn't join me, Spencer. You're too honourable. I needed an assistant and Jack volunteered," said Drake.

Spencer looked at Jack with contempt, "Everything you told me was a lie?"

"Well, no. Not all of it." Jack shrugged his shoulders.

"You both planned this whole thing?"

Drake raised his eyebrows, smiled, and nodded slowly.

Spencer was speechless. The plan worked like a charm, almost to perfection, which is what he would expect from Drake. Knowingly defeated, he backed further away from Jack and stood between them both. "What now?"

Drake paced over to the Portdoor and placed one of his cubes in a small pedestal standing next to it. The Portdoor burst to life. "You must go, quickly, before Tezla sends the troops through. It's programmed for Tezla. You'll be fine, but it won't stay open for long as I'm sure they're already alerted to it on the other side."

Spencer stepped up to Drake, his body and mind weak and exhausted. He looked into his eyes for a sign of remorse, but there was nothing. Drake simply smiled briefly and nodded at the Portdoor.

"Go now," he repeated more urgently. "Here, take this," and pulled out the ecto-phial from his Plasmeriser and handed it to Spencer. "Give it to Albert, he'll know what to do with it. Now go."

Spencer took the phial from Drake and looked into the Portdoor. He hesitated, glanced back at Drake and Jack now standing side by side, then stepped forward into the Portdoor. It was like sticking his head out of a speeding car window. The air rushed all around him. His head spun sickeningly. His limbs were pulled in all directions. With all the determination he could gather, he focused on the grip of the phial. A wash of colour streamed past him.

Then everything stopped as abruptly as it began.

He slumped out of the Portdoor and landed on a white, shiny cold floor.

"Hold your fire," a voice yelled.

His eyes flickered open to bright, white lights. The blurry silhouettes of several people loomed over him. Nausea crept up his throat as the muffled voices and the world around him faded into darkness.

CHAPTER TWENTY SIX

The Numbness

Spencer opened his eyes. The artificial light stung as Frankie's face slowly came into focus. She sat on the edge of his bed, her concerned look slowly changing into a bright, warm smile. "Welcome back. You had us worried there for a while, Spence."

He attempted a smile, but it took a lot of effort. "Hi Fran, it's so good to see you."

He was sure her eyes sparkled with tears. She turned her head and looked up at the others. Spencer rolled his head and saw Hazel and Karl standing behind her.

"Hi guys," he said, but seeing Hazel's face suddenly brought it all back to him and he tried to sit up quickly. The pain in his chest shot through him like he had just been punched in the ribs.

Frankie put her hand on his shoulder and pushed him back down. "Easy," she said.

Angeline appeared at the foot of his bed. "Can you leave us alone for a moment please," she said, looking at Frankie and Hazel.

Frankie stood up. "We'll see you later, Spence," she said softly.

They all left the room, leaving Angeline staring down at

him. "How are you feeling?" she asked.

"Tired and sore," Spencer replied as he slowly pushed himself up. Dizziness took hold for a moment, but cleared when he propped himself against the head of the bed.

"You have done an excellent job, Spencer."

"Thank you," he said, but it didn't seem appropriate. "What about Drake and Jack? Where are they?"

"I don't know this Jack you mention, but Drake is gone. We got a message that he will not be coming back, but we are tracking him. Hazel has explained everything to us."

Spencer sighed with relief. "Where's he gone?"

"To explore new realms. Realms we have no knowledge of. He goes in search of cubes," said Angeline. "But he is behind us now. You have shown great bravery and courage, Spencer. More than I could ever have imagined."

"But Drake saved my life," said Spencer.

"What ever happened in Asgard is with you. What you choose to do with that information is up to you," said Angeline. "I would like to thank you and I hope you will be staying with us after this ordeal. Tezla owes you a great debt, one which I hope we can one day repay," she added.

Spencer suddenly went tense and gasped. "The ecto-Arrawn?" he blurted with sudden realisation.

"Albert has it firmly secured in a chamber," said Angeline. "There is no need to worry."

Spencer sunk back into his pillows. "Drake had been planning this for a very long time."

"Well, we suspected we had a spy in our midst, but we never thought it to be Drake until Hazel explained everything. By that time, you and he were gone."

"What about my parents?" said Spencer.

"They're fine. One of our agents has visited them. But we have not told them the whole story, we will leave that with you," said Angeline with a wry smile. "Is there anything you would like to tell me Spencer?"

Spencer thought for a moment, confused why Angeline would ask such a thing. Was she probing to see if he knew about his ancestors? She surely knew about his father, but he thought he would play innocent for now. After all, he didn't know whom he could trust anymore.

"No, I don't think so," he replied. "But there is one thing I would like to know."

"Yes of course. What is it?"

"If I did such a great job, why do I feel so empty inside?" he asked.

"Spencer, you saved Asgard from extinction. That is something you can be very proud of. But you were also betrayed and that has clouded that achievement. Give it time and you will understand why Drake did what he did. He never harmed anyone intentionally. He simply went after something that he truly believed in. In some ways, that is to be admired."

"I saw Oliver, you know," he began and went on to explain everything that Oliver had told him.

"We will discuss this in more detail at a later date. I would like to hear what actually happened in Asgard. But it can wait until you are strong again. You will need a few days to recover. If there is nothing else, I will leave you with your friends."

"No that's all I have to say," he said.

She then smiled, turned, and walked out of the room. No sooner had she gone his friends return to his bedside. Both girls looked anxious, but Karl held nothing but admiration across his face.

"I can't believe Drake was a Seeper, keeping it secret all that time. Must have taken some doing," Karl said. "What a slime bag."

"I didn't even know he had a twin," Hazel added, bemused.

"How did you find out?"

"That night, after he caught me trying to warn you, he told me everything. He knew I would get into serious trouble after what he did to me, so he made sure I would be okay and told me. He knew he would be long gone before I got a chance to warn anyone."

"Look on the bright side, Head of Seepers is now up for grabs," Karl said, raising his eyebrows and nodding towards Spencer. They all looked at Karl silently as if what he had said was inappropriate.

"What?"

His friends stayed with him as he retold every detail; the missing library files, being sent to the wrong portal, Jack, the Mudheads, the Boargles, the black forest, and the Windigo. But he spent most of his time recalling the events in Arrawn's cave and when he told them about Oliver, the thought of his brother no longer ached in his chest.

Spencer remained in the infirmary for several days as doctors and nurses came and went, bringing him food and a disgusting red liquid medicine that they watched him drink twice daily. It was the fourth day before he got out of bed and was allowed to go home.

Frankie had come to meet him. "You ready to go?"

"Yeah, I think so. I can't take any more of the food or red gunk they keep shoving down my throat," replied Spencer.

Frankie simply smiled.

His ankle was bandaged and he could still feel the dull pain of his bruised ribs where Arrawn had almost squeezed the life out of him, but apart from that, he felt fine provided he didn't move too briskly.

As they walked through the corridors, every cadet they passed stopped and stared at him as if he was a famous pop star. He noticed one boy holding the Paranormal Observer with the Asgard story splashed across the front cover.

When they entered the lobby, there was a large crowd waiting. They began applauding and cheering as more students realised he was there. It ascended until the whole lobby was cheering. Spencer's cheeks burned.

Karl came running out of the throng and hugged him. "Hey man, how are you doing?".

Spencer gasped and flinched.

"Oh sorry," said Karl, quickly stepping back. "I guess it still hurts."

"Yeah, it does a little."

"So, are you leaving us?"

"Well, not entirely. I have to straighten out a few things at home, but I'll be back," replied Spencer. "It's just the beginning," he added and smiled. He looked over Karl's shoulder and noticed Colin was standing behind him.

"Cool thing you did back there," Colin said, briefly glancing at Spencer. "Nice job." He walked away with his hands in his pockets.

"Wow," Karl said. "That's the first time I've ever heard him pay a compliment to anyone."

"There's a first time for everything. Listen, we had better be going. Mum will probably be wondering where I am."

Karl reached out and shook Spencer's hand. "You make sure you come back, do you hear me? Take it easy," he added in a tone of admiration.

Spencer and Frankie entered the Portdoor chamber. Frankie stepped into the silky blackness first, quickly followed by Spencer. It was an easy trip in comparison to the ancient Portdoors and they both seemed to have mastered the travelling. Without uttering a single word to one another, they walked through the old house and stepped out into the warm air. The sun was sitting on the horizon. There was a faint drone of traffic in the distance, and birds chirped in the trees close by. He caught the waft of a barbecue as he strolled along the path at the back of the house. One thing he was sure about, he was glad to be home.

All the way, his mind had been full of rehearsals of what he was going to say to his mother and father. Frankie hadn't spoke a word to him. As they reached his gate, she stopped and turned to face him.

"When I got back from Spain, the first thing I did was come to Tezla," she said quietly. "When they told me what had happened I couldn't believe you had gone."

Spencer looked into her green eyes. Her pupils were large and he saw something new behind the sparkle. It wasn't the tough individual he hung with at school. This was Frankie, the girl next door.

Spencer swallowed.

Frankie continued. "I thought I was never going to see you again."

"Well, here I am." There was a moment of silence between them, as if they were waiting for the other to say or do something.

"I better go," Frankie said and then she leaned over and kissed Spencer on the cheek. "I'm really glad you came back, Spence," she added with a smile, and then took three slow steps back, turned, and started toward her house. Spencer watched her walk to her gate and up the garden path to her back door. She glanced back one last time, smiled, and vanished into her house.

For a moment, Spencer remained rooted to the spot, but his mind turned back to his mother. He ambled slowly up the garden path to his back door. He paused, took a deep breath, and then pushed the door open.

The kitchen was empty and the house was different somehow. He was sure nothing had changed, but it was like he just walked into a stranger's home.

Then he heard footsteps. Somebody was coming down the stairs.

"Spencer? Is that you?" his mother called as she turned the corner.

"Uh, yeah, hi Mum," he replied.

She ran into the kitchen and hugged him like she had never hugged him before. It was affectionate and long. Spencer put his arms around her and he didn't want her to let go.

"Please, come and sit down. There is something I have to

tell you," she said. She seemed different, bright and alive.

"I had a visit from the police," she continued. "He was a nice man, very polite. He came all the way from Hertfordshire to see me. Now, I don't want you to be upset, but they found some of Oliver's things."

"But—" began Spencer.

"Let me finish," she said abruptly. "They have found what they believe to be his clothes. He has truly gone, Spencer."

Spencer knew she was fighting back the tears, but she was making sense and she was composed.

"It's okay, Spencer. Everything is going to be fine." As she said it, she reached out and hugged him again.

"The man that came to see you, when did he come?" asked Spencer.

"This morning, while you were out at Frankie's," she said.

That was when he realised what had happened. Tezla had sent somebody to perform a mind wipe and placed some thoughts into her head. Anger began to rise, but then he noticed how content she seemed. Perhaps it was closure for her and that's all she longed for, one way or another.

His thoughts then turned to his father. "What about Dad?"

"What about him, sweetie?"

"Well, uh, is he going to marry that woman?" he asked, unsure if his mother knew about his true past.

His mother paused and frowned. "How do you know about that?" she said, flatly.

"Uh, I overheard you talking about it on the telephone," he said quickly. It was the first thing that popped into his head.

She smiled and seemed satisfied with his answer. "Oh, of

course. Well, yes, I think he will be. But it's okay. We can all move on with our lives now."

Spencer didn't say another word about what had happened. He left it the way it was.

The weekend went by very quickly. Spencer spent most of his time in bed, sleeping and recovering. He managed to conceal the wounds from his mother and by the time Monday morning came, the pain in his ribs and the wound on his leg had almost healed.

CHAPTER TWENTY SEVEN

Tapping

Monday morning was bright and sunny. It was cool, but the sun warmed Spencer's face as he paced down Oak Lane toward the bus stop with Frankie by his side. They hardly spoke at all and Spencer sensed there was something different between them now. He noticed she looked different too. Her red hair was neat, almost perfect; her eyes seemed brighter; her smile broader and he noticed the sweet fragrance she was wearing.

They had only stood at the bus stop for less than a minute when the bus rolled up. They climbed on and it only had one person on board. The Oak Lane bus stop was the second pick up point on the way to school and they could choose where they sat. They strolled halfway along the aisle. Spencer let Frankie sit next to the window and he dropped into the seat next to her.

"Are you ready for this, Spencer?" she said.

"Ready for what?"

"School, Billy and Arnold. Remember, you put him in a tree at the end of last year."

Spencer looked at Frankie and they both burst out laughing.

Frankie shook her head. "No, stop. We shouldn't laugh, it's not funny, he could have been hurt," she said.

"Well, he deserved it," Spencer reminded her. "Well, okay. Maybe he didn't deserve it, but I couldn't help it."

The journey seemed short, despite the stopping and starting at each bus stop along the way. The bus pulled up alongside the school and juddered to a halt. The bus driver slouched in his seat and stared out of the windscreen with a blank, numb expression as Spencer climbed off.

He didn't feel fear; it was more like uncertainty. He was starting a new year, there were going to be new teachers and new students. He didn't know what to expect.

"Here we go again," Frankie said and she beamed a smile as they both entered the playground together. No sooner had they taken ten steps, did Spencer set eyes on Billy surrounded by his cronies. They were standing next to the main school doors, chest butting the students as they walked past. Arnold wasn't with him.

"Ignore him, don't say a word," Frankie said. Spencer heard what she said, but Billy didn't look like the bully he had feared last year. Physically he was the same, maybe a bit fatter, but he looked smaller somehow, less threatening and more like a boy than a bully.

"Look who it is. Freak Boy and his sidekick. Come back for another bashing, have you?" goaded Billy in his usual offensive manner.

Spencer glanced around looking for fear, but it was nowhere to be found. He walked up to Billy and stood in front of him.

"Spencer, what are you doing?" Frankie blurted.

Spencer knew exactly what he was doing.

"Get away from me, you freak," threatened Billy as he

glared at Spencer.

Spencer remembered what Drake had told him, 'every adversary has a weakness'. Spencer peered into Billy's eyes and wondered what his weakness could be.

He didn't know what made him do it. It was instinctive. He reached out and touched Billy on the shoulder.

Spencer's mind suddenly flooded with Billy's thoughts. He could see a large, round girl who looked similar to Billy, her face blood filled and enraged. She was screaming and lashing out.

As Billy brushed Spencer's hand from his shoulder, a smile spread across Spencer's face. He had realised Billy's weakness. It was his sister. Spencer was certain nobody would know about this.

"What are you smiling at freak boy," barked Billy nervously.

"I'm smiling at you, Billy. Have you told your buddies about your sister?"

"What? What do you mean my sister?"

"You know, the way she—"

Billy interrupted him. "Yeah well, they don't want to hear about that."

"Are you sure?" Spencer insisted.

Billy started backing away.

"I saw what you did to Arnold. You keep away from me, you freak," Billy jabbed the air with his finger. "C'mon lads, let's go," he added and they walked away, into the school.

"What did you do?"

Spencer shrugged. "I tapped him. I saw his sister beating on him." He looked at Frankie and they both laughed again. "I guess I can do that now."

Frankie nodded slowly, smiled and raised her eyebrows. “Come on, let’s get to class,” she said.

They both turned and stepped through the blue doors.

End of Book 1

ACKNOWLEDGMENTS

A big thank you to my family, friends and loved ones for reading the manuscript over and over again; for encouraging me onwards through the bleakest of times and steering me through my minor crises of confidence.

Also to my critique partners, for all of your feedback, without which this may not have been possible. You know who you are.

And a huge nod to Editor Cassandra (EditorCassandra.com) for her sharp eye and doing such a wonderful edit.

Lightning Source UK Ltd.
Milton Keynes UK
UKOW051900240911

179230UK00001B/6/P